I0715983

FIRST FROST

FIRST FROST

A Frost Series Novel

LIZ DeJESUS

BYZANTIUM
Sky Press

Byzantium Sky Press
Ellendale, DE, 19941

This book is dedicated to all the fans.
These books are for you . . . fairy tale lovers.
Believers of magic and wonder.

Acknowledgments

This series has been around for a long time. But it's because of these books that I have been able to go on so many little adventures. Got to meet so many incredible people and have so many opportunities knock on my door.

These characters . . . Bianca, Ming, Terrance, and Prince Ferdinand . . . they all carry a little piece of my friends within them.

Specifically Ming. At the time I started writing this series I reconnected with my best friend, Kristen. Some of you might remember her. She went with me everywhere for so many years.

Ming carries within her everything I loved about Kristen. Her bravery, loyalty, love, joy and laughter. We loved to laugh together.

I want to thank my friends . . . they have come through for me time and again when I needed them most.

I want to thank my husband, Kurt and my family for their love and support.

I especially want to thank Crystal Heidel and Byzantium Sky Press. I was ready to call it quits when she decided to take a chance on me and bring my books back to life.

I'm so lucky and grateful.

FIRST FROST

1

BIANCA SIGHED IN DISMAY. The vacuum cleaner was broken again. She took a quick look at it and didn't see anything wrong on the outside, which meant that the damage was somewhere inside. Probably a fried wire or something that Bianca wouldn't be able to fix with duct tape. It was a black and blue monstrosity. When it did work properly, it pulled Bianca every which way whenever she turned it on. Sometimes she wondered what her mother would say if she bought a saddle for the vacuum cleaner and just rode it around the museum. But lately it was giving her problems. This was the second time this month that it refused to work. Bianca double-checked to make sure it was plugged into the socket properly, placed a new piece of duct tape on the cord, and then tried to turn it on once more . . . still nothing.

"Stupid piece of crap," she muttered under her breath. She would have to tell her mother, Rose, about the broken machine after story time in the Princess Room. "Oh, God," she groaned as she picked up the vacuum and put it back in the utility room.

The Princess Room was every bit as girly as the name entailed. It was a place that catered to little girls with hopes and dreams of being pretty little princesses. The walls were painted in pale pink. A forest was painted on one of the walls and an enchanted, lavender-colored castle on the opposite wall. Small chairs and tables, so the children could color after hearing a story, sat in one corner, and a big round rug covered the floor close to the stage in case the children wanted to sit on the floor. It was a very comfortable set up.

The items in that room were more in the Hans Christian Andersen vein. Rose was worried that the objects from the Grimm stories would frighten the younger kids. That was why Rose went to great lengths to make a miniature set of dolls from "Thumbelina." Inside one of the display cases were items from the story "The Little Mermaid": a comb made from seashells, pearl earrings and bracelet set, and aquamarine fish scales. In the furthest corner of the Princess Room was a huge Plexiglass case containing a few of the feather mattresses from "The Princess and the Pea."

Bianca looked at the clock and sighed. It was nine fifty-five in the morning. She peeked into the room. Ten little girls, with their parents, were waiting for Rose, the Storyteller. Three times a week, Tuesdays, Thursdays, and Saturdays, one could count on hearing a different fairy tale in the Princess Room.

Rose walked into the room wearing a pale pink conical hennin, which was a headdress in the shape of a cone worn by nobility in the Middle Ages. A long and wispy white veil was sown into the tip of the hennin and delicately trailed behind her. It amused Bianca to no end to see her mother wearing their work "uniform" and still appear elegant while wearing a princess hat. Bianca looked down at her own clothes. Their uniform at the museum consisted of khaki pants and a red polo shirt with a name tag pinned above her heart. Rose said it made them look professional. Bianca thought it made them look stupid.

"Good morning, everyone!" Rose said.

"Good morning," all the children and their parents replied in unison.

"How are you on this beautiful summer day?" Rose took a seat and cradled a book of classic fairy tales against her chest. Bianca noticed how peaceful Rose looked when she held it close to her body. Almost as if she wanted to absorb all the words within its pages through osmosis—if that was at all possible she knew Rose would find a way to do it.

Everyone in the crowd replied with different answers.

"Fantastic," she said with a cheerful smile. "Today, I'm going to read the story of 'Snow White and the Seven Dwarves.' This is a personal favorite of mine. I hope you all enjoy it."

Rose and Bianca Frost ran the only children's museum in town: The Museum of Magical and Rare Artifacts. It focused mostly on items that came out of fairy tales and other rarely heard fables from other countries. As far as Bianca knew they were the only museum in the United States that had such pieces.

Bianca pulled herself away from The Princess Room and went to the supply closet. She grabbed the Windex and a huge roll of paper towels. She figured if she couldn't clean the carpet, she could at least clean the windows and the glass cases. She didn't mind doing this menial job. Of course, it wasn't her favorite thing to do, but she liked helping her mother any way she could. Bianca sprayed the blue cleaner on the glass case that held a small green pea, and she listened to her mother's melodic voice as she read the story of Snow White.

Her mother's voice was clear and deep as she sat in front of a tin soldier and a ballerina figurine. For people who didn't know the story about "The Steadfast Tin Soldier," there was a copy of Hans Christian Andersen's book of fairy tales on display inside the case, open to the story about the brave tin soldier who risked everything for love.

"Once upon a time in the middle of winter, when the flakes of snow were falling like feathers from the sky, a queen sat at a window sewing, and the frame of the window was made of black ebony. And whilst she was sewing and looking out the window at the snow, she pricked her finger with the needle, and three drops of blood fell upon the snow. And the red looked pretty upon the white snow, and she thought to herself, 'Would that I had a child as white as snow, as red as blood, and as black as the wood of the window-frame.' Soon after that she had a little daughter, who was as white as snow, with lips as red as blood, and her hair was as black as ebony, and she was therefore called Little Snow White. And when the child was born, the queen died . . .”

Bianca mouthed the words her mother spoke. She knew every single word by heart. Her mother had read every fairy tale imaginable to her since the day Bianca was born. Bianca was amazed how quiet the kids were. She shook her head, unable to understand her mother's ability to calm children down using only the sound of her voice. Anytime Bianca had to step in and take over story time, the children would stand up, talk, or whine. Yet the moment Rose returned and resumed telling the tales, the children magically stopped and listened to her.

Bianca couldn't believe people still came to hear Rose tell stories they'd read hundreds of times, although she had to admit, her mother was an excellent storyteller. It was almost as if nothing else mattered except what she had to say at that moment. People were entranced by the sound of Rose's voice.

Bianca left the Princess Room and headed to the Snow White Room. She wasn't really finished cleaning, but she wanted to be alone for a while. She remembered a time when she had loved the museum her family had run for generations. But this was a place that was passed down to the women in the family. And because she didn't have any brothers or sisters, she would eventually inherit the responsibility of managing the museum on her own when her mother passed away.

She was seventeen years old, and she had spent every free moment of her life working at the museum. She didn't know what it was like to call in sick from work or go on vacation. She wanted to leave, see the world, meet new people, and experience life. Not sit around all day long and tell fairy tales to kids with glazed over eyes. Bianca wanted to go to New York City and study art. She wanted to be an illustrator, a photographer, an artist—anything that required her to use her artistic talents and imagination.

Bianca stopped in front of a bright red apple. She sprayed a bit of Windex on the glass case and wiped it clean in circular motions like her mother had taught her when she was ten years old. The apple was carefully kept inside a Plexiglas case, well-lit and on display for the whole world to see. The fruit was a perfect ruby red, and it was centuries old. It would never rot. A tiny bite mark revealed the perfect fruit that the red skin protected. This was the poisoned apple that had nearly killed Snow White. Bianca wasn't sure if it was real or fake. She didn't know what to believe anymore. It was almost like being agnostic except that the things in the museum had nothing to do with God. What would happen to her if she refused to believe in fairy tales? Would the museum simply crumble to the ground? She hoped that she wasn't so powerful, that her lack of faith would bring down an entire building.

"Excuse me?" a tiny voice spoke.

"Huh?" Bianca looked down.

Standing in front of her was a little girl with bright red hair tied in pigtails. Bianca smiled her best smile. "Yes? How can I help you?"

"I need to use the potty." The girl crossed her legs.

"Follow me, I'll show you the way."

Bianca led the little girl through a maze of fairy tale artifacts: a seven-foot lock of Rapunzel's hair; Puss in Boots' minuscule black leather boots; a feather that belonged to one of the Seven Brothers; a handful of beans from the tale "Jack and the Beanstalk." They walked past several other items until they stopped in front of a door with Princesses in big glitter-covered letters.

"Here you go. Will you be okay to use the potty by yourself? Do you need your mommy to help you?"

"No, thank you. I'm a big girl." The girl gave Bianca a big gap-toothed smile.

"Okay. I'll be close by if you need me."

"Thank you," the little girl replied and walked into the bathroom.

Bianca finished cleaning the glass cases in the Snow White Room, and then she wandered over to the Wicked Wing to clean and straighten things out. This part of the museum always gave her the creeps. This was where they kept all the really dangerous artifacts. No one spent much time in this area—with good reason. Most of the time, it was filled with boys she knew from her school, daring each other to touch some of the artifacts that weren't safe behind the Plexiglass. More often than not they would dare each other to touch the evil queen's magic mirror.

You couldn't pay me enough money to touch that thing. Bianca shuddered. She cleaned the glass case that held the hot iron slippers that Snow White's stepmother was forced to wear on her stepdaughter's wedding day.

Yeah, Disney left out that part of the story.

She went to the next display case and stopped in front of the red dancing shoes. The red leather was worn and scuffed as though they had been to hell and back. It was a Mary Jane-type shoe except that it had two additional straps. Bianca swore that the crimson shoes twitched whenever she looked at them out of the corner of her eye. Every time she re-read the story, she made a point to stay as far away from the dancing shoes as humanly possible.

Then there was the spinning wheel on which Sleeping Beauty had pricked her finger. The wall behind the spinning wheel was covered with the thorny branches all the princes had to go through to try to rescue Sleeping Beauty, as she waited for one hundred years. Bianca was certain that she saw some bones still embedded in there.

The oven Hansel and Gretel pushed the witch into . . . that cooked her . . . alive.

Not real. These things are not real. They're just really good fakes. They're NOT real! Bianca would say that to herself every time she had to be in the Wicked Wing for any length of time. She had forced her mother to remove the needle in the spinning wheel after she had a horrible vision of herself dusting it and accidentally pricking her finger then falling into a hundred-year sleep. Bianca shuddered as she walked past it.

She'd been helping her mother out in the museum for as long as she could remember, and it still freaked her out.

Of course, it didn't help matters when her mother decided to put fake cobwebs in the room and keep it as dark as possible. It was obvious to anyone who set foot in the room that these items were not to be tampered with. And all the other things in the Wicked Wing would send a chill down anyone's spine. Bianca shuddered once more and walked out of the Wicked Wing.

The children were applauding by the time Bianca was finished cleaning the windows and the glass cases in the Snow White Room and the Wicked Wing. That meant that Rose was officially finished with story time. The kids then wandered around the museum with their parents. Child and grown-up alike were in awe over the fact that they could see items from their favorite fairy tales. They didn't appear to care that they weren't real; it seemed to be enough for them that it was something they could see with their own eyes.

Bianca took her place behind the gift shop counter now that people were walking around the museum. They sold everything fairy tale related, from costumes to books. Bianca and Rose put a lot of effort into making sure everything in the gift shop catered to both boys and girls. They painted the walls in a pale lemon yellow and made sure everything was displayed nicely at all times. They had magic wands, plastic swords, stickers, coloring books, anything that was fairy tale or fantasy related.

"Mommy! Mommy! Look! It's Cinderella's slipper!" a little blond girl shrieked. She grabbed her mother's hand and pulled her to the glass case that held Cinderella's famous piece of fragile footwear. The little girl pressed her tiny face on to the glass until her nose was flat. She wore a blue Cinderella costume, the kind they sold at The Disney

Store, with the blue plastic heels to match. It was obvious which tale was her favorite.

"It's always fun to see them get so excited over these things," Rose said as she joined Bianca behind the counter.

"I just cleaned that," Bianca muttered.

Rose chuckled. "Don't worry. We'll have to clean it up again tomorrow anyway."

"Why can't we hire a cleaning lady?" Bianca begged for the millionth time since she started helping out at the museum. Not that she minded cleaning all that much, it just got repetitive after a while, and she didn't want to do it every single day for the rest of her life.

"You know why," her mother replied dryly.

Family only.

Bianca was so sick of that phrase. The two words that had ruled over her life for as long as she could remember. That was the rule. Only family could know the secrets of the museum and ever since Bianca's father, David, had vanished ten years ago, that left only mother and daughter to run the museum's daily upkeep. They had recently bought an automatic ticket machine, so that was one less thing they had to do during the day. They took turns cleaning, vacuuming, counting money from the cash register, and running minor errands. But Rose handled all the important stuff like taxes, accounting, and depositing money in the bank.

Bianca wished she had a brother, or sister, or even cousins. Not just to help lighten the load of the museum, but to have someone to talk to about her father's sudden disappearance. Every time she tried to talk to her mother about it, Rose would clam up and not say another word the entire day. But sometimes . . . at night Bianca heard her mother crying in the bedroom she once shared with Bianca's father. So, she had learned the hard way not to say anything about him. Not even reminisce about memories or funny things he used to say and do. She felt that even thinking about him was enough to hurt her mother.

Anytime Bianca thought she was beginning to forget what he looked like, she would secretly go through their old photo albums. He had been a handsome man, but it was the sort of thing he had never noticed. She always liked that about her father, how easy he was to be around. He wore round, wire-rimmed glasses that hid the ice blue eyes Bianca had inherited. She also had his jet-black hair; the only thing she got from her mother was the pale Irish skin that freckled in the sun and never, ever tanned. He had a dry sense of humor and couldn't tell a joke to save his life; he would stumble through it or deliver the punch-line far too soon. But he had the uncanny ability to make anything fun. She grinned as she remembered the puppets they made one rainy Sunday afternoon. They were classic sock monkey puppets. She still had them carefully placed in the bookshelf in her bedroom. She shook herself out of her nostalgia and dragged herself back to the present.

"Oh, by the way, the vacuum cleaner is broken again."

"Damn it," Rose hissed. "Are you sure?"

"I made sure it was plugged in and everything, too."

Rose muttered under her breath.

"Mom . . . we need a new vacuum cleaner."

Bianca knew that Rose was a little attached to the vacuum cleaner. She'd bought it with David a few weeks before he disappeared. There were times when Bianca wished she was attached to something much more reliable.

"It's just a stupid machine. It doesn't mean anything," Rose muttered.

Bianca wondered who she was trying to convince, her daughter or herself.

"Agh. All right . . . fine. I give in. You win. I'll go to the store tomorrow and buy a new vacuum cleaner," Rose said.

"Yes! Thank you, God." Never in a million years would she have imagined herself getting excited over cleaning materials.

Rose rolled her eyes.

"Excuse me," a tiny voice said.

Bianca looked over the counter; it was the Cinderella girl. "How can I help you?" Bianca smiled sweetly.

"I would like to buy this magic wand and this book," the little girl said.

"You forgot to say please," her mother whispered.

The little girl gasped, and her blue eyes became huge as saucers. "Please, please, please," she added as if fearful she wouldn't be allowed to purchase the items.

"Sure." Bianca took the items and scanned them.

The little girl suddenly became pensive. Her sweet face was serious, and she seemed deep in thought. "Is it really magical?"

"The wand?"

The little girl nodded.

Bianca's first thought was to tell the truth and say that it was just a plastic stick with a glittery star glued on top. There was no chance the girl would ever be able to cast any magic spells with it. But she also didn't want to be the one held responsible for taking away a child's sense of magic and wonderment about the world. She might as well sit down and tell her that Santa Claus wasn't real, that there was also no such thing as the Easter Bunny, and that the Tooth Fairy was just a figment of her imagination. This was the least favorite part of her job. She never knew what to say whenever a child asked her questions. A part of her brain became muddled and tongue-tied. And for some reason people could tell when she wasn't telling the truth. She blamed her blushing cheeks.

"Umm . . ."

"I got this one," Rose whispered and gently patted Bianca on the shoulder.

Rose directed her attention to the little girl and smiled warmly. Bianca let out a sigh of relief; she was off the hook. She took a step back and let her mother take over the delicate situation.

"Hi, what's your name?"

"Clara." She gave a bashful smile and swayed gently from side to side.

"Clara, what a beautiful name. So . . . you want to know if that wand is magical?"

Clara nodded.

"Well . . . what do you think?"

Clara closed her eyes and balanced herself on the balls of her feet. Bianca was impressed with her steadiness, considering how Clara was wearing plastic high heels.

"I think it's magical," she replied shyly.

"Then it is . . . if you really believe in magic," Rose said.

Clara gasped and smiled. Her eyebrows shot up with surprise, making her big blue eyes appear even larger.

"Will it turn my little brother into a frog?" she asked, clearly hoping for a yes.

"No. You see, this particular wand" —Rose held the little plastic wand in her hands and carefully inspected it as though it were made of glass— "can only perform good magic. If you try to do naughty magic or hurt someone, the wand will break, and all of its magic will vanish into the sky until it becomes a star. Now . . . we wouldn't want that to happen, would we?"

Clara slowly shook her head.

Rose smiled and then softly muttered some unintelligible words into the wand. It glowed for the blink of an eye and then she handed it to the little girl. Clara's mother frowned, unable to understand what just happened, but let her daughter enjoy the moment.

"So, what are you going to do, Clara?" Rose met the little girl's eyes.

"Um." Clara tried to think.

"Not turn your brother into a frog," Rose suggested.

Clara nodded and echoed Rose's sage words.

"Good! Glad we agree."

"That'll be twenty dollars," Bianca said.

The little girl opened her little blue purse, pulled out her money, and handed it to Bianca, who then put the items in the plastic bag along with the receipt and gave the bag to her diminutive customer.

"Thank you," Clara said sweetly.

"You're very welcome."

"That was fun," Rose admitted.

"That's not really a magic wand . . . is it?" Bianca whispered.

Rose giggled. "No, of course not. And if it were, the most it could do is shoot a few rainbows into the sky . . . nothing major. Anyway, I wasn't about to ruin the little spark of imagination she has inside of her. That's her mother's job."

"Oh, okay. Just checking."

"Trust me, none of the things we sell in the gift shop are magical."

2

AFTER A VERY BUSY day at the museum, it was finally closing time. At six o'clock on the dot, Rose and Bianca began their end-of-the-day routine. They locked all the doors and windows, double-checked each room to make sure they didn't have any children who wanted to spend the night.

"Clear!" Rose shouted.

"Clear!" Bianca echoed.

"Ready?"

"No, I gotta grab my purse. Hang on a second."

Bianca ran upstairs, grabbed her dark purple hobo purse that was locked in the bottom drawer of her mother's desk, and ran downstairs.

"What do you want for dinner?" Rose locked the bolt on the front door.

"I don't know. I don't care. Whatever you feel like making."

"Okay. I'll see what I can whip up."

They both got in the old Chevy Cavalier that once upon a time had been blue. Now it was faded and rusting in some parts. Bianca diligently put her seatbelt on and waited for Rose to start the car.

On the drive back to their house, Rose asked if spaghetti was all right for dinner.

"Yeah, sure." Bianca looked out the window and watched the buildings and houses pass her by. She was a little relieved that it was Saturday.

She was looking forward to having the next couple of days off. It was tough for her to work all the time while everyone else was going to the beach or going on trips with their family. She wanted to enjoy her summer vacation. They drove past Rita's Water Ice, and she made a mental note to go by there the next day and get a cherry water ice.

I have to ask Ming if she wants to go with me. Maybe we can go to the mall, too.

Bianca tried to remember how much money she had in her checking account when Rose finally pulled into the driveway of their house.

Rose unlocked the front door and hung her purse on the back of one of the chairs in the dining room. Bianca went upstairs and took a quick shower. She wanted to wash the workday off her body. She slipped into her indigo skinny jeans and a cranberry red v-neck T-shirt. While Rose was busy in the kitchen, Bianca went to her bedroom and turned on her laptop. She checked her email, then her Facebook and Twitter page.

Nothing. *Well . . . that sucks.*

Bianca stuck her tongue out at her black laptop and gave it a raspberry, as though it were the machine's fault she had a weak social life. It wasn't her fault she was invisible and socially inept at school. She suffered from foot-in-mouth-itis . . . always said the wrong thing at the wrong time. She made jokes that only she thought were funny. It got to the point where she was forced to become quiet, withdrawn, and introverted. Her hobbies were solitary ones, like reading, drawing, and photography. For some reason, she never did well in team sports or crafts that involved other people.

She spent all her time at the museum or hanging out with her best friend, Ming. She didn't have time to go to any of the football games or be part of any after school programs. Ming and her mother seemed to be the only people on Earth who understood her.

She heard her cell phone buzz—a text message from Ming. *Wanna come over 2nite? New shows on Netflix!*

Bianca texted her back: *Sure. Having dinner in a few. What shows?*
No sooner she pressed send and set her phone down, it buzzed again.
Sailor Moon Crystal and Aggretsuko.

"Sweet," Bianca whispered.

Cool. Will b there in 1 hr.

Bianca went downstairs and kept her mom company in the kitchen. She sat down on a wooden stool and watched her cook. Rose wasn't the best chef, but at least she wasn't the worst. Everything she cooked was edible, and edible was the complimentary word as far as Bianca was concerned.

The kitchen was a mishmash of all of Rose's favorite things. Anytime they traveled Rose bought a tile or other knickknacks to place somewhere in the kitchen. There was the Picasso wind chime that was made entirely out of colored glass; it was something she bought in Spain before Bianca was born. All the tiles were placed as a backsplash behind the stove. Some of them had the Delaware state flag, flower, or animal. Some were tiles hand painted by local artists. This was the most colorful room in the entire house, and it was easily one of Bianca's favorite places to be.

Rose drained the excess water out of the farfalle-shaped pasta using the colander. They were Rose's favorite for some reason Bianca had never understood. Rose then transferred the pasta back into the pot and emptied an entire can of pasta sauce onto the steaming noodles. The steam curled and evanesced as it rose up to greet the ceiling.

"How much do you want?" Rose stirred the contents of the pot.

"Not much." Bianca hopped off the stool and grabbed some plates from the cabinet.

"Thanks." Rose took the plates from her daughter's hands.

"What do you want to drink?" Bianca opened the refrigerator and searched for a beverage among the shelves. Their choices were water, cranberry juice, and Diet Coke.

"Water, please." Rose placed their plates on the dining table.

Bianca grabbed two glasses and filled them both with water, then she sat down to join her mother for a simple meal.

"Don't forget the forks."

"Got 'em." Bianca grabbed a pair from the kitchen drawer.

"Bon appétit." Rose said in a fake French accent.

Bianca smiled and shook her head. "Yes, bon appétit, Mom."

Around a forkful of pasta, Bianca brought up her evening plans. "Is it okay if I go to Ming's house for a while?"

"Yeah, sure. Are you going to spend the night?"

"Nah, we're just going to watch TV."

"Ooh, what are you going to watch?"

"She texted me earlier and we're gonna watch some shows on Netflix together. We'll probably rewatch Sailor Moon all over again, but I don't care. That show's cute and funny."

"Aww. I remember Sailor Moon. That brings back so many memories. She cried A LOT." Rose chuckled softly.

Bianca nodded in agreement. If there was one thing they shared, it was their quirky sense of humor, which cemented the fact that Bianca was in fact her child. Her father had had more of a dry, sarcastic sense of humor, while Rose and Bianca enjoyed slapstick, physical comedy. If someone was falling down or getting pies thrown on their face, it was a sure way of getting them to laugh.

"Back by ten thirty?" Rose asked.

"You know it."

Rose stood and kissed the top of Bianca's head. "Just leave your plate on the table. I'll take care of the dishes." Rose put her plate in the sink.

Score! Fewer chores for me.

Bianca stabbed every bit of her pasta with her fork and stuffed it in her mouth, chewed as fast as she could, then ran upstairs to get her purse.

"Don't choke!" Rose warned.

"Thanks, Mom. I'll see you later!" she shouted with food still in her mouth.

"I love you, kiddo."

"Love you too."

"Drive safe!" Rose followed Bianca as far as the front door.

Bianca waved goodbye to her mother before she got into her old white VW Beetle and pulled out of the driveway.

Bianca knocked on Ming's brick-red door and waited. Mrs. Lee opened the door with a smile on her face. Bianca smiled back; it was impossible not to. She was such a pleasant woman. Her good mood was highly infectious. She could make the nastiest people cheer up. Bianca knew because she had witnessed such miracles firsthand. Her blue-black hair was tied into a loose ponytail. Her dark brown eyes crinkled as she welcomed her.

"Hello, Bianca. How are you?" Her voice was a notch above a whisper. Bianca was amazed she had given birth to Ming, who was the exact opposite of her soft-spoken mother. Ming was loud, honest, and a huge smartass.

"Hello, Mrs. Lee. I'm well, yourself?"

"Busy. Come in. Ming is waiting for you upstairs in her bedroom."

Bianca stepped inside the house and promptly took off her sneakers. She put on the pink fluffy slippers that waited for her by the stairs and went upstairs as fast as she could. Ming's cotton candy pink door was wide open. She was sitting on her bed, painting her toenails in a pale sparkly pink polish.

"Knock, knock."

"Hi! Come on in," Ming said.

Bianca stepped into Ming's pink bedroom and breathed in some of the nail polish fumes that surrounded them. Her best friend was obsessed with the color pink. Bianca's tastes weren't quite so girly. She favored darker colors like sapphire and dark purple. And while Ming loved pop music and anything that played on MTV, Bianca liked indie music and classic punk rock.

"So, how was work?"

"Same as usual, although . . . Mom finally agreed to buy a new vacuum cleaner, so that's kind of a plus."

Ming arched her right eyebrow. "How . . . exciting for you . . . I guess."

"Oh, shut up." Bianca playfully smacked Ming on her arm. "You've never had to do any kind of physical labor in your life, so don't even pretend you know what my day was like."

Ming laughed in response to Bianca's choice of words. She wasn't going to argue; the truth was undeniable. She was a little princess. Her father was a surgeon at the local hospital. He had crazy hours at work, which meant he didn't get to spend as much time at home with Ming and her mother. He made up for that by buying them whatever they wanted. Sometimes Bianca wondered if Ming would rather spend time with her father instead of the things he bought her, but she knew better than to express her opinion out loud.

"I wish she'd let me work there and help you guys out. At least we'd be able to hang out more." Ming pouted as she tucked her black hair behind her ears.

"Yeah, me too. But you know Mom's rule. Family only."

"That's lame. The museum is huge. I don't know how the two of you do it all alone."

Bianca shrugged. It had become routine. They did things so well together that running the museum was a well-oiled machine. At least it was summer, and she could help out full-time. During the school year, Rose did everything on her own, and Bianca could only help out on Saturdays. It was safe to say that Rose looked forward to summer far more than just for warmer weather and the chance to wear cheap flip-flops.

"Anyway, what are we watching tonight?" Bianca changed the subject.

Ming blew air on her toes before answering Bianca's question. She closed her nail polish and placed it on her night table.

"Sailor Moon Crystal is queued up. Season one, episode one," she said.

"Awesome. I stopped at the pharmacy on my way here and bought candy."

"Ooh, what did you bring?" Ming picked up the remote control and pushed the PLAY button.

"Milky Way, licorice, and Sour Patch Kids."

"Sweet!" Ming smiled.

For three hours, Bianca and Ming watched TV, laughed, quoted Sailor Moon to each other, and ate candy. Life was simple for the moment.

Life was, for lack of a better word, perfect.

3

"WHAT TIME IS IT?" Bianca looked at Ming.

"Ten o'clock." Ming took a bite off a string of licorice.

"As soon as this episode is finished, I gotta go home."

"Why don't you spend the night? The museum is closed tomorrow."

Ming had a point. They could go see a movie at the theater and then go to the mall to spend Bianca's meager earnings on things she didn't need.

"Nah. I promised Mom I'd be back by ten-thirty. Besides, I feel like sleeping in my own bed tonight."

"Fair enough." Ming shrugged.

As soon as the episode was finished, Bianca gathered her things. "Good night," Bianca said as they gave each other quick hugs.

"I'll call you tomorrow." Ming promised.

"Okay." Bianca walked out of the Lee's home and remembered to lock the front door behind her.

It was a cool night. She looked up at the stellar view above her. The sky was midnight blue, and the stars twinkled and shimmered.

When had she stopped gazing at the stars with amazement? When had she become cynical about the world? When had life become so completely . . . blah? She shrugged her shoulders and saved those thoughts for another time. All she wanted was to go home and sleep.

She unlocked the door of her car, sat on the driver's seat, and started the engine. Her hand touched the clutch; she was just about to change gears when for some reason she stopped herself. She frowned before putting the car in reverse. A strange feeling spread out from the bottom of her stomach as though something were horribly and terribly wrong. She shook her head and backed out of the driveway.

Even though she knew Rose would yell at her if she found out she was calling while driving, she pulled out her cell and dialed home. With one hand on the steering wheel and the other gripping the cell phone, she waited as the phone rang.

Something isn't right. Rose always answered after one ring. It rarely went to voicemail, but that was exactly what happened. After impatiently listening to the automatic female operator, she left her mother a message.

"Mom? Are you okay? I'm on my way home. Call me."

She ended the call and tossed the phone on the passenger seat. She wove in and out of traffic and stopped at all the stop signs and traffic lights, even though what she really wanted to do was push her little Beetle as fast as it could go. The feelings of unease continued until she parked the car in front of her house. The lights were on, but there was no visible movement coming from behind the curtain in the living room. Rose always waited by the window with a cup of green tea when Bianca was due back home.

What if there's a robber or something inside the house?

She didn't know whether to go inside or call the police first.

But what if someone was attacking her mother at that moment? What if she could stop something terrible from happening by simply opening the door and spooking the attacker away?

"Screw it."

Bianca got out of her car and ran inside the house. She called for her mother as she searched for her upstairs in all the rooms. Nothing. She quickly ran downstairs and was ready to go down to the basement when a strange turquoise light caught her eye.

What was that?

She walked slowly toward the kitchen window; and what she saw would change her life forever.

Her mother was throwing what Bianca could only describe as turquoise fireballs at a woman wearing a black hood. Rose no longer looked like her mom—sweet, kind, with a perpetual smile on her face. Rose looked like a warrior ready for battle. Bianca couldn't see the hooded woman's face, but she could see her pale hands and slender fingers.

Bianca tried to make sense of it all. She kept expecting to see a special effects crew come out from behind the trees and tell her that it was all part of an elaborate prank. But no such thing happened. All she knew was that a strange turquoise flame was coming out of her mother's hands and that she had a ton of questions she needed to ask Rose when this was over.

She knew that her mother sometimes read old, dusty books on witchcraft, but she didn't know she had actual powers. She thought about all the little quirks her mother had. Things that Bianca thought were essentially Rose. Her mother talked to plants and trees. She would sometimes stare off into space as though she were looking at something in another world. Something only she could see. She read tarot cards to random people and would tell them things about his or her life as though she were reading an open book. Bianca always thought she just made really lucky guesses. She chose not to believe in this other world and everything it stood for. Magic represented a life out of the norm, and Bianca desperately wanted to be normal. Just like everyone else.

Bianca pulled herself out of her thoughts. As she looked at the blue and green flashes in the backyard, she quickly realized that this was something she couldn't escape. Normal was no longer a part of her world. Normal was no longer an option for her. Normal was no longer within her grasp.

Bianca didn't know what to do. She was frozen in place. She was afraid to distract her mother for even a second. She ducked behind the screen door; at least this way she could still hear what they were saying to each other.

"Did you really think I wouldn't come?" the hooded woman shouted.

"Oh, I knew you'd be back," Rose snapped.

Bianca slowly peeked above the screen. She saw her mother standing behind the shed on the side of their backyard. The witch—which is what Bianca was calling her—was still too far away to get a good look at, but Bianca saw she was on the opposite corner of their yard.

"Where's the book?" the witch demanded.

"I have no idea what you're talking about." Rose smirked.

Bianca knew that look. Her mother knew exactly where that book was hidden.

"Don't be coy with me. You know very well what I'm talking about."

"Sorry. I can't help you." Rose's breathing was becoming more labored, and Bianca could tell she was drenched in sweat. Rose was showing obvious signs of exhaustion, but Bianca could tell by the look on her mother's face that she wouldn't give up.

"The wards in the museum are impressive. I couldn't get past them. But maybe . . . she'll know where the book is." The witch looked in Bianca's direction and threw a sickly olive-colored fireball at the screen door.

Bianca shrieked and jumped out of the way. The screen door fell off its hinges and landed on the kitchen floor with a loud thud.

"Bianca!" Rose screamed.

The witch cackled as she made her way toward the house.

"Stay away from my daughter!" Rose shouted.

Bianca watched as the witch tried to walk into the house, but then stopped as if held back by an unseen wall. Bianca gasped as Rose struck the witch with a citrine-colored fireball from behind. The witch howled in pain. Bianca wasn't going to wait and see what else would happen. She got up and hid inside the fireplace. It was dark, dirty, and cramped, but she wasn't going to come out of her hiding place until she was sure it was safe.

She heard a scuffle outside and then a loud fizz. Quickly followed by silence.

"Bianca?" Rose cried.

Bianca's heart skipped a beat. She was moments away from calling out to her mother, but she wasn't sure if someone was trying to trick her, so she remained quiet.

"Bianca, it's me, sweetie. Are you okay? Where are you?" Rose asked.

She heard the desperation in her mother's voice as she searched for her in the house.

"Mom?" she whispered.

"Yes, it's me, honey."

Bianca struggled for a few moments to get out of the fireplace. When she finally managed to get out, her hands were black with dust and soot, her clothes were ruined with ashes, dirt, and God only knew what else. Bianca sneezed a few times as she shook off the worst of the mess from her body.

"Oh, thank God. Thank you, God," Rose whispered as she embraced her daughter. She didn't seem to care that Bianca had left a trail of black dust behind her.

"Mom, who was that?" Bianca pulled herself away from her mother's tight embrace.

"Our enemy, Lenore."

"Lenore?" Bianca echoed.

Rose sighed. "Sit down."

"Will she come back?" Bianca looked at the singed screen door. She shuddered to think of how close she had been to being burned to a crisp.

"Yeah, but not tonight. She was distracted for some reason; she's rarely that sloppy. Lucky for us she's as out of shape as I am. She hasn't attacked me in years. But this is good; now I have some time to train you."

Rose closed the kitchen door and locked it behind her.

"Train me? What's going on?" Bianca tried her best to keep her cool. Because what she really wanted to do was grab her mom, shove her inside her car and drive as far away from the house as humanly possible. But a part of her had a feeling that there was no amount of driving that would put distance away from the evil that attacked them.

Bianca pulled a chair and sat down.

"Don't worry I put the ward on the main kitchen door not the screen door. Trust me . . . I won't make that mistake again."

"O . . . okay," Bianca whispered. She was so confused. What was going on?

"Bianca . . ." Rose sat down beside her daughter. She took her hand and held it tightly. "God . . . how am I supposed to cram hundreds of years of family history into one conversation?" she wondered aloud. "I've never spoken of your grandmother, have I?"

Bianca shook her head. It was a taboo subject. What little she did know was fairly unpleasant. Based on what Rose had told her, Alice Phillips, her grandmother, had been a woman who'd been rough around the edges. She'd had patience only for her garden and animals. There had been very little left over for her only daughter, Rose. Bianca had always been curious about her mysterious grandmother, but she'd kept all questions to herself. She knew talking about the past caused her mother pain.

Rose took a deep breath. "My mother was a witch. And so are we."

"I'm a what now?" Bianca was trying to wrap her head around what Rose just said.

"A witch," Rose said.

"I don't understand," she whispered.

"I felt the same way when the time finally came for me to learn of our history. It was the only time in my life that I saw pity in my mother's eyes. Almost as if she felt sorry for the load she was about to place on my shoulders, just as I'm about to do with you. It all started with one question. I remember that question all too well. That's how everything began."

Bianca held her breath and waited.

What could she possibly be about to ask me?

"You remember the story of Snow White?" Rose met Bianca's eyes.

Bianca arched her eyebrow and nodded. That was the big question? Of course she knew the story. What person in the world didn't? Someone had to have lived under a rock to not know about the most famous brunette in the world.

"It's true. It's all true," Rose said.

Bianca frowned, unable to process the words her mother had just spoken. Rose had mentioned something along those lines to her before, but she'd thought she meant that it was based on a true story. That perhaps there had been a grain of truth to the story of Snow White. That there may have been a queen somewhere who had been jealous of her stepdaughter and banished her, making the story so scandalous at the time that it took on a life of its own, thus ending up a fairy tale. But never in a million years would Bianca have believed that Snow White was an actual true story, along with magic, poisoned apples, dwarves, and the handsome prince who broke the spell with true love's kiss.

"Come on, Mom. Really?" Bianca waited for her mother to smirk like she normally did when she was ready to burst into a fit of giggles, but Rose's face remained stoic.

"A lot of these stories are actually true. Not so much with the Hans Christian Andersen stories. He made a lot of them up . . . thankfully. But most of the fairy tales in the Grimm books have spells woven into the stories. For example, 'Mirror, Mirror on the wall, who is the fairest of them all' is only half a spell. The Brothers Grimm left the other half out because they didn't want other people using the spell on the queen's mirror. At the time they published their book, the mirror was still missing along with other items from their now famous fairy tales. That would just cause too much trouble. People don't really want to hear the truth about certain things. Look at what happened to the queen."

"Oh, my God. Are you serious?"

"I am very serious. This isn't a joke. Magic is real. The stories are very real," Rose said.

"But why print these stories at all? Why not just keep it all a secret?"

"Because it forced a lot of the witches to go into hiding, especially the evil ones. They were out of control. Children went missing almost every day, and beautiful young girls were locked away for fear that witches would become mad with jealousy and try to kill them. People lived in constant fear. The Brothers Grimm helped put a stop to it. By telling their stories, they were able to expose the worst of them and sharing how they could be defeated."

"Witches? Like the one that just attacked us?"

Rose nodded.

"When did she get here?"

"Around ten. I was ready to make my cup of tea and wait for you to come home."

Bianca smiled. That was what she had expected to see when she had come home that evening. She thought about what her life would become now that she knew this huge family secret.

"Mom?"

"Yeah?"

"We're witches? For real?"

"Yes," Rose replied.

"Does that mean I have magical powers too? Like you?"

"I'm sure you have some natural abilities, maybe even some things that only you are capable of doing," Rose said. "Your grandmother, Alice, was good with offensive spells and potions. My talents lie with healing spells and some defensive spells, for obvious reasons. I'm no good at potions, which makes sense because I'm not a very good cook."

Bianca opened her mouth to say something, but nothing came out. She felt like a fish out of water.

What am I good at?

What sort of magic would be her forte? Would she be good at potions like her grandmother? Or would she be a healer like her mother? Or perhaps she would have a completely different talent? The possibilities seemed endless. Then another fear crept up. What if she wasn't any good at magic? What would happen to her then?

On the kitchen table was a deck of tarot cards. The box was missing some of the flaps and the corners were worn. This was the deck her mother had used from the time she had been thirteen years old. Bianca reached for the cards and pulled them out of the box. She tried to keep her mind clear as she shuffled them. She pulled a card from the middle of the deck. Bianca held her breath as she turned the card over.

The Tower. The illustration was that of a tower being struck by lightning and several people falling to the ground. The illustrator had drawn people covering their eyes as they fell headfirst toward the rocky ground. The Tower represented chaos, sudden change, revelation, disruption, hard times, and realizing the truth.

Nothing good will come of this, Bianca thought grimly as she gazed into her mother's emerald eyes. "Why didn't you tell me sooner?"

Rose took a deep breath. "Selfish. I was being selfish. I wanted to keep you innocent for as long as possible. I should've started training you the moment you turned twelve. Also . . . I didn't want to repeat the same mistakes my mother made. I wanted to be the exact opposite of the woman my mother had been. I mean, sure she was an excellent witch and had defeated many evil witches . . . but it was almost as though she didn't know how to take that armor off around me."

Bianca was a little relieved that her mother hadn't broken this bit of news to her on her birthday. She wasn't sure she would have wanted to hear she was a witch right after blowing the candles on her chocolate birthday cake.

"So . . . what happens now?"

"We get some rest. We have an early day tomorrow."

Bianca's heart skipped a beat. She would have to learn how to defend herself with magic. She couldn't imagine being able to go to sleep.

"Okay." Bianca nodded reluctantly in agreement.

"Good night."

"Yeah . . . night," Bianca muttered.

Bianca went to the bathroom to take another hot shower and change her clothes. It was like she was in a bit of a daze. She wanted to stay up and talk to her mother all night long, but she knew that wasn't going to happen. She knew Rose would wake her up at the crack of dawn and continue where they left off.

After Bianca turned off the lights in her bedroom, she lay in her bed, and thought about everything that had happened that night. Eventually sleep found her, but she had dreams of rotting apples, pale hands reaching out to her in the darkness, and sharp white teeth.

4

THE FOLLOWING MORNING—five o'clock to be exact—after a quick breakfast of green tea and buttered toast, mother and daughter went downstairs.

There was a corner of the basement that was covered with boxes. Some of them were full of Christmas decorations—at least ten boxes dedicated to that holiday alone. Rose loved Christmas; it was her favorite holiday. Halloween was a close second.

A few boxes were full of Bianca's old baby clothes, and there was yet another set of boxes dedicated to her father's clothes. Bianca used to ask Rose why she kept them, and her mother would shrug her shoulders and say, "He might come back." And they'd leave it at that. A different subject they would ignore for years to come.

The rest of the basement had been turned into a craft room for Rose's little projects. Sometimes she would make wreaths and give them as Christmas presents. Or she would buy fruits and make jam. Rose spent a lot of her spare time in the basement. Bianca glanced at the table and noticed that her mother was halfway finished making a Christmas wreath. All the materials she needed were laid out and waiting to be used: the hunter-green plastic wreath, the little bright red hollies, the yards of cranberry red ribbon, and the can of silver glitter spray. Bianca wondered who that would be gifted to.

"So, where do we start?" Bianca tied her hair into a ponytail.

"Your grandmother was the one who taught me everything I know, and she was pretty brutal when she started training me."

"How so?"

"She threw every spell imaginable at me until I learned how to block them and attack back. I remember shielding myself from her spells and dodging fireballs and every other spell she felt like throwing at me that day," Rose whispered.

"Whoa."

Rose lifted her white T-shirt halfway and showed Bianca some of the scars she had on her back and stomach. She had never seen these marks on her mother before. Now Bianca understood why Rose only wore one-piece bathing suits in the summer. And why she went to great lengths to make sure her shirt was always tucked in. She didn't want anyone seeing her scars. Bianca gently touched one of the scars on her mother's back. It was the size of Bianca's fist. The scar was the palest silver she had ever seen, barely noticeable next to Rose's alabaster skin. Angry tears shot out from her eyes. She wiped them away with the back of her hand and tried to stop more tears from coming.

"I got that on my first day of training. I learned the hard way never to turn my back on my attacker. I never thought she'd throw a freaking fireball at me. Safe to say I never made that mistake again."

Bianca thought back on every conversation she'd had with Rose about Grandmother Alice. She knew next to nothing about her because Rose rarely spoke of her. She didn't share any memories of her or quirky details that she assumed most grandmothers had. And now she had proof, right on her mother's skin, of how far Alice's cruelty went. Suddenly, Bianca hated her grandmother.

How could she do such a thing to her daughter? Was she *insane*?

"I swore to myself that I wouldn't teach my daughter that way."

Bianca thanked her mother. She was grateful that Rose wouldn't do any of that to her. Now that she knew a little more about her past, she understood why Rose was better with healing magic.

"Let's start with fire spells. Those are easy," Rose suggested.

Bianca nodded. She chewed on her thumb while she waited.

What if I'm a dud? What if I completely suck? What if I'm the first one in the family who can't do magic? What will happen then? Oh, God . . . please don't let me be a dud.

"All right, first rule is to relax. Fire is the easiest form of defense, but it takes a lot out of you, which is why you should learn other spells. I know it's going to be tough to do when someone is attacking you, but you must learn to ignore everything that's going on around you. Guide all of your energy, every thought, feeling . . . everything you've got into your hands. Then you direct it wherever you want it to go."

Rose demonstrated by showing her a tiny turquoise ball of fire that hovered on the palm of her hand. Rose played with it by making it dance and bounce from her right hand over to the left hand. Then she divided it into three miniature fireballs. Rose grinned and gave Bianca a playful wink as she started to juggle them with both hands.

"Wow . . . that's so cool," Bianca said. "Why are yours that color?"

"It depends on the color of your aura," Rose explained. With a flick of her wrist the three fire balls vanished in a puff of smoke.

"Does that mean that Lenore has a green aura?"

"Not necessarily. Lenore's aura isn't the green of life. It is more of a brownish green . . . almost sick looking, like bile. It's her spirit rotting from the inside out."

"Ew." Bianca couldn't imagine having something like that happen to her. She pictured fruit going bad. All covered in mold, wrinkled, and decomposed to the point where it was unrecognizable. She shuddered at the thought and tried to clear her mind, which was easier said than done. Bianca closed her eyes and tried to do what her mother suggested. For a long time, nothing happened . . . until she started thinking about her father. No specific memories, just the man she remembered. Handsome, kind, always trying to make Bianca laugh. Then she felt a tingling in her fingertips.

"That's it!" Rose beamed.

A smile bloomed on Bianca's face when she heard the pride in her mother's voice.

"What are you thinking about?" Rose spoke a notch above a whisper.

"Nothing," Bianca lied.

As soon as the lie passed her lips the feeling in her hands vanished, and the magic was gone. Bianca opened her eyes. Rose's mouth flattened into a thin line. "Don't lie. Magic . . . at least good magic . . . doesn't help liars." Rose's voice held a warning.

"I'm sorry." Bianca lowered her head in shame.

"It's okay. We're here to learn, not judge one another. Wanna try again?"

"Yeah," Bianca whispered.

The awkward moment passed, and they turned their attention back to Bianca's training. She thought of her father once more. She remembered the time they had all gone to the aquarium together. She had been six years old, and at that time she'd wanted to be a marine biologist. She loved the water and stingrays. She thought they were odd and graceful. All she could see was her father's handsome face as he'd pointed to one of the creatures as it swam.

"Did you know that stingrays are usually docile and curious? They sometimes brush their fins past any new object they come across," her father, David, said.

"Really?" Bianca looked up at him.

"Yep." He nodded.

"Cool." She pressed her tiny hands on the cool glass.

Bianca opened her eyes and watched in awe as both her hands glowed bright white. She cried in surprise and looked at her mother for guidance. "What do I do?"

"Okay. Now direct it somewhere. Anywhere," Rose instructed gently.

Bianca looked around and threw her fireball towards a box of old papers.

She honestly didn't think that the box would catch fire. She didn't think her magic was powerful enough to make something burst into flames. But that was exactly what happened.

"Oh, crap!" Rose ran upstairs, grabbed the fire extinguisher from the kitchen, then back to the basement, and put the fire out.

"I'm so sorry," Bianca said, rooted to the spot. She was shocked. She stared at her hands as though seeing them for the first time in her life.

"No, no. That's okay. You were great." Rose wiped the sweat off her forehead.

"Mom?"

"Yes?"

"When you asked me what I was thinking about earlier and I said nothing . . . "

"Yeah?"

"I was thinking about Daddy," she admitted.

"Oh." Rose spoke so softly Bianca wondered if she'd really heard her speak or if she had imagined it. 'Oh' was such a small word, yet it filled the room.

"I'm sorry."

"Don't be. You're not forbidden to think about him."

"But you always cry and get so sad when I mention him."

"I know. I'm so sorry for that. It's just . . . it's hard living without him. God . . . it's been ten years, and I still can't get used to it. He is the love of my life."

Bianca almost corrected her and said was. It was as though Rose were implying that David was still alive. But if he were alive, Bianca knew that her father would do everything in his power to come home to his family.

If her mother's implication were true, where is he? Why hasn't he found a way to come back to us?

She had been seven years old when her father had disappeared. The first year he was gone she'd cried nearly every day. With time she'd cried less and less until she had gotten used to not having her father around. She had become accustomed to having that huge gaping hole in her heart.

"We were trying for another baby when he disappeared," Rose said.

"Really?"

Rose wiped at a runaway tear with her fingertips and nodded.

Wow. We're actually talking about Dad without Mom running from me.

With everything that happened last night, there was a question she wanted to ask. It was burning in the back of her throat, begging to be released. She almost didn't ask for fear of her mother reverting back to her old ways and shutting her out once more, but Bianca decided to take a chance. It was now or never.

"Does Lenore have anything to do with Daddy's disappearance?"

Rose nodded once more.

"What happened?"

Rose got a faraway look in her eyes, as though she were someplace else, in another time altogether. "Lenore turned your father into a bear right before my very eyes," she whispered.

Bianca's jaw literally dropped. She couldn't believe what she heard.

"A bear?" Bianca heard the disbelief in her own voice. After she had taken a moment to digest, she gazed at her mother. "When did this happen?"

"You don't remember?" Rose's voice held surprise.

Bianca tried to remember that day. It was foggy . . . at best. "I remember coming home from school, and you sat me down on the couch and told me that Daddy was missing. But what I meant to ask was when, as in was it during the day? At night? Was it here at home or at the museum? Details, Mom. You've never given me the details behind Daddy's disappearance."

Rose ran her fingers through her hair and looked around the room, desperate for an answer. "How could I possibly tell you? How on earth was I supposed to explain to a seven-year-old that a witch turned her father into a bear? I couldn't tell you then, sweetheart. And I'm sorry I kept so much from you."

"I guess that makes sense," Bianca replied as she nibbled on her thumbnail.

"Anyway . . . David was working late at the museum. He had some paperwork he wanted to take care of, some tax forms or something like that. At that time, we were sharing the car, so I told him to stay and wait for me to come pick him up. I needed to come home to take care of you and get dinner started. I knew he would be safe as long as he stayed inside the museum because of the wards I had placed on the building.

"I left you at Ming's house because you were spending the weekend with her. Then I drove up to the museum to get your dad. David came out of the museum, locked the doors behind him, and walked toward me. He smiled and winked at me like he did every time I picked him up. That was when Lenore stepped out of the shadows and cast her spell on him. I froze, watching in horror as he transformed into a bear right before my very eyes. Before I could mutter a single spell, he was gone. I can still hear her cackle as she took him from me . . . from us."

A sudden hush fell between them. Bianca was at a loss for words.

"What a horrible thing to do to a person," Bianca said finally.

"She said she wanted to help turn my life into a real-life fairy tale."

"I don't understand. Why would she want to do that?"

"You know my full name is Rose Red Frost," she said.

"Yeah, I know. Still not getting it, Mom." Bianca tapped on the side of her head.

"Haven't you ever read the story of Snow White and Rose Red?"

Bianca frowned as she searched her memory for the story and vaguely remembered having read a fairy tale with those names at some point in her life. It made sense because most of the women in the family were named after a fairy tale character. "Did Grandma name you after the story?"

"Yeah." Rose smiled. "It was her favorite story."

"Is that why you named me Bianca?" She had wondered about the story behind her name, Bianca Silver Frost. Sure, it took some twisting and turning, but it was almost like being named Snow White.

"Yes. I didn't want to go so far as to name you Snow White, I thought people might make fun of you, and I didn't want you to go through that," she admitted. "Anyway, Lenore thought that since our names were so similar to the ones in the fairy tale, she wanted to make it come true. She has a thing for torturing people. She wants to see what they're capable of and how much they can withstand before finally breaking down. That's the part she loves the most: watching someone break. I guess she wanted to see how far she could push me. I don't know . . . maybe she wanted me to kill myself since she had failed so many times in the past."

Bianca couldn't stand the thought of losing her mother. That was one scenario she didn't want to imagine.

Bianca took a deep breath. "Where is he? Where is Daddy?"

"I don't know. I've looked everywhere for him. He isn't in the forest or in a zoo. I've tried scrying for him."

"Scrying?"

"Scrying . . . how do I explain it?" Rose took a moment and gathered her thoughts before saying, "It's a form of fortune telling and divination. You try to contact the spirit and sometimes if you're lucky they give you a vision or the answer to your question."

"Woah. Okay." Bianca nodded. "Did it work?"

Rose shook her head. "No, I've tried everything. I even asked the magic mirror in the museum if it knows where he is."

"Wait a second . . . the mirror talks? That thing is the *real* mirror? As in 'Mirror, mirror on the wall . . . ' all that?"

Rose nodded. "Yes. All of the items, except for the stuff in the gift shop, are very real."

"But . . . some of that stuff on display is very dangerous. What if someone accidentally touches it? Oh my God, I have to clean and dust some of that stuff. What if I had accidentally pricked my finger on the spinning wheel?" Bianca was trying hard not to freak out . . . and quickly failing.

"Don't worry. That's why I took the needle out of the spinning wheel and put it in the attic. And there's a reason a lot of that stuff is behind protective glass," Rose explained.

"Geez. You think you know a person," Bianca whispered. "Anyway, what did the mirror say?"

"*Across the world, The man you seek, In another realm, His language you cannot speak.*"

"What the hell is that supposed to mean?"

"I'm not sure. It could mean he's in another world altogether, or he's now part of the animal kingdom, which technically is a different realm because animals abide from different rules than humans do. I just don't know."

"Why is the mirror so cryptic? Why can't it just say what it means? Why can't it say 'Hey, your father is in Yellow Stone Park next to the maple tree' or something like that?" Bianca snapped.

"Trust me, sweetheart, I've been asking that mirror questions my whole life, and it's never given me a straight answer."

"Well, it sucks." Bianca pouted as she crossed her arms across her chest.

"It's better than nothing."

Bianca wondered how she would feel if the love of her life had been transformed into a bear and then kidnapped by an evil witch.

Devastated. That was the only word that came to mind.

Bianca lifted her gaze to ask Rose another question and saw that her mother was in tears. "Oh, Mom." Bianca walked up to her and hugged her. "It wasn't your fault."

Rose sobbed and covered her mouth as though wanting to take back the sound that escaped her lips.

"Mom, don't cry. Please stop crying."

Rose shook her head and dried her tears from her bloodshot eyes. "I think about that night every single day."

"We'll find him, Mom. Don't worry, we'll find him," Bianca said, trying to comfort her.

"It's been ten years. For all I know, he's probably dead," Rose whispered.

"We'll find him," Bianca repeated the words in a louder voice. She was fiercely determined to make this statement come true—no matter what. She had no idea how she was going to find her father, but she would do everything she could.

"I'm sorry I didn't tell you sooner," Rose said between tears.

"Yeah . . . me too."

Rose wiped her cheeks and tried pull herself together. She took a deep breath. "Come on, let's practice a little more, and then I'll make us some lunch."

"Okay." Bianca nodded.

They stayed down in the basement for several hours, practicing magic spells, creating fireballs and other defensive spells. By the end of the day, Bianca had learned how to shield herself from another witch's magic. Although it hadn't felt like she'd been doing any rigorous activity, she was drenched with sweat by the time they were done.

5

AT EIGHT O'CLOCK IN the morning on Tuesday, mother and daughter opened the doors to the museum. Bianca's life had been altered in one day. She was glad she'd had all day Monday to sit and let everything sink in. It was hard for her to look at the items in the museum the same way. Would putting on Cinderella's glass slipper make her want to dance? Would pricking her finger on the spinning wheel cause her to go to sleep for one hundred years? What about Snow White's apple? Was it even real? If so . . . was it really poisoned?

All this stuff is real. She'd gone from not believing in magic to being completely surrounded by every magical item known (or unknown) in the fairy tale world.

As she stepped into the Wicked Wing, her eyes widened in horror, her mind running through the list of the items in that particular room.

The oven from Hansel and Gretel. How they managed to get a hold of that monstrosity will always remain a mystery.

The spinning wheel from Sleeping Beauty. The Red Dancing Shoes.

Another spinning wheel from Rumpelstiltskin, the one he used to turn the straw into gold.

A golden cage with a fake nightingale inside; it was the one from the story Jorinde and Joringel.

The evil queen's magic mirror.

What is that thing even doing on display? Bianca wondered as she walked past it.

Oh, my God! Those things are real!

Bianca tried not to freak out in the middle of the museum while there were people roaming around. She plastered a big fake smile on her face as she left the room in search of her mother. She checked the gift shop—not there. She went upstairs, hoping Rose would be in her office.

"Not here," she muttered as she opened the door and found the chair behind her desk empty.

Her face hurt from smiling so much. She rubbed her cheeks as she walked down the stairs. She let out a sigh of relief when she found her mother in the art gallery, struggling with a twenty-four by thirty-six framed painting of a mermaid lovingly gazing at an unconscious sailor. It was all done in pencil and a series of blue and green markers. Bianca had always been blown away with the art that had been collected in this room. A lot of the paintings in the gallery were done by local artists. And some of the artwork were reprints of famous illustrations from popular artists like Arthur Rackham, W. Heath Robinson, and John Tenniel.

"Mom?" she whispered.

"Yes?" Rose grunted as she balanced the heavy frame in her hands.

"This stuff is real."

"Yeah, I know," she replied as she looked behind the frame and tried to line up the wire hanger to the nail on the wall.

"No . . . Mom. I mean . . . this is real," Bianca repeated her words slowly.

"Ah, I see where this is going." Rose smiled. She carefully let go of the frame and stepped back to make sure it was straight. "Don't worry, a lot of this stuff is harmless, but maybe I'll give you the unofficial tour once we're closed."

"That would be great."

"Does it look straight to you?" Rose murmured.

Bianca tilted her head left and right as she studied the newly framed piece of art. "It looks good to me," she replied.

"Works for me."

At six o'clock, they closed the doors of the museum. They went through their usual routine and made sure they didn't have any stowaways in the building.

"I'll be right back. I gotta grab something from my office," Rose said.

"Okey dokey."

When Rose returned, she had a large brown leather book in her hands. Together, they went into the Snow White Room, stopping in front of a portrait of the room's namesake. Bianca studied the painting. Snow White stared back at her with indigo-colored eyes and the ghost of a smile, as though she had just told the artist a dirty joke and was doing everything she could to remain composed.

Rose took a deep breath and whispered, "This is harder than I thought."

"Are you okay?"

"Yeah . . . I'm okay. I just . . . I always expected your father to be here when the time came to tell you about your family history."

Bianca teared up at the mention of her father. She wasn't sure she could get used to talking about her father as though it were perfectly normal to do so.

She looked at her beautiful mother and noticed the white hairs scattered over her bright red hair. The fine lines on the corners of her eyes. Bianca realized for the first time how tired Rose looked.

Has she always looked like that and I just failed to notice? Or is it that Mom is really good at hiding how she feels from everyone . . . even me?

Rose pulled Bianca out of her thoughts when she said, "I really need you to pay attention to everything that I say to you from this moment forward. If Lenore attacks again, I want you to be ready. I need you to be ready, in case I'm not around. Your grandmother killed Lenore's mother, Gertrude, but what no one suspected was that she would throw a death curse at my mother with her dying breath." Rose looked into Bianca's eyes and gently said, "The good guys don't always win."

Bianca's stomach dropped. This was becoming more and more real by the second. She took a deep breath and prepared herself for what came next.

"Anyway . . . this is your great-great-great-grandmother . . . Snow White."

"She's my what?" How was that possible? There was no way that Bianca was a descendant of the most beautiful woman in the world.

Bianca gazed up at the portrait, half expecting it to come to life.

Snow White wasn't real, it's a fairy tale. Stories that happened in a different time and in a different world. At least that's what Bianca kept saying to herself over and over again.

Rose and Bianca sat down on the floor in front of the portrait. Rose softly touched the edge of the book she had brought down from her office. On the cover, in Old English gold lettering, it said Our Family. The book also had gold edging; it was beautiful. Priceless.

"Whoa," Bianca whispered. "May I?"

Rose handed the book to her daughter. Bianca carefully took the tome in her hands and placed it on her lap, then opened it ever so carefully. The very first page was a piece of tissue paper. She turned the page and hiding behind the tissue paper was Snow White. It a professional portrait like the one hanging on the wall of the museum, but instead it was a drawing done in pencil. The Snow White looking back at her was slightly older but still strong, proud, and confident. The look in Snow White's eyes told Bianca that she could do anything if she just believed in herself.

Underneath the drawing was information about her.

Snow White von Waldeck

Born January 14th, 1750 in Everafter.

Snow White married Frederic von Waldeck on October 8th, 1770 in Brussels. She bore him four children: Mason, Leonard, Grace, and Katina.

Died July 20th, 1830.

"Everafter?" Bianca felt a world of confusion, which was probably evident on her face.

"It's where she's from. Where a lot of the fairy tales you've read took place," Rose explained.

"But . . . how?"

"Long ago, people sometimes would wander into fairy rings and go to another world . . . almost like a portal. And sometimes fairies would come into our world, steal human babies, and take them to their world to raise them as their own. Eventually there were enough humans in Everafter to populate that small world. The humans created their own kingdoms and villages, much to the fairies' annoyance. They didn't like the humans taking over their world, so they would often play tricks on the royals and local folk. Sometimes . . . with tragic endings.

"The Brothers Grimm accidentally stepped into a fairy ring and it was during their stay in Everafter that they collected all of their stories. In fact, the whole 'and they lived happily ever after' is a typo. It's supposed to be 'and they lived happily in Everafter.' Anyway, some of the people from Everafter followed the two brothers here to our world."

"Really? Like who?"

"Snow White, obviously." Rose pointed to the book. "Rapunzel, Jack from Jack and the Beanstalk, Briar Rose, and a few others."

"But . . . why?"

"The fae aren't necessarily known for their kindness, Bianca. Life in Everafter isn't easy. The men and women who came here wanted normal and peaceful lives. Some got it . . . others weren't so lucky."

"How so?"

"Magic will follow you no matter where you are. Magic has no boundaries."

"Is that what happened to Snow White? Magic followed her here?" Bianca studied the artist's depiction of her ancestor.

"Yes," Rose replied.

She suddenly felt very sad for Snow White. A lifetime of searching for peace, and she never got it. Bianca felt tears stinging her eyes . . . she silently cried for her. She wondered if Snow White had found the peace she was looking for when she passed away . . . or had the magic followed her into the afterlife, too?

Bianca wiped her tears away and turned her attention back to the book. Inside the book were portraits and photographs of everyone in the family. But other than a birthday, number of children and date of death there wasn't much more information.

"Why isn't there more about her in the book?"

"In case it should fall into the wrong hands. We wouldn't want anyone else knowing all of our most intimate secrets or our weaknesses," Rose explained.

Bianca turned to the page that had Grandmother Alice's photograph. The woman looking back at her had a hard face, almost as though she had never smiled a day in her life. Bianca made it her mission to remember the woman staring back at her. There were no pictures of Alice in her house. Her dark brown hair was gathered into a loose bun. She had thin, stern lips. Bianca marveled over the fact that her beautiful, caring mother had come out of someone who seemed so completely joyless. She read the notes below the image.

Alice Phillips. Born October 11th, 1940 in Newark, Delaware.

Married Victor Phillips on July 14th, 1970 in Wilmington, Delaware. She bore him a daughter they named Rose Red.

Died April 25th, 1994.

"I think there should be more in this book besides birthday, who was married to whom, how many children he or she had and when they died. How can you put someone's life into a single page like that? It just seems unfair." Bianca closed the book.

"That's why the journals are kept in the safe," Rose said.

Bianca turned to Rose with a huge grin on her face. "Journals? Did Snow White keep a journal?"

"She sure did." Rose smiled.

"And everyone else in the family?"

"Some were more diligent than others, but yeah we have everyone's journal. One of these days you can sit and read them all. I'm still working my way through them."

"Wow." Bianca was eager to read Snow White's journal. She was dying to know the true story . . . what really happened to her. Were there really seven dwarves? What did the prince look like? Was he really handsome? Was he kind? What happened to her after happily ever after?

She glanced at the poisoned apple. It was the most beautiful shade of red she had ever seen. It was no wonder Snow White had been tempted to take a bite.

"Is that really the apple that almost killed her? I always thought it was a fake." Bianca pointed at the red apple on display.

"Trust me . . . it's real. Don't worry though . . . lots of people think it's fake."

"But . . . how has it stayed intact for so long?" She stared at the bright red apple with a mixture of fear and awe.

"Magic. It's a very good stasis spell."

"Who cast it?"

"Snow White cast the spell the first time around. She wanted to keep it to remember how close she had been to death. She wanted to remind others that life was fragile. Of course, the spell wears off once you pass away, so the task of casting a new stasis spell falls on the daughter or granddaughter. The next in line to inherit this history, the museum, and all the trouble that follows along with it," Rose said.

Bianca thought she heard a bit of spitefulness in her mother's last phrase. She nodded, understanding the importance of the items in this room. This was her heritage and her inheritance. She stood up and took a closer look at the items on display in the Snow White Room.

In another display case, Bianca saw the poisoned comb. It was made out of fourteen carat gold. It was adorned with oval-shaped amethysts and emeralds. Each sharp tooth on the comb had been soaked with poison. It was the comb that the evil queen had used to try to kill Snow White.

How can something so beautiful be so deadly? Bianca wondered.

There was another glass case that had a small tree made of bronze wires. The metal tree was covered with ribbons. Their color had faded many, many years ago. They no longer looked vibrant and eager to be used. The ribbons hung limply on the bronze branches as though ashamed of the way they had been used.

Rose and Bianca walked to yet another item displayed in glass. In it were seven little bowls, cups and eating utensils. Bianca was looking at everything with new eyes. These things before her were no longer just tiny and cute and possibly made in China. They were proof that there was true magic in the world.

"How much of the story is true?" Bianca looked to her mother.

"Almost everything except the ending," Rose said.

"The prince didn't wake her up with a kiss?"

"There was a prince, but he woke her up with a spell, not a kiss. Although . . . I'm sure there was some kissing afterward."

"The prince was a wizard?" Bianca giggled as she imagined the prince wearing a wizard's hat.

Rose rolled her eyes. "No, but he found another very powerful sorcerer who could wake up Snow White and undo the evil queen's magic."

"Did they know each other?"

"No. The prince heard about her because of the dwarves. The seven brothers put her in a glass coffin because they weren't convinced that she was actually dead. They took turns traveling across the country, searching for someone who could break the spell. Six of them stood guard while one searched." Rose took a deep breath. "It was the seventh brother who found the prince who would eventually wake up Snow White from her slumber."

"What happened once Snow White woke up?"

"Well . . . she was angry, to say the least. Mostly at herself for eating the apple. She felt very foolish. She, of course, went after Queen Mirabel and defeated her. To complete the humiliation, she forced her to wear hot iron shoes to walk herself to the executioner. Pretty gruesome, don't you think? Forcing someone to drag their burned and blistered feet to meet their death?"

"But if she was powerful enough to defeat her, why didn't she do it the first time around? Why did she run away at all?"

"Snow White was a little girl when she ran away. She was only twelve or thirteen years old when her emerging beauty caused the queen to go mad with jealousy. She lived with the dwarves for several years in hiding, practicing her magic and growing stronger."

"Hang on . . . if Snow White defeated Mirabel, then who are we fighting now? Who have we been fighting all these years?"

"Ah. Good question. What Snow White didn't know was that the queen had an apprentice named Tara who swore to avenge Queen Mirabel."

"Well, that sucks."

"Yeah, and ever since then, we've been fighting each other. Daughters of Snow White fighting against Tara's daughters. Ruining each other's lives." Rose then sighed. "Such a waste."

Bianca was a little depressed after hearing the true story. It wasn't at all what she had expected, but then what seventeen-year-old expects to learn that fairy tales are real? Or that she was related to the most famous fairy tale princess in the world?

"Come on, I'll show you something else. I think you'll like this," Rose said.

Bianca nodded and followed her mother until they stopped in front of a seven-foot-long lock of Rapunzel's hair. It was the color of golden wheat, incredibly silky and thick. She knew this because her mother had let her touch it once when she was ten years old. When she was younger, she would take the hair out of the glass case, without her mother's permission, and play with it.

"Rapunzel isn't just some girl with really, really long hair," Rose said.

"Who was she really? Was there really a witch involved?"

"Oh, yes, everything in the story of Rapunzel is one hundred percent true. One little tidbit they left out of the story is that Rapunzel's hair was enchanted.

"A spell?"

Rose nodded. "Rapunzel's hair was always long . . . but it needed the witch's help to get long enough to reach her at the bottom of the tower."

"That's nuts," Bianca whispered.

"You think that's nuts? Wait till you hear this. The spell on Rapunzel's hair never died after the witch cut off her hair."

"Really?"

Rose unlocked the glass case and pulled out the long blond braid.

"*Rapunzel, Rapunzel, Let down your hair, So that I may climb, The golden stair,*" Rose chanted the spell and then threw the hair across the floor, and before a single lock of hair touched the black and white marble floor, it grew four times in length.

"What the—" Bianca's eyebrows shot up in surprise.

"Pretty cool, huh? I've climbed all the way up to the roof with this thing. Trust me, nothing can cut it. Not scissors, not a knife, and it won't burn. It's basically indestructible."

"But how did the witch cut off Rapunzel's hair if it's supposed to be indestructible?"

"Magic, obviously."

Rose chanted another spell. Bianca was lost in thought and didn't pay any attention to what her mother was saying or doing. By the time she snapped out of it, Rose had put the hair back inside the glass case.

"What else is there?"

"Follow me." Rose had that twinkle in her eyes that let Bianca know she was in for the night of her life.

Bianca followed Rose up to the attic.

"Why are we up here?" Bianca waited as Rose closed the door behind them. A tiny moth flew around Bianca's hair. She gently swatted it away as she searched for a place to sit in the tiny and cramped attic.

"It's not wise to put everything we own out on display. Some things really should be kept secret," Rose said.

"Oh."

Rose opened a huge cedar trunk and pulled out several items. Among one of the items was a small jar filled with pumpkin seeds.

"Guess." Rose held the jar in front of Bianca for closer inspection.

Bianca took it in her hands and peered inside. "Umm . . . really old pumpkin seeds?"

Rose arched an eyebrow and pursed her lips. "Please be a bit more imaginative."

Then it dawned on Bianca what the seeds were. She gasped. "Holy crap! Are these from Cinderella's pumpkin? The one that the fairy godmother turned into a coach?"

"Bingo," Rose replied with a wink.

"What do they do?"

"They turn into a coach when you put them on the ground. All you have to do is add water."

"That is so cool." Bianca dove into the open trunk and rummaged through it. "What else is in here?"

Bianca felt something so soft it made her gasp in surprise. *What's this?* she wondered as she pulled out the item in question. It was blood red and made out of a rich velvet cloth. "Is this what I think it is?" Bianca whispered. She studied the fabric and then she realized that what she held in her hands was indeed Red Riding Hood's cape. "Why isn't this on display?"

"Honestly? I don't know. I think there's a reason why it's been hiding in this trunk all these years. I've left the museum pretty much intact. Not much has changed since my mother passed away."

"Does it do anything? I mean, besides look really awesome?" Bianca tried on the famous red cape. She loved how it felt over her shoulders. Soft, but heavy, almost like armor. She now understood why Red Riding Hood had felt safe in the middle of the dark and dangerous forest. Why she had felt brave enough to fight a wolf. Why she wore this cape everywhere she went.

"If I'm not mistaken . . . " Rose's words brought Bianca back to the present. "I think it shows you which path to take. The safest and quickest way to your destination."

"Awesome," Bianca whispered as she took off the cape and carefully folded it before putting it back inside the trunk. There were other things that caught her eye. Among the items in the trunk were a coat made of different types of fur, three dresses, and the golden ring.

"This coat smells weird." Bianca wrinkled her nose as she sniffed the coat.

"Yeah, it still smells a little like onions and soot. Nothing I can do about it though." Rose shrugged.

Bianca pulled out a gold dress. It looked as though someone had beaten sheets of gold into a fabric so soft it made silk feel like bark from a tree. The dress shimmered and sparkled so much it would've put the sun to shame.

Bianca caressed the dress with her fingertips. She couldn't believe the story was true, yet . . . here was the proof. She pulled another dress out and this one was made entirely out of silver. It was just as soft as the golden dress, if such a thing were even possible. It was as bright as the full moon in a midnight sky. The third and final dress was made of dark blue velvet, and upon closer inspection Bianca could see tiny diamonds stitched into the velvet fabric.

"This is beautiful."

"I think those all belonged to Allerleirauh," Rose explained.

"Who?"

Rose smiled and repeated the name slowly. "Allerleirauh, it means All-Kinds-of-Fur or Thousand-furs. The story is a little similar to Cinderella except that Allerleirauh's father tried to marry his daughter, and there was no fairy godmother to help her out of that sticky situation . . . also no glass slipper. She was a clever girl and used her own wits to save herself. I like her story."

"Interesting," Bianca muttered as she found another item that tied the three dresses and the fur coat together. It was a thick gold ring. Bianca studied it and found that there was something engraved inside the band.

"I do," Bianca read aloud.

"Hmm?"

"It says, 'I do' in this ring," Bianca explained as she handed the ring to her mother so she could see.

Rose smiled as she looked at the engraved words.

"So?" Bianca encouraged her mother.

"So what?"

"So . . . what's the story behind this ring?" Bianca waited eagerly for her mother to answer her question.

"I don't know," she replied.

"Come on, Mom. You can tell me."

"I'm not kidding. I don't know why it says 'I do' in this ring."

"What a rip off," Bianca muttered.

Rose chuckled and told Bianca there was no way for one person to know every story ever written in the world. Bianca was still disappointed that her mother didn't know about the ring.

"What's this?" Bianca pulled a maroon-colored brick out of the trunk.

"Ooooh." Rose's eyes twinkled with excitement. "Follow me."

Rose grabbed the brick with one hand and with the other, she took Bianca's hand. Rose pulled Bianca up to her feet before she could utter a word in protest. They left the attic, wound their way through the museum to the backyard. Bianca looked up at the sky; it was starting to get dark. She could already see some stars beginning to peep through. It was one of those rare, cool summer nights.

"Okay, you might want to take a few steps back," Rose warned.

Bianca frowned, but she knew better than to ask too many questions and followed her mother's instructions.

"*Not by the hair of my chiny, chin, chin,*" Rose chanted the spell. The brick glowed with a lovely shade of red-orange and moments later it multiplied itself over and over again. It looked as though a hundred invisible hands were putting together a small building at rapid speeds. Within moments, a cottage had been built.

"What the what?" Bianca walked around the tiny home. Every brick had been perfectly placed, windows, a door, and a chimney. Bianca touched it . . . wondering if it was all an illusion, but no, it was warm to the touch and radiating a homey energy. Safe. That's how she felt being nearby. "What is . . . I mean . . . seriously? A brick house?" she stammered.

"Not just any brick house. This was the house of the third little pig."

"Awesome." It was a very simple house with one window and one door. "Can I go inside?"

"Yeah, just a heads-up though, only the person who cast the spell can open the door." Rose pointed at the brick house's door. "No one else can come inside unless you allow it."

"Not even if you huff and puff?" Bianca joked.

"Not even if you use a machine gun. Trust me, my dad tried it once. Nothing will go in."

"That's so cool."

Rose opened the door and together mother and daughter stepped inside the small brick house. There was a tiny bed, a rocking chair next to the fireplace, and a small stove. Everything a person could need. Bianca was amazed by its simplicity.

"Um, where's the bathroom?" She noticed the lack of a toilet.

"Back in the day, they did their business outside or in a latrine if they were lucky," Rose explained.

"Ew," Bianca said. "How come there's only one bed?"

"The brick thinks I'm alone. You have to hold hands with the person or people who are with you."

"The brick *thinks*?"

"You'd be surprised what else it can do." Rose chuckled.

"How do you make it go back to being a brick?"

"Watch and learn."

Rose plucked a single strand of red hair from her head and tied it around the doorknob. In the blink of an eye, the small brick house reverted back to its original single brick.

Bianca's eyebrows shot up in surprise.

"Well . . . I don't have hairs on my chin, thank God . . . so this is the best I can do, and it works, which is all that matters. Anyway, I think this concludes Part One of the museum tour." Rose gave a s soft smile to Bianca. "I'm starting to get hungry. Time to take a short dinner break."

"Aw, man," Bianca whined.

"Don't worry, we can go over some more things tomorrow," Rose promised.

"Okay."

Rose checked the time on her watch and gasped. "Holy mackerel, it's getting late. Come on, let's go home."

"What time is it?"

"It's a quarter after seven. Hungry?"

"Starving." Bianca admitted.

"Come on. We'll get tacos on our way home."

"Sounds good to me."

Bianca was halfway done eating her chicken burrito when she said, "You know . . . I've been thinking. I can understand where the Snow White stuff comes from, but . . . how do you explain all the other items in the museum?"

Rose chewed her food and then swallowed before answering Bianca's question. "When the museum opened its doors in nineteen twenty-one, all we had were the items you see in the Snow White Room and a few of the things in the Wicked Wing. Little by little, people sold or donated items to the museum. A lot of people thought the items were cursed, so they were happy to get rid of them. Lucky for us, Great Grandma Frances was very good at calming the items down."

"Calming them down?"

"Well, you can't disenchant them because then they wouldn't be magical. All she did was put the more dangerous items in a magical form of sleep. You know what I mean?"

"Yeah, I think so."

"Anyway, Frances opened the museum. I'm sure you skimmed through her picture in the book I showed you this evening. If not, I have a box full of old photos—you can also see what the museum looked like when it opened its doors."

"I don't understand," Bianca said. "Why not keep all this secret? Why put these things on display at all?"

"The family was broke. They lost everything during the Great Depression. They were going to lose the house. They had children to take care of. Her husband lost his job as a professor at the local university, and they were running out of ideas. She knew about all the treasures she had in the attic, so she decided to open a part of the house to the public and charge half a penny to anyone who could afford it. Those who couldn't pay would barter their goods or services. She was able to feed her family and get a lot of repairs made on their house. Lots of people wanted to see Snow White's items, if only to forget about life for a while," Rose said. "They didn't care whether they were real or not. People drove for miles just to come and visit the 'Fairy Tale Museum' as they lovingly called it back then. When Great Grandma Frances had enough money to save the house, she let people come in for free once a week. Once the Great Depression was over, she started acquiring newer items for the museum."

"How?"

"She went to Europe a lot. There was a lot of stuff there, especially in Ireland. The fairies love it there for some reason. And then after World War II, a lot of soldiers came back with items they had found. They would go to Great Grandma Frances and sell the items, not knowing what they were. They only wanted the money, and she paid well for those items." Rose finished off her taco. "Word spread quickly that she was purchasing unusual items, and that's how we got a lot of the things that are in the museum now."

"Wow."

"Yeah, it's amazing what you can learn when you sit down and read the journals. Everyone who ran the museum kept a journal. Great Grandma Frances, Grandma Paulette, Aunt Rosie, my mother, and now me. Hopefully you'll run it when you're ready to take over the reins."

Bianca nodded. She had never thought she would ever want to run the museum when her mother passed away. She had wanted to live a life that was her own, not a hand-me-down of her ancestors. But now that she knew and understood the history of the museum, she would never be able to sell the place or let anyone else run it.

She was beginning to understand why Rose had the "family only" rule when it came to working the museum.

Who else but family would understand?

6

THE NEXT THREE WEEKS passed by in a blur as Bianca learned everything Rose knew about magic and their family history. She learned that Rose still used chants and incantations to call upon her magic. It was a crutch but that was all Rose knew. Bianca was learning how to use her own energy to call upon her magic. It took a lot longer, but it was getting easier for her to concentrate and focusing on specific memories.

Bianca knew that the next attack would come soon by the way Rose was constantly looking over her shoulder and the way she tensed up whenever she heard a loud sound. The last thing they needed was to fall into a false sense of security.

One night while Rose and Bianca were eating dinner, a huge brick sailed through the window. Glass rained all over the hardwood floor.

"What the hell?" Rose stood up and ran to the window.

Bianca followed closely behind her mother. Rose studied the brick without touching it. Then, with a flash of light, the brick turned into a bright red snake. Rose took a step toward it and the snake hissed at her, baring its sharp white fangs and recoiled as though it were getting ready to spring at her. Rose narrowed her emerald green eyes at it. To Bianca her mother was a lioness trying to protect her home and her young.

Bianca gasped and took a step back. Just as the snake was about to lunge at Rose, she muttered a spell, waved her right hand, and used her magic to turn the snake into a handful of roses. She stared at the shadow standing outside her house.

Bianca followed her mother's steady gaze and found Lenore's pale and haunting face glaring at them. Bianca was taken aback by the anger and hatred that was evident on their enemy's face. Thanks to the wards Rose had set on their home, there was no way that Lenore could physically enter and wreak havoc inside the house. Other items? That was an entirely different matter.

"Bianca, go upstairs," Rose whispered.

"But, Mom—"

"Now, Bianca," Rose said in a loud, firm voice that Bianca rarely heard.

Mother and daughter looked into each other's eyes for a moment. She felt ready to fight alongside her mother and actually be of some assistance. Bianca wanted to argue with Rose, but instead she reluctantly obeyed and went upstairs. She made it as far as the top of the steps.

"Come out, you coward!" Lenore shouted.

If there was one thing Bianca knew for sure, it was that her mother would never, ever back out of a fight. She slowly inched her way down the stairs. Rose stepped out of the house, moving far away from the safety of her wards. Bianca tried to call as little attention to herself as humanly possible. She duck-walked across the living room until she was directly underneath the broken window, peeking now and then to watch her mother in action.

"Where's the book?" Lenore barked.

"Where is my husband?" Rose demanded.

"How about we make a trade? Your husband for the book."

Rose remained silent. Bianca knew that somewhere in her mother's mind she was seriously considering trading whatever book Lenore was talking about for her father.

"You're not getting anywhere near that book," Rose replied.

Lenore snarled and contorted her face in anger as she created a fireball and threw it at Rose.

Her mother muttered a spell as she threw her hands up, creating a wall of water around her, and the fireball vanished with a loud hiss. She then used the water that surrounded her and attacked her adversary.

Lenore used an ice spell and froze the water, causing it to crash around her with soft clinks.

"You have to learn to control your brat. I can smell her better now that she's downstairs," Lenore said with a cackle.

"You shut your filthy mouth about my daughter," Rose shouted.

"Want to come out and play, little one?" Lenore taunted.

"Bianca! Stay inside the house. Do you hear me?"

"Mom, let me help," Bianca pleaded.

"You do as I say!" Rose snapped.

Bianca's heart skipped a beat as she ducked underneath the window. She knew she was safe inside the house because of the wards. Bianca risked a peek at the battle. The two were fighting viciously, doing everything in their power to destroy each other with their spells.

At one point, Lenore had Rose trapped in a small tornado. Bianca saw her mother's bright red hair whipping in every direction imaginable as Rose struggled to counter the spell. It was enough time for the dark witch to reach in and take something out of her pocket. Lenore pulled out a tiny glass vial and drank a black potion that swam inside the container.

What is *that*?

Lenore flashed her sharp yellowed teeth at Bianca, then turned her attention to Rose. Bianca gazed at her mother—she had finally countered Lenore's tornado spell. Before Rose could cast her next spell, Lenore took a deep breath then blew black fire at Rose. The dark flames took the shape of a sinister dragon. It narrowed its yellow eyes at Rose, its chosen target, and slithered its way toward her.

Bianca gasped. She had never seen anything so menacing in her life. It launched itself at her mother and wrapped around her body. Rose struggled to free herself from the black dragon but nothing she did worked. It had a firm grip on her and wouldn't let her go. The dragon pried Rose's mouth open and shoved its clawed hand down her throat. When it pulled its dark claws out of her mouth, Bianca saw that the creature held a tiny ball of turquoise light between its thumb and index finger.

"No!" Bianca shouted. The blood in her veins froze, her stomach dropped, and her heart leaped to her throat. She watched in horror as her mother did everything she could to fight off Lenore's monster . . . and failed. The dragon let out a chuckle and vanished with the light it had taken from Rose.

"Mom!" Bianca dashed to the front door and stopped herself from running into the front yard.

Lenore kicked Rose in the stomach and grabbed a fistful of her red hair. The smoke dragon had taken away Rose's voice and with it . . . her magic. She was now mute. She looked like a fish out of water as she tried to cast a counter spell, but it was no use. The damage had been done. Her mother had lost her voice and the battle. Rose turned to Bianca, and for the first time she saw actual fear in her mother's green eyes.

"There, now we can have a little chat . . . no interruptions. Come on out here and sit with me a while." The false saccharine in her voice was obvious.

Rose shook her head violently. Bianca knew what her mother wanted her to do. She wasn't sure she could obey Rose's request to stay inside the house now that her mother was in danger of losing her life.

I can't just sit here and do nothing. God . . . what do I do? What do I do?

"Come here!" Lenore roared as her face contorted with rage, making her look uglier and older than she was. Lenore yanked on Rose's hair so hard she opened her mouth as though she were screaming . . . except no sound came out of her lips.

Bianca tried to remember everything she had learned with Rose. She tried to concentrate on a spell, a thought, anything that could help her mother. She closed her eyes and tried to conjure up a fire spell . . . or anything that would work for her at the moment.

Lenore laughed. "You're joking. All right, I'll play. Let's see what you're made of."

Bianca thought her heart was going to burst out of her chest. She took several deep breaths before stepping out of her house and into the front yard. She put every thought, every ounce of energy she had into her hands, just like Rose had taught her.

"Humph. Looks like I have to crush a little fly," Lenore said to Rose. "Don't go anywhere." She muttered a spell and vines sprouted from the ground, covering Rose's body.

Rose struggled to free herself, but the more she fought the tighter the vines held on to her.

Bianca took a deep breath and opened herself to the magic that coursed through her veins. Without realizing what she had unlocked within herself, she was suddenly able to feel everything around her: the grass beneath her feet, the wind flowing all around her, the blood rushing through Lenore's body, and her mother's beating heart. Bianca's breath quickened. She didn't understand any of what she was feeling. What did it mean? This was without a doubt a brand-new sensation to her, one she wished wasn't happening in the middle of her first real fight. She wanted so desperately to be able to speak to her mother about what she was experiencing and why, but it would have to wait for another day. If she succeeded, then she and Rose would be able to speak about it that same night.

Bianca wasted no time. She attacked. She threw every spell she could think of at Lenore.

The witch was able to deflect Bianca's spells, save for one, which hit her squarely in the chest. It knocked her down momentarily. Lenore snarled as she got up, showing off row after row of yellowed crooked teeth.

A shiver ran down Bianca's spine as her eyes locked with Lenore's. She had never seen anyone so devoid of humanity and compassion. This wasn't a woman anymore; this creature before her was more monster than human.

Bianca used a fire spell and instead of directing it at Lenore, she threw the spell at the vines that had ensnared her mother. The vines were ablaze within moments. Rose was free, but it was short lived. As soon as Rose got up, Lenore leapt and landed on top of her knocking them both on the ground. Lenore tried to claw Rose's eyes out, but she grabbed the evil witch's wrists, and they struggled with each other for what felt like an eternity.

Bianca grabbed the shovel that rested on the fence and hit Lenore on the back. The witch howled but kept her attention on Rose. The hatred she had for Bianca's mother oozed out of her. If she hadn't been thrashing as she was, Bianca was certain she could touch the feelings that surrounded Lenore. Bianca was ready to strike her once more, but all of a sudden she was blinded by a bright green flash that knocked her back several feet.

Bianca landed gracelessly on the ground with a heavy thud.

"Not bad, little one. But I don't have time to play with you anymore," Lenore said.

Lenore muttered a spell under her breath and opened a portal. A swirl of shadows sucked up what little light there was around them.

"Find the spell book and you will get your mother back, though I can't guarantee she'll be in one piece when you do," she said, dragging Rose by her hair.

"No! Wait! I don't know where it is," Bianca shouted. She tried to stand up, but her legs gave out. She was still trying to recover from the impact of being thrown several feet in the air.

"Find it," Lenore snapped.

"No!" Bianca shouted as she struggled to walk toward the portal. Her knees buckled several times as she fought to reach Rose. But the portal closed before she could go through it and save her mother.

"Oh, God. What do I do? What do I do?" Bianca muttered.

Losing all sensation in her legs, she fell to the ground, unable to do anything except breathe. The night felt colder, the crickets seemed to mock her. She looked up at the sky and the stars laughed at her. They no longer seemed to wink at her playfully like she had always thought as a child.

Everything just seemed wrong, distorted, and ruined, as though she were in an alternate universe.

Then she heard a little tinkling sound. It took her a moment to realize that it was her cellphone ringing. Her fingers were numb as she pulled it out of her pocket.

She answered it. "Hello."

"Hey, B. Did you wanna come over and watch some more Sailor Moon? My mom bought popcorn and I think there are still some Sour Patch Kids from the last time you were here."

It was Ming.

"Ming, I can't . . . I can't go anywhere right now." Bianca didn't even know how to explain what had happened.

"What's wrong?"

"Mom . . . Mom's been kidnapped."

"What? By who? Have you called the police?" Ming shrieked.

All of these were valid questions, only Bianca didn't know how to answer any of them.

"I can't call the police. They won't find her. I don't even know where to start looking for her."

"Umm . . . have you seen CSI? They can find anyone."

"This isn't a TV show, Ming." Bianca tried very hard not to scream at her friend.

"Sorry, just trying to help. Why would someone kidnap your mom? She wouldn't hurt a fly," she said.

"You wouldn't believe me if I told you." Never in a million years, did Bianca think she would ever have to use that sentence.

"I'm your best friend. If you can't tell me, who can you tell?"

Bianca remained silent as she thought about whether she should tell Ming everything.

"Helloooo? Bianca? You still there? I can hear you breathing."

"Fine. You wanna know what happened?"

"Yes, please."

"A witch took my mother. A freaking evil witch took my mom and told me she'd kill her if I don't give her a spell book. And to top it off? I don't know where the stupid book is, so my mom may as well be dead!"

Her confession was met with silence. "Hello? Ming?"

"Sorry. Yeah . . . umm . . . I'll be right over."

"Okay, but come alone," Bianca said.

"Okay."

Bianca looked at the spot where her mother had vanished. There were black singe marks where Lenore had attacked Rose using her fireballs and the second singe mark from where Bianca had used fire to free her mother. It'd worked, but the more she thought about it, the more she wondered if it would have changed anything had she just let her mother free herself. She cried out in frustration. No matter how she played it out in her mind, she still would've done everything the exact same way.

Even though she had seen it happen firsthand, she still couldn't believe it. How could Rose be there one moment and gone the next. Poof! Just like that. Gone.

"This can't be real," she whispered.

Bianca closed her eyes tightly and thought to herself, *Wake up. Wake up from this nightmare. Mom is gone. Dad is gone. I'm all alone. Wake up. This has to be a nightmare. Wake up!*

She opened her eyes and half expected to appear in her bed with the bright morning sun shooing all the bad things back into their hiding places. Instead, all she saw was the pale moon hanging overhead, reminding her of the things that were wrong in the world.

She went inside and waited for Ming to arrive. The house felt empty and vacant of the love and soul that made it a home. Without her mother, the house was nothing but walls and a roof.

Everywhere she looked she was reminded of her mother's absence. Helpless. That was how she felt, completely and utterly helpless. She had no one to turn to. No one to tell her what she should do next. No one to tell her that everything would be okay. She burst into tears and sobbed, her body folding itself in half. She watched as her tears pooled on the hardwood floor. After what seemed like hours, she finally heard Ming's car pull up on the driveway.

She wiped her tears away and tried to pull herself together. Ming turned the car off, and Bianca heard her friend's footsteps as she ran to the front door. Before she could lift her hand to knock, Bianca opened the door and urged her best friend inside the house. Bianca locked the door behind them, then she fell into Ming's arms. Ming hugged Bianca and did her best to sooth her dearest and oldest friend.

"What happened?" Ming pulled away from Bianca's arms.

Bianca wiped her tears away again and after gaining her composure told Ming everything that had happened. Ming remained quiet and listened to Bianca intently. But Ming's eyebrows slowly climbed higher and higher as Bianca told her story. They got high enough that they almost reached Ming's hairline by the time Bianca finally finished speaking.

"That's just . . . " Ming struggled to find the right word.

"Incredible?" Bianca said.

"Crazy. This is just twenty different kinds of crazy, B. I mean . . . I believe you because there's no way you'd make something like this up, but that's all I can say about it."

"Yeah . . . it's definitely crazy." Bianca agreed.

"What do we do now?"

Bianca looked at the clock on the living room wall. It was already eleven. She was bruised and dirty. Every bone in her body ached. Her head was pounding, and her temples throbbed. She kept massaging them, hoping that it would somehow help to ease the pain, but it was hopeless. Besides it wasn't like she could go lie down and sleep it off, she had work to do.

"Right now? I gotta cover that broken window with a tarp or something and I need to tear this house apart and find that book."

"Well . . . I'm gonna help you."

"Really?"

"Of course," Ming said.

"Thanks." Bianca smiled.

"Do you want me to stay the night?"

Bianca nodded. She didn't want to be alone in the house. Not after everything that had happened. Even with Ming close by, she was terrified. Every noise made her want to leap out of her skin. Then the air conditioner turned itself on, making the loud clanking sound it did whenever it started. Bianca flinched and began to tremble. She shoved her hands into her pockets to see if that would help her stop trembling, but it didn't do a thing.

Ming gently patted Bianca on the shoulder, whispering, "It's just the AC. Calm down."

"Sorry, it's just . . . you didn't see it happen. You have no idea what I'm up against." Bianca rubbed her arms to try to get rid of the goose bumps that riddled her skin.

"Don't worry, we'll figure it out." Ming tried to reassure her.

Bianca wished she could make Ming understand, but she didn't have the patience at that moment.

"You wanna call your mom?"

"Nah, I already told her I'd crash here."

"Thanks." Bianca did her best to smile.

"No problem. That's what best friends are for."

Ming went to her car and grabbed her overnight bag. Bianca remembered that they had an old black tarp at the bottom of the pantry from the last time they'd painted the living room. She grabbed a roll of duct-tape and together they taped the old paint spattered tarp to the broken window. Bianca double-checked the doors and windows to make sure everything was locked. It was something her mother did every night before she went to bed. Bianca took some comfort in keeping that routine in place. She knew that the protective spell her mother placed on the house would keep them safe for a while.

Bianca threw herself on the couch and took a moment to catch her breath. She thought about where the book could be. Where should she start looking? What did it even look like? These thoughts plagued her mind.

What if I don't find the book? What happens then? What if Mom dies because I failed? I'll be an orphan. I'll be all alone. What will happen then?

The thought of being an orphan terrified her. Losing her father had been awful, but it was bearable because at least she still had her mother. But losing Rose? She couldn't bear to think of that for a single moment. She was going to find her mother . . . no matter what. Her mind was filled with questions, worries, and other random thoughts.

Eventually . . . sleep found her. She didn't even realize it had happened. Her face slumped on the armrest. Her black hair fanned across her eyes like a makeshift mask. That night she dreamt of dying animals, a tangle of spider webs, and Lenore's cruel laughter.

7

BIANCA WOKE WITH A start. She looked around . . . confused. She had a cranberry red blanket draped over her. It slid off her body as she sat up and rubbed her eyes. She glanced out the window and saw that it was still dark. The neon green numbers on the Blu Ray player told her that it was five o'clock in the morning. Ming had made herself at home, falling asleep right next to her. Bianca smiled when she saw that Ming was using her pink Hello Kitty sleeping bag.

Bianca groaned, unable to believe that she had let herself fall asleep when they had so much work to do. She rolled her neck and shoulders, doing her best to get rid of the kinks from having fallen asleep at such an odd angle, not to mention being thrown around by Lenore.

"Ming," she whispered.

"Hmm?"

"Ming, wake up."

"Five more minutes," Ming muttered and then turned to her side.

"Fine. Five more minutes and then we need to start looking for that book."

"Okey dokey."

While Ming slept, Bianca went into her mother's bedroom and did a quick search for the book. The more she thought about it, the less likely it seemed that the book would be in her house.

What would Mom do? "Hmm."

If I had my daughter in my house, I would do everything possible to keep her safe. So I would keep the book as far away from her as humanly possible.

And that was when Bianca knew that the book was at the museum. It was the only other place it could be.

As soon as the sun rose, Bianca and Ming went to the museum. Bianca figured it would be best to keep the museum open at least part time since it was their only source of income. She went through the motions of opening the museum while Ming sat behind the gift shop counter and stayed out of Bianca's way. This was fine with Bianca since she didn't have time to teach Ming the ropes of running the museum in such a short amount of time. Bianca turned on the cash register, turned on the lights and unlocked the front doors. For the first time in fifty years, there was no story time. Bianca waited until everyone arrived and gathered in the Princess Room to make the announcement.

She stood by the doorframe and listened to everyone's happy chatter. The kids were so excited about story time . . . they always were. And now Bianca had to go in and tell everyone that it wasn't happening today.

"Good morning, everyone," Bianca said.

"Good morning," everyone replied.

"Where's Miss Rose?" a little girl in the crowd asked.

"Umm, she's not coming today," Bianca replied nervously.

"Oh? What happened?" It was one of the moms.

"My grandmother is sick. My mom had to go away for a while and take care of her until she gets better," Bianca lied. She had practiced what she was going to say until it felt natural and almost true. Ming had even coached her while they'd driven to the museum that morning. Still . . . she could feel her cheeks burning as the lie slipped out of her mouth.

"Anyway . . . if you need anything, I'll be in the gift shop." Bianca then ran away as fast as she could before anyone could ask her any more questions. She tried to suppress the urge to cover her ears as they spoke to each other in hushed tones and the moms tried to soothe their disappointed children.

She hid behind the counter and groaned.

"You okay?" Ming was perched on the stool, reading a fashion magazine.

"This is a disaster. It feels so wrong to lie," Bianca whispered to Ming, who was happy to be behind the counter of the gift shop. Ming had wasted no time exploring every inch of the museum, especially now that Rose wasn't around to tell her not to touch anything.

"Well, what are you going to do? Tell the truth?" Ming closed the magazine and tucked it between the cash register and the wall.

"Yeah . . . like that's gonna happen any time this century. I may as well take myself to the psych ward."

"Do you want me to read the kids a story? How hard can it be?"

"Ming, have you ever had my mother tell you a story?"

"I don't think so."

"Trust me. They won't want anyone but her."

"Why?" Ming sounded confused.

"I don't even know how to describe how she does it. All I know is that she has a way of bringing stories to life. Almost as if she were playing a movie inside your head. She takes these fairy tales and adds more to them somehow. You can smell the river, see every leaf twitching in the wind, see the characters, and for a moment, it's almost as though you can feel what they are feeling."

"Wow."

"Yeah, it's hard to describe what it's like to be on the receiving end of that."

"I bet."

Bianca grabbed the phone book. It had a thin layer of dust over it. "Ew," she muttered as she picked up a rag and wiped the dust off.

"Whatcha lookin' for?"

"A repairman, I need to have the front window of my house fixed," Bianca replied as she flipped through the pages of the phonebook. Eventually, she came across an ad that looked somewhat professional. She grabbed the phone on the wall and dialed the number. Normally she would've used her cellphone to look it up, but this was how Rose usually looked up a really good handyman.

"Moore Repairs. If it's broken, we can fix it. This is Bill. How can I help you?"

"Yes . . . hi . . . I need to have the front window in my house repaired," Bianca said.

He asked several questions, and after a few minutes of talking back and forth, they settled on a day and the price to have her window fixed.

"Cool. Thank you so much," Bianca said politely.

"No problem. We'll send someone over tomorrow morning," Bill replied.

Bianca thanked him once more and then hung up.

"How are you going to pay for the window?"

"I know where Mom keeps her credit card. I'm authorized to use it, only if it's an emergency. I think this counts as an emergency."

A woman approached the counter and purchased a few items from the gift shop. Ming smiled, hopped off the stool, and scanned her items. Bianca was going to be sure to tell Rose about Ming helping her out in the museum. Maybe she would break her rule and let her work here.

"What did the witch want again? I forgot." Ming looked to Bianca after she finished taking care of the customer.

"A spell book."

"Why?"

"I think it belonged to Queen Mirabel. Mom told me that the witches we've been fighting all these years are descendants of the queen's apprentice. I'm guessing that the spell book belonged to her," Bianca explained.

"The one from Snow White . . . right?"

"Yep."

"Okay. Do you know where it is?"

"Nope."

"Then we have nothing else to bargain with," Ming said.

"Well, there are other things in the museum that belonged to the queen, but she specifically asked for the spell book," Bianca said.

"Is there an attic or a basement in this place?"

"Yeah, an attic and a basement."

"And you think it's hidden somewhere in the museum?"

"I know it's here somewhere," Bianca said.

Ming's chocolate brown eyes widened as a thought occurred to her. "Ooh, maybe there are clues to follow, like in *The DaVinci Code*."

"Except without Tom Hanks' weird hair."

"Yeah . . . no bad hair allowed." They both nodded in agreement.

"Okay, do we split up?" Bianca met Ming's eyes.

"Hell, no! I've seen enough horror movies to know that's a bad, bad idea. We stick together the entire time."

"Fair enough. I'm going to check in Mom's office and see if I find anything there. It should be safe enough with you here and the museum full of people."

"Don't you have walkie-talkies or anything like that just in case you see anything suspicious?"

"Umm . . . we have cell phones. They should be good enough for now."

"As long as you're okay with that," Ming said.

"All right. I'm gonna take a look around and if I don't find anything, we'll go to the attic together when I close the museum."

"Okey dokey. Oooh, look a wand! I'm totally buying this," Ming said as she picked up a pink, sparkly, plastic wand.

Bianca sighed. It was going to be a long day.

At four in the afternoon, they closed the doors of the museum, a couple of hours earlier than usual. Thankfully no one complained. Bianca locked the doors, counted the money in the cash register, and locked it in the safe underneath Rose's desk. Unfortunately, she hadn't found anything in her mother's office or in any other room in the museum, at least nothing that seemed like an obvious place to hide a really old spell book.

"Done?" Ming was waiting as Bianca stepped out of Rose's office.

"Almost. I have to set the alarm before we leave here tonight," Bianca said.

"Okay. I'll try to remind you." Ming promised.

Bianca went to the utility closet and grabbed two flashlights. She handed one to Ming and led the way up to the attic. She thought about the last time she had been that room. Rose and Bianca had explored one of the trunks and had found a treasure trove. She hoped that she would find what she was desperately searching for.

"So what does this book look like? Any idea?"

"I have no clue what it looks like." Bianca took a deep breath and added sarcastically, "This should be fun."

"Well . . . I'm sure it's not going to say Evil Queen's Spell Book on the cover of it. Right?"

"Right."

Bianca wondered why no one had recognized that Queen Mirabel was evil sooner. How was it that she had hidden her true nature for so many years? Most people can sense when there's something wrong with a person. Yet . . . Queen Mirabel was able to hide her intentions very well. The only one who saw right through the charade was Snow White.

Maybe that's why she hated Snow White so much. Maybe it had

nothing to do with Mirabel's jealousy of her beauty and everything to do with the fact that Snow White saw right through her.

"Right!" Bianca shouted.

"What?" Ming asked with a frown.

"It's not going to be some big creepy book. She was a queen. She needed to hide her true nature from her husband, the king, and everyone else. It has to be a book that looks harmless and possibly even . . . boring."

"Boring, huh?"

"Yeah."

"Ye Olde Knitting Book?" Ming joked.

Bianca giggled. "Probably something along those lines."

"Ye Olde Cooking Book?" Ming suggested.

"Ye Olde Cleaning Book."

They made more jokes that involved "Ye Olde" as they looked through the boxes in the attic.

After an hour of searching, Ming suddenly let out a blood curdling scream. Bianca tripped over her shoelaces, scrambled up to her feet, and ran to Ming, expecting to see the worst.

"What? What is it?"

"Spider," Ming squeaked. A tiny spider crawled underneath a box that Ming had been searching through.

"A spider? You screamed as though someone were trying to kill you." Bianca took off her shoe and killed the spider with a single stroke.

"Next time you feel like screaming, save it for when the bad guys show up." Bianca put her shoe back on.

Ming stuck her tongue out at Bianca, and they resumed their search for the spell book.

"I don't think it's up here, B," Ming said.

Bianca sighed, disappointed. They looked in every box and trunk in the attic and still . . . nothing.

"Yeah, I'm not finding anything either."

"Basement?"

"Yeah."

So off to the basement they went. This time they didn't need flashlights because they were able to turn on some lights. There were boxes everywhere, twice as many as in the attic. Bianca massaged her temples and let out a heavy sigh.

"Don't worry. We'll find it. Stop looking as though someone just ran over your puppy," Ming said.

"I wish," Bianca muttered. She was worried that they would never find the book in this mess. Nothing was labeled. It would take all night to look through all the stuff in the basement.

"If you were an evil spell book, where would you be?" Ming wondered aloud.

"In my hands so we could get my mom back," Bianca replied.

"Well, it's not in your hands yet, and we're not going to find it by standing around looking depressed."

"You're right."

"Of course, I'm right. Come on, you take that half and I'll take this one." Ming went to the left side of the room.

Bianca took a deep breath and continued her search for the spell book.

It was several hours before either of them realized what time it was. They had missed dinner and were getting more and more frustrated as time crawled by. Bianca took a quick break and stretched her back.

It was beginning to cramp from all the time she had spent hunched over the boxes on the floor. She wiped the sweat off her forehead when she noticed a loose brick on the wall. Bianca squinted as she tried to figure out what it was.

Ming noticed her squinting and gently chided, "Put your glasses on, Bianca."

"I don't like them," Bianca complained. She had been nearsighted her whole life. It wasn't until she was eight years old that her mother had realized she couldn't see things very well. The doctor had called it "low congenital myopia"; Bianca, however, liked to call it "a pain in the butt."

"Then wear contacts," Ming argued.

"Yeah, not gonna happen. Can't see the point of poking myself in the eye . . . on purpose . . . with glass." Bianca shuddered as she thought of wearing contact lenses. She made a point to leave her glasses at home whenever she could. She hated wearing them; she thought it made her look nerdy. Of course, Rose always carried a spare pair of glasses with her in case Bianca "forgot" them.

"You're hopeless." Ming rolled her eyes.

"Enough about me, come here and take a look at this." Bianca pointed at the brick on the wall.

The brick was the exact same color as the others. The only difference was that it was slightly loose. She could tell that it was separated from the others because there was no cement around the edges.

She pulled on the brick until it came out and found a letter resting in the empty space. As careful as possible she took the paper and unfolded it. She immediately recognized her mother's handwriting and her heart dropped to her stomach as she began to read.

> *Dearest Bianca:*
>
> *I'm afraid if you've found this letter, then the worst has happened. I wish we had more time together and more time to prepare you for what's to come. If you find my journals, they may offer*

you some advice and further insight to what you may face in the future. They are in the small trunk under my bed.

As for the spell book . . . you can't let Lenore have it, no matter what she says. She's a vicious woman and will stop at nothing to get what she wants. The spell book was written by Queen Mirabel herself and the contents will bring chaos should it fall into the wrong hands. Guard the book, keep it hidden and keep it safe.

I can't tell you exactly where it is in case this letter falls into the wrong hands, but I will leave you with a clue so that you know where it is for future generations to come. This is all I can give you right now. Remember that I love you. You are and always will be the greatest joy of my life.

Love, Mom

The letter trembled in her hands. Her vision blurred as tears pooled in her eyes. A single teardrop splashed onto the letter. The black ink swam inside the little tear as Bianca reread the letter a few more times.

She carefully folded the letter and put it in her back pocket. She wasn't going to show it to Ming. It was something that was too private to share with anyone . . . even if she was her best friend.

On a separate piece of paper, there was this sentence.

"Black veins are hidden under the First Frost," Bianca whispered.

"What's that supposed to mean?" Ming stood behind Bianca and looked over her shoulder.

"I don't know. That's why we have to figure it out," she replied.

They went back upstairs to the museum and searched through the Wicked Wing. Bianca looked behind the magic mirror. For a moment, she thought this was where the spell book would be, mostly because of the frame that decorated the mirror. It was made of ebony with vines, thorns, and withered roses carved into the ancient wood.

"Anything?" Ming's hands shook slightly.

"No . . . nothing." Bianca's disappointment was evident in her voice.

"This room is creepy at night."

"I know." Bianca gently put the mirror back in its place.

"Stupid spell book. Where else do you want to look?" Ming stood next to Bianca.

Bianca opened her mouth to reply, but instead of her response to the question, all that came out was a deep male voice that said:

"That which you seek,

Hides beneath

Red lips that can

No longer speak."

Ming shrieked. Bianca let out a string of curse words that her mother would frown upon and probably ground her for, as she stepped away from the mirror. Ming pointed to the mirror, but all they saw were their own reflections. Bianca frowned and took a tentative step toward the mirror. She put her hand on the looking glass and waited for something to happen. After a moment of waiting . . . nothing happened.

"Maybe we should ask it another question," Bianca said.

"I don't know, B. This is all you . . . you know what I mean?"

"Yeah," Bianca whispered. She took a moment to think of a question in the form of a rhyme.

"Mirror, mirror on the wall

where in the world is my mother?

Can you make sense of it all?"

She wasn't good at poetry but it was the best she could come up with on short notice. She didn't know if the mirror only replied to questions in rhyme . . . but she figured it was worth a try.

Whatever, it's worth a shot.

An ivory white face emerged from a fog deep within the darkness. He stretched his jaw as though he hadn't used it in centuries. He opened his pitch-black eyes and stared at Bianca with a bored expression on his pale face. It took every ounce of strength within her to meet his gaze.

"Rose Red is held against her will

in another land

by a witch who wishes you ill."

"I already know that," Bianca said.

Ming eagerly patted Bianca on the shoulder and said, "Umm, okay. How about . . .

"Mirror, mirror on the wall,

how can we get Rose Red

Back to us

Give us a suggestion . . . instead?"

Ming shrugged. Bianca knew that Ming wasn't very good at rhyming either; she hoped the mirror would reply.

The face inside the mirror curled his thin lips as though getting ready to growl at them. Bianca wondered if the mirror was going to answer Ming's question or tell them to leave him alone.

"Queen Mirabel's book you must find,

within it is a spell

that will take you

to where the witch dwells."

"Okay." Bianca thought about asking the mirror another question, but she already had the clue her mother had given her in the letter. All she had to do was figure it out.

"Thank you, Magic Mirror," Bianca said and then gave it a quick bow.

The bone white face inside the mirror gave her a single short nod in return and then vanished in a puff of smoke.

"That was twenty different kinds of creepy, B."

"You say that a lot. Are you sure there are twenty different kinds, Ming?"

"Yep."

"You're going to have to list them for me one of these days," Bianca said.

"I can do that right now."

"You really don't have to."

"I'm going to prove my point once and for all."

Bianca groaned.

"There's creepy, obviously, quickly followed by kooky, spooky, mysterious, ookey," Ming said.

Bianca raised her hand and said, "That's the beginning of The Addams Family song."

"Those words still make my list," Ming argued. "Sinister, eerie, weird, strange, abnormal, uncanny, frightening, odd, scary, unnerving, chilling, unsettling, disturbing, bizarre, and abominable."

Bianca blinked several times and waited for Ming to say something else. "Are you officially finished?"

"I am," Ming replied, looking really pleased with herself. "You know it took me weeks to memorize all of those words in case I needed to list them someday."

"So that's what you do with your spare time?"

"Oh, shut up." Ming stuck her tongue out and gave Bianca a raspberry.

Bianca thought about the clue and tried to piece everything together.

Black veins . . . that's definitely the spell book. No doubt about it. But what did Mom mean by "the First Frost"?

Then she gasped.

"What?" Ming shrieked.

"Snow White! The First Frost is Snow White! God, I can't believe it took me this long to figure it out. I'm so stupid," Bianca shouted as she threw her hands up in the air.

"Okay . . . the riddle says hiding under the First Frost, does she mean Snow White's apple? Where she's buried? What?"

"I don't think it's in a cemetery, Mom wouldn't do that to me . . . at least I don't think she would. But I'm pretty sure it'll be in the Snow White Room. So we'll try there first. If we don't find anything there, we'll ask the magic mirror for more clues."

They each took a side of the Snow White Room and explored every nook and cranny they could think of. Ming examined the glass case that held the ribbons while Bianca took on the case with the poisoned apple.

Then Bianca wandered over to the portrait of Snow White. She gazed into her blue eyes and whispered, "You know where the book is, don't you?"

The portrait only looked back at her. It said nothing. No matter how many times Bianca asked, it would never reveal its secrets. Snow White was after all—a painting.

"Humph. Fine. I'll take that as a yes," Bianca replied. "Ming?"

"Yeah?"

"I need you to help me bring this painting down, please," she said.

Together they struggled to pull the heavy portrait off the wall. After a few minutes of swearing and struggling with the bulky frame, they managed to rest the painting against the massive table in the corner of the room. Bianca wiped the cobwebs off the wall with her hands and looked for something out of the ordinary. But all she saw was a smooth wall. Bianca ran her hands over it, hoping to find something . . . anything. It took several tries, but eventually she felt a loose minuscule corner, almost as though someone had painted over wallpaper with pale pink paint. She picked at the corner until she had a large piece to pull on. Little by little, the wallpaper came off and revealed a wooden box neatly tucked between two bricks.

"Whoa," Ming said.

"Why didn't we think of this in the first place?" Bianca gazed at the box.

"Because we have no idea what's really going on?" Ming replied.

"Very true." Bianca pried the box out of its hiding place.

"If my face melts off like that guy from the Indiana Jones movie, I'm gonna be one very pissed off ghost," Ming warned.

"Duly noted."

Bianca took several deep breaths and opened the little wooden box. And there it was: a thick, brown leather book. It looked so harmless. No title on the cover. Nothing to let anyone know its true contents, which probably didn't matter because not everyone could read in the seventeenth century.

"Ye Olde Spell Book?" Ming whispered.

"Yeah."

"Not what I expected it to look like."

"Me neither," Bianca said.

Don't worry, Mom. I'm gonna save you. After this is over, I'm going to burn this book. This ends with me. Bianca made that silent oath to herself. She was going to make everything right again even if she died trying.

8

BIANCA PUT THE WOODEN box in her bag and said, "Come on. Let's go home."

Bianca punched in the code to activate the alarm system for the museum.

She pulled her keys out of her bag and locked the doors.

"I'm hungry," Ming said.

"Me too," Bianca said as she stood by Ming's car and waited for her to unlock the door.

Ming pointed her key chain and pushed a button at her brand-new light blue hybrid. A loud clunk sound let them know that the car doors were unlocked. Bianca sat on the passenger seat and waited for Ming to start the car.

"You got anything in your house that's edible?" Ming asked as she pulled out of the museum's parking lot.

"Not really. You know I can't cook, maybe we should pick something up on our way to my house," Bianca suggested.

"Good idea. I've never met anyone who can burn water. Seriously, B. It wouldn't kill you to watch the Food Network instead of Nickelodeon."

Bianca rolled her eyes and made a face at Ming.

"I'd appreciate it if you didn't distract me from my driving," her friend scolded.

"Oh, suddenly you're Miss Careful?"

"Yeah."

"Since when?"

"Since my dad bought me this brand-new car, and he'd murder me if I got a scratch on it. So if you would please cut it out, I'd appreciate it."

"Fine, then let's talk about what to eat."

After much debate, they decided to stop at McDonald's. As soon as they got home, they ate their food as quickly as possible. They were both curious as to what the contents of the spell book were. Mostly, Bianca wanted to see what it was that Lenore wanted so badly that she was willing to sacrifice a person's life for it.

Bianca retrieved the wooden box from her purse and placed it gently on the dining room table. She used a damp paper towel and wiped the thin film of dust and dirt that covered it, then opened the wooden box that held Mirabel's spell book. She half expected an evil looking skull or a pentacle of some sort to suddenly appear on the cover. But all she saw was a plain brown, leather book that could've easily belonged to anyone. The book smelled like leather and wood.

"Are you sure you want to do this now? I mean . . . what if there's something in there that makes me wanna throw up? I just ate, B. You know?"

"I have to know," Bianca replied.

Ming took a deep breath and sat beside her friend. "If I blow chunks on the table, I'll expect you to go get more chicken nuggets to replace the ones I lost."

"Deal."

Bianca carefully opened the book before she had a moment to change her mind. She found that the yellowed pages smelled like herbs and lavender. Once more, she had expected to see something horrible but instead found a tiny inscription on the first page.

Remember, my child, magic is all around you. In the herbs we use, the ground we walk upon, and the intangible feelings that swim inside our hearts. Beware of whom you share your secrets with.

Love, Mother

Bianca couldn't believe it. Mirabel's mother gave this book to her? It seemed to her that it was Mirabel's mother who had taught her everything the wicked queen knew.

She turned another page and found the first official entry of Mirabel's spell book. In it, Mirabel described some of the herbs she discovered in the castle's garden and some of their basic uses and ailments they could cure.

"That's not so bad," Ming whispered.

"I guess we have to keep reading it to see what happens next," Bianca muttered.

"I don't like where this is going, Bianca," Ming warned.

"Then go watch TV or something. I'll call you if I find anything interesting."

"Sounds good to me." Ming got up and headed to the family room.

Bianca ignored the voices coming from the television and focused all of her attention on the spell book. The book started out innocently enough with spells like Banish Evil Spell, Luck Oil, Happy Harmony Spell, Blessing Oil, and Destroy All Evil Bath. Bianca wondered if she had the wrong spell book because she had read a third of the book and had yet to find anything that led her to believe that the spell book was evil until she noticed a change. It was a subtle change . . . very gradual, but some of the spells took on a slightly darker aspect. Spells on how to give someone nightmares, how to command a magic mirror, and the proper usage of mirror charms. Once the book began taking a more sinister turn, Bianca slammed the book shut and walked away from it.

She joined Ming in the living room, took the remote control and changed the channel.

"Hey! I was watching that," Ming protested.

"*Gossip Girl* can suck it," Bianca said.

"You suck," Ming pouted.

"This whole situation sucks," Bianca said as she clicked the buttons on the remote so fast it was difficult to tell what was playing on the television screen.

"You okay?"

"No."

"I can tell. You've usually settled on a show by now."

Bianca groaned in frustration, turned the television off and threw the remote control on the floor so hard it shattered. She ran her fingers through her hair several times.

"She was a good person, Ming. She was a good witch . . . who practiced good, healing magic, and she just lost it. How can someone lose their way like that?" Bianca turned to Ming, hoping that her friend would give her the answer.

She was met with a blank stare. Once more, she found herself wishing for her mother.

Ming's eyes softened. "That bad?"

"It's like watching someone spiral into the darkness and feeling helpless . . . like . . . I can't do anything to stop it."

"Have you found the spell to open the portal?"

"Not yet. I'm scared to read the rest of that book, Ming. I don't want to know what was inside that woman's mind."

For a while neither said anything. They just sat on the couch and stared off into space. Bianca was afraid of voicing her worries for fear that they would somehow come true, that the universe would be cruel enough to turn her thoughts into a reality.

I don't have a choice. I either read that book or resign myself to a life without Mom.

The following morning, Bianca and Ming discussed what they were going to do that day while having breakfast.

"Isn't the repairman supposed to come today?" Ming broke the yolk on her sunny-side-up eggs with a corner of her toast.

"Yeah, at nine o'clock," Bianca replied.

"What are you going to do about the museum?"

"I dunno. I was thinking about asking you to stay here while I go to the museum and open the doors and get everything ready for the day. Then we'll switch, you stay in the museum, and I'll come home and deal with the repairman."

"Why don't I just go to the museum and you stay here?"

"Because I have to disarm the alarm system, put money in the cash register, turn on all the lights, and make sure the credit card machine isn't on the fritz again."

"I think I'll stay here and wait for the repairman," Ming said before taking a bite of her buttered toast.

"Good." Bianca gave her friend a tight-lipped smile and ate her breakfast, which consisted of Cinnamon Chex with lots of ice cold milk.

"Did you find anything in the book last night?"

"I forced myself to stop. It was just too creepy. It gave me nightmares," Bianca said.

"Really?" Ming had a worried look on her face as she waited for Bianca to reply.

"That book is seriously evil."

"But we need to use it. Do you think you can handle it?"

"I hope so," Bianca whispered.

"You're not leaving me alone with the book, are you?"

"I have to leave it here. It's the only place I know where it'll be safe. If I take it with me, who knows what could happen to it."

"Can you tell me where it is? I really don't want to touch it," Ming said.

"It's in my mom's room."

"Good to know."

They finished their breakfast, and Bianca headed to the museum. Most of the time there would be a line of people at the entrance waiting to go inside. But on that Wednesday morning . . . it was completely deserted. Bianca sighed, unlocked the doors and got everything ready for the day. Once she took her post behind the gift shop counter, she called Ming and asked if the repairman had arrived yet.

"Yeah, he's here. Got here about five minutes ago," Ming replied.

"Okay. Tell him I'll be there soon. I'll leave as soon as you get here," Bianca said.

"You want me to leave him alone in the house?" Ming whispered.

"If he meant any harm, the wards Mom placed on the house wouldn't have let him walk in. Trust me, it'll be okay. Just tell him you're going out and that I'll be there soon."

"Okay . . . if you say so." Bianca heard the hesitation in Ming's voice. Once more she reassured her that everything would be okay.

"See you later," Bianca said.

"Bye."

Twenty minutes later, Ming appeared.

"Wow. This place is dead," Ming said as she took in her surroundings.

"Yeah, word spreads real quickly around here. Now everyone knows that Mom won't be doing story time for a while. Anyway, I'm gonna go home and make sure everything is okay with the repairman," Bianca said.

"Okay."

Bianca paused for a moment and asked, "Does he . . . you know . . . does he seem nice to you?" Bianca fidgeted with her car keys.

"Oh. My. God. He was super cute, and yeah, he seemed nice and polite. Very professional looking," Ming replied.

"Cool. I'll see you later." She waved at Ming and walked away.

Bianca drove back home and found the repairman outside by his black pickup truck unloading supplies and materials he needed to fix the window.

"Hi," Bianca said as she approached.

"Hello, you must be Bianca." He set down his toolbox and extended his free hand to her.

She shook his hand and smiled. Ming was right; he was very cute. He had dark blond hair, chocolate brown eyes and dimples. He looked like the sort of man that liked to spend all of his free time outdoors, which was a stark contrast to Bianca, who loved nothing more than to be in her room, drawing or reading a book.

"I'm Don Carlson, and I'll be fixing your window today," he said and then flashed her a smile.

"Great. Do I need to do anything?"

"We'll, if you wanna stick around that's up to you. I do need you to sign some papers before I get started, and then once I'm finished, I'll need you to sign some more paperwork. But other than that I'm good to go," Don said.

"Okay, I'm going to stay here in the house. I have some reading to catch up on anyway," she said.

"Cool."

"How long should this take?"

"A few hours give or take. I have to replace some of the frame and put in the new glass."

Bianca nodded. "Sounds good to me. Do you need any help carrying stuff in?"

He grinned and shook his head as though amused at her offer to help him. "Nah, I'm good. Thanks, though."

Bianca nodded and went inside the house. She asked Don if he wanted anything to drink as he set his stuff up in the living room. He politely declined. Bianca then retrieved the spell book from its new hiding place and sat on a stool in the kitchen.

She sighed as she looked out the window. It was a glorious day. The sky was a perfect light blue with ivory white clouds that slowly drifted from one end of the sky to the other. It was a great day to sit in the hammock with a glass of lemonade and read the collection of short stories she'd borrowed from Ming a few months ago. It was a shame that she had to spend it with her nose buried in an evil spell book that gave her more questions than answers. She spent several hours reading page after page until she found what she was looking for. Bianca gasped as she read the title of the spell, Everafter Portal Spell.

I found it.

"All done," Don said. He had been working quietly for several hours.

"Oh, wow. It looks brand new. Thank you so much."

Bianca let out a sigh of relief. She felt a lot safer knowing that the window was fixed.

"No problem. Here's the total and I need you to sign here, here and here." He pointed to several Xs on three pieces of paper. "And if you have any other repairs you need taking care of, here's my card. Call me anytime." He gave her a playful wink.

Bianca blushed and signed on the Xs and handed him her mother's credit card. He jotted down all the numbers as well as the security code on the back of the card. He handed her another piece of paper to sign and gave her copies of the paperwork as well as a receipt.

"Cool. Thanks again," Bianca said.

"You're welcome. Have a nice day." And just like that he was gone.

Bianca grabbed the spell book and raced back to the museum. She needed to share this with Ming.

9

"PLEASE TELL ME WE don't need eyes of a newt or kitten paws for this; otherwise I'm going home," Ming said as she put down the magazine she was reading.

"No. It's just a spell. Look," Bianca replied. She opened her mouth to chant the spell, but Ming put her hand over Bianca's mouth and stopped her.

"Wait," she said.

Bianca pulled Ming's hand off. "What?"

"You can't just go there without being prepared, and you definitely can't open a portal to another world in the middle of the museum you and your mother run. Plus, you don't know where you're going or what you're going to find on the other side of whatever it is you're opening."

"You're right," Bianca admitted.

She was lucky she had Ming with her. Had she been all by herself, she would've thrown herself headfirst into the portal. She thought about the things in the museum and made a quick mental list of the items she would need.

She made her way to Rapunzel's hair and carefully took it out the glass case. Then, went to her mother's office and collected the brick from the Third Little Pig's house. She felt it was better than taking a tent with her. She wasn't exactly the camping type anyway.

When she wandered into the Wicked Wing, she wondered if there was anything in the room that would be useful to her. Out of the corner of her eye, she saw the red dancing shoes quivering with excitement as she walked past them. The worn red leather shoes seemed eager to get out of the glass case and cause all sorts of mischief. They looked as though they had literally been to hell and back.

What good would they be to me?

It wasn't as if she could force someone to wear them . . . or could she?

"Hmmm." Bianca finally decided to take the shoes with her. She also picked up a little hand mirror; it was supposed to be like Mirabel's magic mirror . . . only smaller.

The evil queen's version of an iPod Shuffle . . . only . . . evil . . . I guess.

She climbed up the stairs and headed to the attic. For some reason, Rose had never gotten around to putting lights in the attic and there was a faint smell of mothballs. Bianca hated mothballs; it reminded her of old people and not in a good way. She opened the trunk that contained Red Riding Hood's cape. She pushed several items and dresses out of the way until she found the famous blood red cape, then carefully placed it in her backpack, zipped it shut and rejoined Ming downstairs at the gift shop counter.

"Got some good stuff?" Ming looked at the stuffed pack.

"I hope so," Bianca replied.

"Any magic carpets?"

"We don't have that here. Most of the Arabian Nights collection is somewhere in the Middle East."

"Ohhh."

"Most of the stuff we have here are from European fairy tales. You know, like the Brothers Grimm, Hans Christian Andersen, and old English fairy tales."

"Huh." Ming wrinkled her nose.

"What?"

"Nothing. It's just surprising how much you know about this place."

"Well . . . I grew up around all this stuff," Bianca said.

"Anyway, what do you wanna do now?"

"Well, there's no one here. May as well close up for the day and go home."

"Okay."

"Can't afford to waste any more time."

"True."

"Mom is going to kill me when she finds out I've been closing early, but since I'm trying to save her butt, I think she'll forgive me."

"I call dibs on your stuff," Ming said.

"I don't think she's going to literally kill me."

"Well if you die, I still call dibs on your stuff."

"You really know how to inspire confidence," Bianca said sarcastically.

Ming gave her a bright smile. "I do what I can."

At noon—the earliest they had ever closed the museum since it had opened—both friends headed back to Bianca's house.

"What are you going to tell your mom?" Bianca glanced at Ming as they walked through the front door.

"I have no idea. I'll come up with something," Ming promised.

Bianca sighed. She didn't like lying to the soft spoken Mrs. Lee. "Let me know what she says."

"Will do." And with that Ming went to her house to pack for their unexpected adventure.

Bianca's heart skipped a beat when she heard the door close behind her best friend. She was alone again. She was overwhelmed with the feelings of sadness and guilt that washed over her. At least with Ming around she could hide it and try to pretend that she was fine.

But on her own . . . she felt as though the sky was collapsing over her. *Stop thinking that way!* She scolded herself. *Mom doesn't need that.*

She climbed the stairs and went into her mother's room. She wanted to pack a fresh set of clothes for when they rescued her. It had been two days since her mother had been kidnapped.

She pushed down the lump that formed in her throat and opened her mother's drawers then grabbed some underwear, a bra, T-shirt, and a pair of jeans. Bianca carefully folded these pieces of clothing and put them in her black backpack which was beginning to get full and heavy. She wasn't sure what more she could fit into it. She went to her room and packed a couple of things for herself as well.

By the time Ming returned to her house, she was finished packing. Ming unlocked the door, using the key that Bianca had given her several days ago.

"Hey!" Ming called out.

"Hey."

"Where are you?"

"My room," Bianca replied.

Ming pounded up the stairs and joined Bianca in her bedroom. Ming dropped her pink backpack by the door and sat on the corner of Bianca's bed.

"So what did you tell your mom?"

"I told her you had to join your mom in Florida to help with your sick grandma and that you asked me to go with you to keep you company on the flight over," Ming said.

"She believed you?" Bianca wondered if Ming had elaborated more on the story. Ming was known to be a bit of a drama queen.

"Yep."

"That's crazy." Bianca shook her head in disbelief.

"Yep, it sure is. I guess it helps that I only lie in case of an emergency. Most of the time, I'm actually telling her the truth. What are you bringing?"

"I got clothes for me and Mom. A few things from the museum, a couple of flashlights, batteries, Pop-Pastries, and soup. You?"

"I got clothes, water, ramen noodles, waterproof matches, and a first aid kit."

"Cool."

"Ready?"

Ming said, "Yeah."

Bianca opened the spell book and chanted the spell:

"Find the shortest distance between

This place and the faeries' green.

A place for weird-less days and weary nights,

Put this door within my sight."

At first nothing happened. They stood silently side by side, waiting for a magic door to appear out of thin air, but that didn't happen. Magic . . . at least the magic that came forth was much more subtle. She felt a surge of power coming from the middle of the living room. Bianca saw a very pale hand use a silver knife to cut through space and time. The door that appeared was translucent, almost ghost-like, except that the frame and the doorknob were highlighted with blue-white light.

Bianca examined it before touching it; there was nothing behind the doorframe. She touched the doorknob and was amazed to find it was just as solid as everything in her house.

"Ready?" Bianca repeated her earlier question.

Ming was pale and looked like she was ready to throw up what she'd had for lunch, but she nodded and stepped toward the door.

"Okay, here goes nothing," Bianca whispered and opened the door.

Bianca and Ming held hands as they walked into the unknown. They went a very short distance into a hallway filled with bright light and then fell several feet down until they landed on the ground. Bianca couldn't contain the scream that escaped her lips.

10

BIANCA LANDED FEET FIRST and stumbled gracelessly onto the ground. Sharp pain rushed up her leg, but thankfully subsided within seconds. At least she didn't break her ankle with that landing.

"Ow." Ming whined as she massaged pain from her right knee.

"You okay?" Bianca crawled toward her friend. It would certainly be a bad way to start this bizarre adventure if Ming was injured in the first five seconds of being in this strange new land.

"Yeah. I'll probably get a bruise, but I'll live. You?"

"I'm okay," Bianca replied. She muttered while she wiped the dirt and grime off her light blue jeans.

"Where are we?" Ming whispered.

"I have no idea. I hope we're in the right place," Bianca replied. She studied her surroundings. Everywhere she looked was a series of earth tones: emerald, jade, lime, pine, and hunter green. The tree trunks were a mix between chocolate brown and auburn. Bianca turned her gaze to the sky. It was a perfect light blue with not a single cloud to be found. She heard birds singing and chirping. She couldn't tell what types of birds they were. Not like she was an expert in that sort of thing.

"What now?" Ming stood, dusting off her jeans then moaned when she noticed the grass stain on her left knee.

"I guess we start walking until we find a village or someone who can help us," Bianca replied.

After several hours of wandering in the woods, they had yet to meet a single person. There was nothing but miles and miles of forest and a dirt path that seemed to take them nowhere fast.

"Do you have any idea where you're going?" Ming said just before a tree branch smacked her on the jaw. She spat a few leaves out of her mouth and pulled more from her hair.

"Depends," Bianca said.

"On what?"

"On whether you want me to lie to you." Bianca stepped over a huge pile of poop left behind by an animal she hoped she never had to meet face to face. "Watch your step."

"Ew." Ming covered her nose and jumped over the huge pile of animal dung. "Fine, tell me the truth."

"I have no idea where we're going," Bianca said.

Ming groaned. It was obvious that wasn't the answer she was looking for. "So, what's the plan?"

"Find a castle or something equally creepy," Bianca replied.

"I think you're just hoping we stumble into a creepy castle with a big neon sign that says Bianca's mother is in this room."

"Yep."

"This place gives me the creeps," Ming said.

"Ditto. But it's good that we're walking. Better than staying still and letting the bad guys find us."

"I thought the only bad guy after you was a mean ol' witch."

"Yeah, but she could have an evil minion or something."

"You have a point. God . . . I hope we find your mom soon."

"Me too."

"I wanna go home," Ming whined.

"Yeah, me too," Bianca whispered.

They walked in silence for several minutes when Bianca heard a branch break. She grabbed Ming's arm and stopped her.

"What?" Ming's dark brown eyes became big as saucers as they darted nervously from side to side.

"Did you hear that?"

"No. What is it?"

"I think someone or something is following us," Bianca whispered.

"Oh, God." Ming turned pale green.

They heard more branches breaking and the rustling of leaves. Bianca felt her heartbeat hammering against her ribcage. It was going so fast she thought it was going to burst out of her chest.

She grabbed Ming's hand and whispered, "Run."

Ming nodded and took off like a shot. Hand in hand they ran through the woods. Whatever it was that was chasing them began to run as well. Within moments, Bianca's lungs started to burn and her thighs ached. She hadn't expected to do this amount of running so soon. Just when Bianca thought about surrendering to whatever it was that was chasing them, she heard an even louder sound, almost as though thunder had sprouted legs and decided to join them for a jog.

"What is that?" Ming managed between pants, but not once did she slow down to look over her shoulder to see for herself.

Bianca, who was still running, replied, "Sounds like a horse."

As soon as the words escaped her mouth, a bright white horse appeared in front of them. Ming and Bianca fell as they tried to avoid crashing into the four-legged beast. The horse reared up when the man that rode him forced the creature to come to a complete stop. Another man appeared moments afterward, riding a black horse.

"Do not worry, fair maidens. I shall save you!" the man on the white horse shouted and then rode off into the forest.

The other man muttered something unintelligible under his breath and followed his companion.

Bianca spotted a hollow tree a few feet away from where they stood.

"Come on." She grabbed Ming's hand and led her to the hiding place she had discovered.

"This is crazy, B," Ming hissed once they were safe inside the tree.

"I know. I'm sorry I dragged you into this. I'll make it up to you if we make it out of here alive. I promise."

Ming's ears perked up. "Really? How?"

"I'll buy you that tokidoki purse you've been drooling over for months. The big one."

Ming's eyes widened and she whispered, "Ooooh. Deal."

Bianca and Ming heard the men shouting. Whatever was chasing after them was big.

Then . . . silence.

"Oh, God. They're dead, aren't they? They're dead because they were trying to help us," Ming muttered as she covered her ears and shook her head.

"Shh," Bianca said gently. She was trying not to freak out. One of them had to keep a clear head.

After several minutes of waiting in silence, she heard a soft rustle. Then Bianca saw the bright white legs of the horse.

"Hello? Maidens? Where are you?" the man on the white horse called out in a singsong voice.

He sounds harmless enough.

The man and his friend were the only people they had encountered since their arrival. She hoped that her instincts were correct, and that they were trustworthy.

Bianca slowly crawled out of her hiding place. Ming soon followed. She looked up at the man sitting on top of the horse. She smirked when she realized that he looked to be her age and he was gorgeous, a man who belonged in one of the many fairy tales she had read. He had blond hair that was curled to perfection, bright blue eyes, and a dimple on his chin. Bianca had never seen anyone with an actual dimple on their chin. She noticed his style of clothing and wondered what century they were in. He wore a navy-blue coat, with a form fitting vest and matching trousers. His shirt was so white it was almost blinding. He looked like he belonged in the Victorian Era

"Ah, there you are," he said with a kind smile.

"Thank you for rescuing us," Bianca said.

"Yes, thank you," Ming echoed.

The man openly stared at Ming. Bianca guessed he had never seen an Asian girl before.

Ming noticed the way he stared at her and blushed. "Something wrong? Do I have a bug crawling in my hair or something?" She combed her hair with her fingers, searching for something that wasn't there.

"Maybe he just thinks you're pretty," Bianca said softly.

"Oh," Ming replied.

"Sir?" Bianca said. "Can you please tell me . . . what was after us?"

"A buck," he replied.

"A what now?" Bianca raised a brow.

"What's a buck?" Ming looked at her.

"I think it's a deer," Bianca replied.

"A deer?"

Bianca sighed. "Afraid so."

"We're so friggin' doomed. Doomed, I tell ya." Ming made a point to stretch out the oo in doomed for as long as possible. It didn't help Bianca with her self-confidence.

"How am I supposed to save my mom when I'm running away from friggin' Bambi?" Bianca said out loud.

The man smiled and hopped off his amazing horse. "Please allow me to introduce myself. I am Prince Ferdinand, future king of Everafter."

"At least now we know we're in the right place," Bianca told Ming.

"Yeah . . . but are we in the right century? Do you see what he's wearing?" Ming whispered.

"Yes, I can see that. Let me . . . just give me a minute," Bianca replied. She was trying not to get flustered or let her anxiety get the best of her.

She then turned her attention back to the prince. "I'm Bianca Frost, and this is my friend Ming Lee." Bianca did a mix between a bow and a curtsy since she wasn't certain which was acceptable. Ming settled on a curtsy and stifled a giggle.

"Your Highness, the beast has been slain," a young man said as he emerged from the woods and stepped into the clearing. It was the man she had seen on the black horse. He had the huge buck tied to the stallion by its antlers and was dragging the animal's corpse through the woods.

"Oh, and this is my steward, Terrance Connor," Prince Ferdinand said.

Bianca was shocked to see that Terrance's hands and arms were covered in blood. He had rolled up the sleeves of what had once been a white shirt that was now stained with dirt and blood. Oddly enough . . . he didn't seem to mind. He wore a suit similar to Ferdinand's except that the pants and vest he wore over his shirt were black. His matching jacket was draped over the midnight-colored horse that followed closely behind him. She quickly realized that the prince hadn't killed anything, it was Terrance who had done all the dirty work.

"You're both welcome to join us. There's plenty of food for everyone," Prince Ferdinand offered graciously.

Bianca turned to Ming. No words were necessary; the question she wanted to ask was plain to see in her eyes. Ming nodded. They didn't need to speak to know that neither one of them wanted to spend the night alone in the woods in a world they knew nothing about.

"Thank you. We would like that very much," Bianca replied to the prince.

"We will eat well tonight," Terrance said with a wicked smile.

It didn't take Bianca much to guess that he had enjoyed killing the buck. There was a slight glimmer in his dark brown eyes. Bianca couldn't explain it, but there was something both primal and civilized about him, almost as if there were something more to this steward than met the eye.

Terrance seemed to feel her stare and met her gaze. Bianca didn't look away. Her heart skipped a beat when she saw his bright white teeth as he grinned. He had long brown hair that she wanted to curl around her fingers. She didn't know what it was about Terrance. She couldn't quite put her finger on it, but she was determined to find out.

Yeah . . . there's something more to him.

Bianca shook herself out of his unfaltering gaze and took a deep breath. She was relieved that they weren't running anymore. She looked toward the mountains and watched the sun slowly sink into the horizon. She had never seen a more glorious sunset. The sky was tinged pink, peach, and red. The sky changed from the deep blush to a cool blue, and slowly the stars began to peep through.

Bianca saw something glowing in the trees. She squinted, but that didn't help. She reluctantly reached into her backpack and put her glasses on, gasping in surprise when she saw a small group of fairies shimmering high in the trees.

Bianca tapped Ming on the shoulder and pointed to the trees. "Hey! You put your glasses on. Good for you, B," Ming said.

"Shh. Look up there," Bianca whispered.

"What am I looking at?" She looked in the direction Bianca pointed.

"Fairies."

"No way."

The fairies squeaked and danced from branch to branch. Bianca didn't dare get any closer for fear of scaring them away. Some of them had wings that looked like the ones on a butterfly while others had wings that made Bianca think of dragonflies.

"So many colors." Ming marveled.

She was right. The fairies glowed in soft sapphire blue, emerald green, light pink, and some were ruby red.

"Ah, yes. Fairies." Prince Ferdinand stood beside them and gave the fairies a tightlipped grin.

"They're beautiful," Bianca said.

"They're dangerous. Stay away from them," he warned.

"Why? They're so tiny," Ming said.

The fairies sensed that they were talking about them and began to curl and uncurl their fingers at them, as though beckoning them to follow them deeper into the woods. Part of her wanted to throw caution to the wind and follow the fairies, but Ferdinand's warning forced her to stay with the group. The fairies covered their lips with their hands and giggled wickedly at Bianca.

"They are one of the most powerful beings known to mankind. Tiny doesn't mean weak," the prince explained.

"Point taken. Ming, stay away from the fairies," Bianca said.

"Aw." Ming pouted.

"Come on, let's see if we can help Terrance with something."

They found Terrance behind a tree, skinning the buck. Ming gagged and turned away from the awful scene. The buck's skin was halfway down its torso.

"Umm, hi . . . Terrance," Bianca stammered.

"Hello" He continued to work on the task at hand.

"We were wondering—" Bianca forced herself to look away and regain her composure "—if you needed any help with dinner."

He wiped the sweat off his forehead. Without realizing it, he had smeared blood on his skin. He gave Bianca a puzzling look and then replied, "You could gather some wood."

"Okey dokey. We'll go do that."

"That was so gross," Ming whined.

"How do you think we get meat?"

"I swear to God, I'm going to become a vegetarian when we get back home," Ming vowed.

"Whatever you say," Bianca said dismissively. She knew that Ming wouldn't stick to being a vegetarian. The moment she smelled a cheese-burger back home that would be the end of it. "Come on, help me gather wood."

Ming was surprised to see that Terrance was able to build a fire using rocks and dry leaves because she whispered to Bianca, "No matches? How is he doing that?"

She could tell her friend was impressed by Terrance's skills. "Excuse me, I have a question," Ming said.

"Yes?" Prince Ferdinand smiled at Ming.

"Where are we exactly?"

"You don't know where you are?"

"We know we're in Everafter. But where exactly?" Bianca replied.

"We are in the Enchanted Forest not far from my summer cottage," Prince Ferdinand said.

"Forgive my boldness, but I couldn't help but notice that your choice of dress is very strange," Terrance said as he studied Bianca and Ming's clothing. He reached out and touched Bianca's black T-shirt. "And you do not behave as maidens should. You are not from our land . . . are you?"

Bianca noticed that Terrance seemed amazed over the softness of her shirt. She gazed at his long fingers. She could see the dirt and caked blood underneath his nails. But she didn't pull away from him. In fact, she was surprised by how little it bothered her.

"You're right. We're not from here," Bianca replied.

Terrance realized what he was doing and quickly pulled away. Bianca tried to look away when she saw a bit of color on his cheeks. So . . . he can blush. She put her hands over her mouth and covered her smile. She didn't want to embarrass him.

"We had heard rumors for many years that there was a way to travel to another world, but I didn't think they were true," Terrance said.

"Yeah . . . we're definitely not in Kansas anymore," Bianca said.

"What is Kansas?" The prince met Bianca's eyes.

"Nothing, nowhere, never mind," Bianca replied quickly. She didn't want to tell them too much about where they came from in case it changed the way of life in Everafter. She didn't want to be responsible for the fall of a civilization.

Definitely don't need to add that to my already-guilty conscience.

"What brings you to our world?" Prince Ferdinand sat on a log.

"I'm looking for my mother." Bianca found herself unsure how much she should tell them. She decided to remain silent until she figured it out.

"Don't fret. All will be well." Terrance gave her a kind smile. He then pulled out his knife, cut a huge slab of deer meat, and placed it on a plate. He handed the first serving to Prince Ferdinand, the second to Bianca, and the third to Ming, saving the last piece for himself.

"It smells delicious," Bianca said.

Ming sat beside Bianca, leaned over and whispered, "We're not really eating this, are we?"

"Better than using up our food supply. We have to make it last as long as possible. We don't know how long we're going to be here," Bianca explained.

"True, but hopefully not more than a week, otherwise my mom will freak out."

"Don't worry, I'll get you back home," she promised.

Bianca turned her attention back to their rescuers. "I'm curious, why are you out here in the middle of the woods?"

Terrance chuckled. "Prince Ferdinand is looking for a princess."

"Really?" Bianca couldn't help but smile. She never thought she'd be trapped in her very own fairy tale . . . except for the fact that she wasn't a princess.

"Or a damsel in distress. Either one will do . . . so long as the damsel in distress is a princess trapped in a tower by an evil witch," the prince said.

"I guess we weren't what you had in mind," Ming said after she swallowed a bite of her venison.

Prince Ferdinand grinned. "Not exactly princesses, or in distress, but you are certainly maidens who were running away from something. It was my duty to step in and rescue you."

"So . . . where's your castle?" Ming looked around.

"Several days' walk from here," Ferdinand replied.

Bianca nodded.

Ming turned her attention to Bianca and whispered. "Why can't we go to his castle, get an army, and then go to the witch's castle?"

"There's no time, Ming. My mom could be dead by then. I can't risk it. Besides I already have what she wants," Bianca whispered trying hard not to be rude in front of their new friends.

Terrance, however, frowned softly as though trying hard to look away . . . could he hear them?

"Yeah, but . . . " Ming whispered.

"Don't even finish that sentence," Bianca warned.

She knew exactly what Ming was thinking: *What if we die getting there? What if your mother is already dead? What if it's all a trap?*

Too many what-ifs. If Bianca let herself go down that train of thought, she wouldn't be able to take another step forward. It was like having to go down the dark, foggy, and creepy path even though you just wanted to turn around and go home.

"I have to go, Ming, with or without you. I have to do this," Bianca said.

"Don't say that. I'll go with you as far as I can. I'm not going to pretend to be a hero. I'm not. You of all people know that I cry if I break a nail. But for you . . . " Ming placed a hand on Bianca's arm. "I'll go as far as I can."

"I know, Ming. Thanks."

"No problem."

"Where will you be staying?" Terrance had just finished a bite of the deer meat.

"Out here . . . I guess," Bianca said as she patted the soft earth by her feet.

She had the third little pig's brick in her backpack, so she knew that they would be safe in the middle of the forest. She would be able to rest easy knowing that nothing would get through the indestructible brick house. Still . . . she wasn't sure how much of her treasures she wanted to share with their new friends. Until she got to know them better, she decided to keep mum on the items she had in her possession. They were going to be the aces up her sleeve.

Terrance shook his head. "No, absolutely not. That simply won't do. Your Highness?"

"Yes?"

"What say you? I think we should allow them to stay in the cottage."

Prince Ferdinand opened his mouth. It looked to Bianca as though he was going to say no. Before the prince could respond, Bianca said, "We're on a quest."

"Really?" Prince Ferdinand's ears perked up once he heard the word quest.

It was exactly why he was out in the woods.

"Yes. We're searching for my mother, Rose Frost, and seek to . . . " Bianca struggled to find the right words. Whatever was necessary to get them to help her.

"Defeat the evil witch, Lenore," Ming added dramatically, trying to be helpful.

"Defeat a witch! Oh! This is a mighty quest indeed!" Ferdinand exclaimed.

"We could really use your help with this," Bianca admitted.

"Is there a princess involved?" the prince asked.

She thought about lying just to get him and Terrance to come along with her, but she decided against it at the very last moment. "Not really . . . but we could find one along the way . . . you never know."

He stood up and drew his sword out of its scabbard as he spoke. "Terrance, I feel as though it is our duty . . . nay . . . our destiny . . . to make certain that they succeed in their quest."

Bianca was certain that if he had been able to, he would've had the sun shining all around him with angels singing hymns to add to the drama.

"I agree, Your Highness," Terrance said. He winked at Bianca, who in turn blushed. She knew that he would've convinced him to help her had he decided differently.

"Are you sure about this?" Ming whispered to Bianca while the prince pretended to fight the shadow of a tree with his sword.

"Better to have them both with us and know where we're going than wandering all alone without a clue in the middle of the woods by ourselves," Bianca said.

Ming reluctantly nodded in agreement and turned her attention to Prince Ferdinand. "I'm not too sure about having him tag along. But if you trust him and his friend, then I guess I can too."

11

AFTER DINNER, THEY DECIDED to go to Prince Ferdinand's cottage in the forest. Bianca got on the black horse with Terrance, and Ming rode on the prince's white horse. Bianca wrapped her arms around Terrance's waist and held on as though her life depended on it when the horse whinnied.

"The horse can tell you're nervous," Terrance whispered and then gently patted her hand. "Calm down. I won't let you fall."

She took several deep breaths and did her best to relax.

"How long have you been with the prince?" Bianca hoped talking would keep her mind off of falling.

"My whole life. We were playmates as children."

"So . . . you were born in the castle?"

"Yes. My mother, Lady Claire, is Queen Felicia's lady-in-waiting and closest confidante."

"Life in the castle must be interesting."

"I don't know if interesting is the word I would use. I suppose it's normal for me since I've been there my whole life."

There was a lull in the conversation. After a few minutes, Terrance spoke. "What about you? Can you tell me about where you live?"

"I live in my grandmother's old house with my mom. My dad used to live there with us too, but he's been missing for the past ten years."

"Missing?"

"Yeah . . . the witch who kidnapped my mother turned my father into a bear and then vanished." Bianca sighed and rested her cheek on Terrance's wide shoulders. It was weird saying it out loud, now that she knew the truth.

"That's awful."

"Yeah . . . Yes, it is," she replied in a soft voice.

They finally came to a clearing in the woods and Bianca watched in wonderment as a quaint little cottage came into view.

Bianca gasped.

"We're here," Terrance said.

"Wow."

It's like something in a fairy tale.

"Um . . . are you sure this is a cottage? This is more like a really, really big house or a tiny mansion. I thought cottages were supposed to be small and quaint," Ming said loudly from the prince's horse.

"At least we know there's room for us somewhere," Bianca replied.

"True."

Terrance gracefully dismounted his horse. He held out his arms to Bianca and helped her climb off the horse.

"Wait here while I take the horses to the stable and feed them," he said and then walked away.

Prince Ferdinand didn't wait. He walked into his "cottage" and left Bianca and Ming alone outside.

"So . . . what did you and Terrance talk about?" Ming half-teased.

Bianca rolled her eyes. "Nothing. Just chatting a little. No harm in getting to know someone while we're here. What about you? Change your mind about Prince Ferdinand yet?"

"Prince I-Love-Myself-More-Than-Anyone? Blah, blah, blah, I'm a prince. Blah, blah, blah, I have a castle. Yeah, right. I'd rather deal with the Neanderthals in school than the prince . . . even if he is royalty."

Bianca couldn't help but laugh. "You are going to marry him so hard," she said with a mischievous grin.

"I am not," Ming argued.

"Whatever you say . . . Mrs. Charming." Bianca giggled.

Ming gave her a dirty look and pinched her arm.

"Ow! That hurt." Bianca rubbed the sore spot on her right arm.

"Good. I hope that'll get you to shut up about who I'm NOT going to marry."

"Who's getting married?" Terrance walked up to them.

"No one. I'm just teasing Ming," Bianca said.

"Sorry to have interrupted." Terrance smiled. "Where is the prince?"

"He went inside."

"Well . . . no use standing out here. Come on I'll show you to your room," he said.

They stepped inside, and Bianca had to suppress the urge to gasp. The cottage was breathtakingly beautiful. There were white lace curtains on the windows, glossy wood floors, and a deer head above the fireplace. She could imagine her mother drooling over the antique furniture and wanting to get back home to redecorate their house.

"Wow," Bianca whispered as she took in her surroundings. She didn't know if Prince Ferdinand had been resourceful or cold enough to build the fire himself, but there was a cozy blaze burning in the fireplace. All Bianca wanted was a hot cup of cocoa and to sit by the fire, but she knew there was no point in relaxing at this moment. There was still so much that needed to be done.

"You may use the two rooms downstairs. Prince Ferdinand and I will be in the rooms upstairs. Please let me know if there is anything I can do to help." Terrance guided them to the rooms.

"Thank you so much," Bianca said.

"You're very welcome," he replied.

Bianca and Ming went to their assigned bedrooms as soon as Terrance retired upstairs to join the prince. Bianca's room was plainly decorated. It had a small bed with two white pillows and a white comforter. There was a wooden night table on the one side of the bed with a ceramic bowl filled with water and a silver pitcher beside it. There was also a wooden trunk at the foot of the bed. The hardwood floor gleamed under the gentle light that entered the room through the only window.

"This is really nice," Bianca said.

"Yeah," Ming replied.

"Do you wanna share the room, or do you want this one to yourself?"

"I think we should stick together. There's plenty of room for both of us in here."

"Cool." Bianca sighed as she put her backpack on the floor.

"You okay?"

"Yeah, I'm fine. It's just . . . it's just really weird being here, you know what I mean?"

"Yep." Ming sighed. "I wonder if there's any warm water here. I sure could use a bath."

"Why don't you ask Terrance?" Bianca suggested.

"All right. What are you going to do?"

"I'm going to read for a bit. I want to see if there's anything else I can learn from that spell book that will help me rescue Mom."

Ming nodded and walked out of their room.

Bianca sat on the corner of the bed and looked around. She was amazed at how much had changed in such a short amount of time. She took a deep breath and pulled the spell book out of her backpack. She had stopped reading the book once she'd found the portal spell. She was still curious as to why Lenore was so desperate to have the book in her possession. The following page told her why.

There in front of Bianca, Mirabel gave precise details as to how you could bring someone back from the dead. As she continued to read, a chill ran up and down her spine. Bianca then remembered what Rose had said to her: "Your grandmother killed Lenore's mother, Gertrude."

Oh, my God . . . she's trying to bring her mother back from the dead.

12

"YOUR LITTLE BRAT is here," Lenore said.

Rose took a raspy breath and muttered a prayer for her daughter's safety. Lenore sneered when she heard what she was doing but said nothing. The spell Lenore had cast to remove her voice had worn off. Rose now had her voice back . . . much to Lenore's annoyance.

Lenore cackled. She already knew Bianca had the spell book with her. She could feel its pull—its power. The girl was foolish enough to think that she could trade the book for her mother's life.

Mistress told me so.

She knew that Queen Mirabel had a spell that could bring back the dead. She'd spent a year trying to contact her spirit and just when she had been close to giving up, Mirabel had appeared inside her bedroom mirror.

Lenore thought about the promises that Mirabel had made to her when she'd decided to attack Rose and steal the book from them ten years ago.

"I'll tell you everything you need to know to bring your mother back to life. But . . . you must promise me that you will destroy the Frost women. They are the only ones left with Snow White's blood still running in their veins. Once they are dead, my vengeance will be complete and I will finally be able to rest."

Lenore had only nodded and agreed to her demands. All she'd

wanted was her mother back. Rose's estranged mother, Alice, had fought and killed Gertrude before her very eyes. The only thing that helped her sleep at night was the fact that Gertrude's death curse had fallen upon Alice and killed her instantly.

Lenore looked into Rose's eyes. They were the same shade of emerald green as her mother's. All it did was remind her of her loss and how much she abhorred Rose and her family and everything they represented. She tried to keep her hatred in check. No matter how much she wanted to kill her, she needed her alive for a while longer.

Mistress said she wanted her alive. But she didn't say I couldn't have a bit of fun with her.

"Hungry?" Lenore asked.

Rose didn't answer. In the three days she since she'd captured the witch, Lenore had only given her stale bread and dirty water. Lenore was amazed she hadn't gotten sick.

Lenore pulled a bright red apple out of her pocket. "Here."

Rose tightened her lips and moved her face away from the apple. Lenore hissed and grabbed Rose by the jaw. She pried Rose's mouth open and shoved the apple in her mouth. Rose squirmed and spat the piece of apple she had bitten. She could see Rose trying hard to resist the crisp and juicy apple. She probably suspected that the apple was poisoned.

Lenore leaned over and whispered into Rose's ear, "I want you to know . . . the only reason you're even still breathing is because I want to see the look on your face when I extinguish the light from your daughter's eyes."

Angry tears escaped Rose's eyes. Lenore saw the impotent rage in her enemy's face and delighted in it. Rose shrieked and screamed as she struggled against the ropes that bound her. She knew what would happen to her should Rose break free. The sounds coming out of her were so animalistic, so primal . . . a mother protecting her young. Well, too bad it wouldn't do her any good.

"Don't bother. Even if you do manage to get out of those ropes, you won't be able to leave."

Lenore cackled and walked out of the room. She closed the door behind her and then pressed her ear against it.

She listened as Rose burst into tears once she thought Lenore was gone.

"Oh, God, help me. David . . . I don't know where you are . . . if you're even alive, but please hear me. I need your help. Don't let Bianca anywhere near this place. This place reeks of envy and death. Please find me . . . I don't want to die here."

Lenore walked away and chuckled. There was no one that would hear her plea. She was going to see to it that Rose died in that room. Alone. In the darkness. With no one to hear her scream.

Lenore walked into her room feeling pleased with herself. She had finally gotten inside Rose's head.

To most people, their bedroom was a getaway, a sanctuary. With Lenore's bedroom, this was not the case. Her bedchamber was more dungeon than sanctuary. Her bed was unmade and dirty. The sheets were tattered and filthy. Her night table was covered with black candles and spider webs. The stone floor hadn't been swept in ages. Lenore heard the cockroaches skittering across the floor, hiding from her view.

She walked toward her vanity and stood before her mirror. This was the only item in her room that she kept clean. This was the mirror she used to communicate with her mistress. It had an elaborately designed black frame, with roses, thorns and skulls carved into the ebony wood. She polished the wooden frame carefully every week.

"Mistress? Are you there?" Her dark eyes desperately searched her reflection for any sign of Queen Mirabel.

She studied her likeness while she waited for Mirabel to appear. Her dark brown hair was greasy and beginning to show signs of graying. Her skin was sickly and pale. Lenore was starting to look like an old woman, and she was barely forty years old. Yet Rose, who was the same age she was, looked like she was still in her early thirties.

"Bitch! Stupid hateful, bitch! I hate her! I hate them all!" she screamed. She picked up her perfume bottle and threw it on the floor so hard that it shattered into thousands of pieces.

"That's the spirit," a female voice whispered.

Lenore gasped and turned her attention to the mirror. She no longer saw her reflection in the looking glass. All she saw was a tall and lithe blond woman. The air of royalty could be felt even from where Lenore stood. Mirabel had long blond hair that cascaded over her shoulders. She had small, thin lips that remained hard and unsmiling. Her dark brown eyes assessed everything harshly as she looked past Lenore and gazed at her bedroom. It was the only time Lenore felt ashamed of the way she kept her room.

"Mistress," Lenore said and then bowed her head. She struggled to regain her composure, but her chest rose and fell rapidly as she fought to catch her breath.

"Have you captured Rose Frost?" Queen Mirabel demanded from within the mirror.

"I have."

"Does she have my book with her?"

Lenore was afraid to answer the question for fear of Mirabel's reaction to the news. She took a deep breath. "No, Mistress. She does not."

"Damnation!" she shouted. The glass vibrated with her anger. For a moment Lenore though that the mirror would fall to the floor and join her perfume bottle's fate.

"Why does that family always get in the way of my plans? Why?" Mirabel stomped her feet from one side of the mirror to the other.

"I'm doing everything I can, Mistress," Lenore replied.

"Get the book, and you will find a way to bring your mother back to life."

"I did manage to get Rose's daughter to follow us here. I believe she has your book."

Mirabel arched an eyebrow and grinned. "Really? Interesting . . . perhaps I'll have a bit of fun with her before she arrives."

"What do you want me to do?" Lenore gazed at the mirror.

Mirabel turned back to Lenore as though remembering she was still standing before the mirror awaiting further instructions. "Wait for her. She'll come on her own. I know one thing for certain and that is that no matter how hard you try to extinguish them they always find a way to save their own . . . but not this time . . . Not. This. Time."

13

BIANCA SAT IN THE living room hunched over Mirabel's spell book, trying to figure out if there was anything she could use to her advantage. But after a while, all the words just jumbled into one another and nothing made any sense. When she had started reading, there had been plenty of great light to read by, but as the day slipped away and the night became dark, she had to use a couple of flashlights to see the words scribbled in the book.

She couldn't help but feel curious. She wanted to know what it was that had made Mirabel go mad. Why had she allowed herself to be seduced by the darkness? What had happened to ultimately make her snap? So many questions . . . never enough answers. A part of her wanted to sit and talk to Mirabel, another part of her wanted to throw the book into the fire and run away as fast as humanly possible.

As she went to turn the page, an angry green spark shot out from the book as though warning her to go no further. The spark stung her in the middle of her palm. Bianca shrieked and pulled her hands away. She quickly inspected her left hand. Nothing. Her heart was pounding so hard she thought it was going to burst out of her chest. She had expected to see a burn mark or something along those lines, but her skin was perfectly clear.

What the hell was that all about?

She tried to turn the page once more and was met with the same treatment. When she inspected the palm of her hand again, she found a tiny apple-shaped bruise the size of a fingernail.

"What the what?" she whispered.

She rubbed the imprint on her hand with her thumb, hoping that it would somehow make it go away. She even tried scratching it off with her fingernails but all it did was aggravate her skin. It was dark pink by the time she decided to stop.

Bianca slammed the book shut and placed it back inside its wooden box. She then put the box in her backpack. She did her best to calm down. Bianca thought about going to sleep, but she knew that she wouldn't have a restful slumber that night. She also didn't want her tossing and turning to wake Ming.

So Bianca grabbed her sketch book and pencil. Drawing always had a way of getting her to relax. At first she drew the shape that had now taken permanent residence on the palm of her left hand. But the more she drew it, the more it stressed her out. She thought about Terrance and without realizing it she began to sketch him on a new sheet of paper. She thought about his dark brown, deep-set eyes. His square jaw, thin lips, and long brown hair that barely grazed his shoulders. She let herself fall into the soft scratchy rhythm of the pencil against the paper. By the time she was finished drawing his face, she was exhausted and ready to go to sleep. Still . . . the mark on the palm of her hand haunted her while she slept.

What did it mean?

A ray of sunshine landed on Bianca's eyes. She turned over and tried to ignore the internal alarm clock that let her know it was time to wake up.

Growl . . . growl . . . growl . . .

What now? She sat up and rubbed the sleep out of her eyes.

Her eyes felt heavy, and she had a slight throbbing in her head that she knew would last all day long. She needed to check and see if there was any aspirin in the first aid kit.

"Ming?" Bianca whispered as she gently shook her friend. But nothing she did could wake Ming from her deep slumber.

Who am I kidding? I should know better. She sleeps like she's in a coma.

Bianca quickly got dressed and went outside. Immediately after stepping outside, she wished she had put on her jacket.

It must be at least fifty degrees outside. Hopefully it'll get warmer throughout the day.

Bianca searched for the source of the sound from where she stood. She knew better than to wander off alone in the forest. She rubbed her arms and tried to warm herself. Bianca could see the sun peeking through the mountains, the sky losing the dark inky color and slowly changing into a light blue. The cool morning breeze made the trees sway from side to side. They rustled softly, greeting the new day.

"I must be losing my friggin' mind," Bianca muttered. She started to turn around to go back inside the cottage, but stopped when she heard the growl once more.

"Okay . . . that was definitely something," Bianca whispered. She gasped when she heard the breaking of branches and the ground tremble softly. "Oh, my God." Bianca's eyes almost fell out of her sockets when she saw a huge black bear appear. It was definitely the last thing she had expected to see.

"Help," Bianca squeaked. She tried saying it a little louder, but it only made the bear move closer toward her. "Oh, God," she gasped and jumped a step backward.

The bear growled softly and took another step toward her. It was then that Bianca noticed his eyes. They were ice blue . . . just like hers. The bear groaned. He moved his mouth as though he were trying to speak to her.

It couldn't be . . .

Impossible.

"Daddy?" She quickly covered her mouth, almost as if she wanted to force the word back inside her mouth. A lump formed in her throat—she tried to push that down too.

The bear nodded.

"How is this even possible?" Bianca wondered aloud as she walked closer to the creature she believed to be her father. Even though she knew exactly how it had happened, it was still hard to accept the circumstances as true.

He covered his eyes with his paws and shook his head as though embarrassed.

"It's okay. Don't worry. We'll find a way to get you back to normal. Then we can all go back home." Bianca hugged her father. She felt him put a giant paw around her. She pulled herself away and gazed into those soulful blue eyes. There was no denying that her father was trapped in there, somewhere. Bianca studied the creature her father had become. He was massive and heavy bodied—all muscle. Her gaze traveled down to his huge paws; they ended with long, sharp, and curved black claws. She gently patted him on the shoulder, taking a moment to feel his thick black fur.

"How did you find me?"

He lifted his head and sniffed.

"You could smell me?"

He grunted as he nodded.

Ten years. Bianca stifled a sob as she thought of everything he had missed. All the times she had needed him at home to . . . just be there. Ten years. Tears spilled forth, and the dark brown soil swallowed it greedily. So this is where he had been all this time.

"Can you stay?"

He nodded.

"Do you know where Mom is?"

He shook his head and grunted.

"That's all right, we'll find her." She patted him on the head gently and tried to sound confident.

He nodded once more.

"Okay . . . stay here." Bianca used her hands and motioned for him to sit. "Just don't go anywhere . . . don't move. I need to go inside and wake Ming up."

Bianca ran back inside the cottage. She tripped over the rug and hit her shin on the coffee table. She grabbed her leg and massaged the pain away as she hopped on one foot, still trying to make her way toward their room. She knew that she would have a black and blue bruise in a few hours. She prayed that she wasn't hallucinating as she burst into the room she shared with Ming.

"Ming! Wake up, wake up, wake up!" Bianca shook her friend so hard that she almost fell off the bed.

"Holy crap, what! Are we being attacked?" Ming she sat up and finally opened her eyes.

"I–I think I found my dad," Bianca stammered, still unable to believe the words she'd just uttered.

"Are you serious?" Ming rubbed her eyes.

"Yeah."

"Where is he?"

"Outside."

"What are you waiting for? Let's go see him."

Ming got out of bed and followed Bianca outside.

"Oh, my God," Ming said as soon as she caught a glimpse of Mr. David Frost—the bear.

"Did I also mention that he's a bear?" Bianca muttered while she chewed her thumbnail.

"You could've given me a little heads-up," Ming said.

"Sorry."

"Hi, Mr. Frost." Ming gave David a tiny awkward wave.

David grunted in response.

"Halt! Who goes there?" Prince Ferdinand burst out the front door, sword in hand.

"Wait! Stop!" Bianca threw herself in front of her father. She tried to protect him from the overzealous prince and his very sharp sword.

"Unhand her foul beast." Prince Ferdinand pointed his sword at Bianca's face. It was a breath away from her nose.

"Ming?" Bianca whispered. She did her best not to move. She was practically cross-eyed as she stared at the blade hovering at her nose.

"Yes?" Ming whispered in return.

"Find Terrance, please . . . and hurry." Bianca was afraid to move for fear of encouraging Prince Ferdinand further into action.

Ming swiftly ran into the cottage and returned with Terrance moments later.

"Yes? What is it?" Terrance stifled a yawn. He was clearly half asleep and hadn't noticed the scene before him.

"A little help here, please." Bianca pointed at the prince.

His eyes widened in surprise. He sputtered a few times, trying to find the right thing to say. It took him a moment, but he managed to speak. "Your Highness, please lower your weapon. It really is quite unnecessary, and if I may be so bold as to say that it is far too early to begin the day with bloodshed."

The prince narrowed his eyes and tightened his lips. He clearly wanted to argue with Terrance but in the end he listened to reason.

"Very well, Terrance. If you say so . . . but I still think that this bear is searching for his next meal." Prince Ferdinand reluctantly lowered his sword and returned it to its scabbard with one smooth movement.

Bianca realized she had been holding her breath when she finally took a deep lungful of fresh air.

"Prince Ferdinand, Terrance, I want you to meet my father, David Frost."

Bianca stepped aside, and the bear that was once her father bowed to the prince.

"But he's a bear," the prince said.

"Your Highness is very observant, but it's obvious that Mr. Frost wasn't always a bear," Terrance said.

"A spell perhaps?" The prince wrinkled his face as though it physically hurt him to think and ask questions.

"Yes, Your Highness," Bianca replied.

"A quest and a spell to break? A mighty adventure indeed! The minstrels will sing songs about me," Prince Ferdinand said, unable to hide the smile from his face.

"Glad you think so," Bianca muttered. "Dad? Do you know how to break the spell?" She turned her attention to her father.

He shook his head.

"Great. Just . . . great," she whispered.

"Now what?" Ming looked to Bianca.

"We have to find a way to get him back to normal," she said.

"Do you think there's something in Mirabel's spell book?" Ming asked.

"I don't know. I haven't gotten that far into it yet. Plus . . . I feel weird every time I touch it. I think the book wants me to stay away," Bianca said.

She avoided mentioning that the book had literally attacked her and left a strange mark on the palm of her hand. She resisted the urge to inspect her hand for fear that someone might notice.

"That's ridiculous. It's just a book," Ming said, dismissing the importance of what Bianca was trying to say.

"I wouldn't be so quick to misjudge it, Ming. I don't trust it. Not one bit," Bianca said. "I'm going to have a quick breakfast and then we'll be on our way." Bianca turned to her father. "Dad? Can you wait here while we get ready?"

David nodded and sat down on the ground. The dirt and leaves floated and swirled all around him. It all slowly drifted back to the soil underneath him.

Everyone went inside and had breakfast. Bianca and Ming had some cold Pop-Pastries while they changed out of their pajamas and into their jeans, long sleeved T-shirts, and hiking boots.

"Are you okay?"

"I'm fine," Bianca replied quickly. She knew what that question was going to lead to. She wasn't ready to talk about it just yet.

"Yeah, you look fine." Ming arched her eyebrow.

"Ming . . . not now. Please."

"Okay." Ming put her hands up in surrender. "But . . . if you change your mind and you do wanna talk about it, you know I'm here for you, okay?"

Bianca nodded. She wanted to say something more, but she felt that if she opened her mouth to speak she would burst into tears and not be able to follow through with the rest of their journey.

"Come on. We've got a long way to go," Ming said.

"Yeah." Bianca nodded.

They both went outside and waited for Prince Ferdinand and Terrance. She went up to her father, who unfortunately was still a bear. She sighed and sat next to him. David grumbled and buried his nose into her neck. She was surprised that his nose was so cold.

"Oh, Daddy," she whispered.

He shook his head, but remained silent. She patted his head and still couldn't get over the fact that she was touching thick, black fur and not the soft silky hair she remembered him having.

She looked up and saw Prince Ferdinand and Terrance emerge from the cottage. She gave her father a kiss on the nose and stood up.

"So, which way do we go?" Bianca asked.

"I believe the witch you speak of lives north of here, but I don't know the castle's exact location," Terrance said.

"How long do you think it'll take us to get there?" Ming asked.

"I'm not certain. Perhaps five days if we only rest at night," Terrance guessed.

What if we end up going the wrong way? Bianca wanted to be absolutely certain that they were heading in the right direction. She remembered that she had Red Riding Hood's cape in her backpack. She glanced over at her best friend. They had seen each other in some pretty embarrassing outfits, but she wasn't sure she wanted anyone to see her wearing the famous blood red cape.

"I'm never going to live this one down," she muttered.

"What?" Ming asked when she saw the annoyed look on Bianca's face.

"If you tell anyone about this, I'll kill you," she warned.

"Tell anyone about what?"

Bianca remained silent and instead pulled Red Riding Hood's cape out of her backpack.

"Oh . . . my . . . God." Ming stifled a giggle.

"Shut up," Bianca hissed.

Ming pretended to zip her lips shut and covered her mouth with her hands.

Bianca took a deep breath and put the red cape on, tying the silk ribbons into a knot around her neck. The cape swished from side to side, seemingly of its own volition. Bianca felt like an upside-down red rose.

"What are you doing?" Terrance glanced from Bianca to the cape.

"This was Red Riding Hood's cape. I'm going to see if it still works the way it's supposed to," Bianca explained.

"How did you get your hands on this?" Prince Ferdinand narrowed his eyes.

"We've had this at the museum for ages."

"It has been lost for centuries. Among other precious items from myth and lore," Prince Ferdinand said.

"I'll have to show you our inventory list one day," Bianca said.

"I thought it would be longer," Ming said.

"Well . . . remember it was worn by a little girl in the original story." Bianca tugged at the end of the cape. No matter what she did it wouldn't go past her waist.

Bianca knew she looked silly, yet she couldn't help but love the feel of the velvety cape over her shoulders. It was almost as though she was putting on a piece of red armor. She felt the soft veil of magic fall over her body, closed her eyes, and immersed herself in the feeling.

Okay, Red Riding Hood . . . show me the way to my mother. Help me find the right path.

She wasn't sure that would work. Rose had never taught her how to use the cape, but she hoped that being honest was enough to get the cape to work for her. When Bianca opened her eyes, she saw blue footprints softly glowing on the ground.

"That way." Bianca pointed to northeast.

"Are you sure?" Ming followed her fingers.

Bianca nodded.

"Very well then, off we go," Prince Ferdinand said as he mounted his white horse. He extended his hand out to Ming and helped her mount the four-legged beast.

Terrance did the same for Bianca although she barely noticed Terrance picking her up and placing her on the saddle. She was almost in a trance. All she saw was the path before her, the bright blue footsteps beckoning her, urging her to follow them to the destination she had politely demanded from the cape.

David whined and sniffed Bianca's feet. She could tell that he was worried about her. The horse neighed and took a few steps back, but Terrance took control of the stallion. He managed to calm the creature down by whispering a few soft words and patting it gently on the neck. David did his best to stay away from the horses.

"Are you all right?" Terrance had noticed the state she was in.

"Just follow the path. Stay on the path," she said in a soft voice.

"Very well," he replied.

One by one, the witch, her friend, the prince, the steward, and the bear marched into the unknown.

14

BIANCA OPENED HER EYES. Darkness. All around her was dark, dark, dark.

Where am I? Bianca wondered.

"Nowhere," a soft voice replied.

Bianca gasped and turned around searching for the voice that had answered her silent question.

"Who's there?"

"Who's there? Who is there?" the voice echoed, mocking her.

Bianca wondered if it was possible to have a heart attack at seventeen.

She took a deep breath and decided to try again. "Hello? Is someone there?"

"Here, I'm in here," the female voice said.

Suddenly, a spotlight zeroed in on Bianca and temporarily blinded her. When her eyes readjusted to the light, she saw a mirror. Bianca furrowed her brows, she recognized the looking glass. It was the one they had in the museum.

Either the same one or its twin, she thought as she took a step toward the mirror. Bianca had expected to see her own reflection in the looking glass, but instead all that looked back at her was that of an angry beautiful woman. She was tall and blond, her face in a permanent state of anger and anguish.

Before Bianca could utter a single word, the woman stepped out of the mirror and physically attacked her. She screamed and tried to fight back with her magic, but for some reason her magic wasn't working here.

Who are you? Bianca asked as she fought off the surprisingly strong woman from the mirror.

"I am Queen Mirabel," she hissed into Bianca's ear.

"Impossible," Bianca whispered as she shook her head and continued to fight off Mirabel.

The evil queen put her hands around Bianca's throat and began to strangle her. Bianca tried to pry the hands from her neck, but her hands went through them as if they were smoke.

What did I ever do to you?

"Bianca. Wake up." She heard Terrance's voice. It was distant, but she heard him. That's when it dawned on her . . . she was dreaming. She struggled to open her eyes, but something in the dream continued to pull her against her will. She could feel her body fighting to wake up and stay alive.

Terrance shook her until she opened her eyes and gasped for air.

"Are you all right?" he whispered. He had a tight grip on her hands. Her entire being shook violently. She was drenched in sweat.

She looked around, temporarily disoriented. It was still dark outside; her friends and her father were sleeping peacefully beside her under the stars. She envied their peaceful slumber. The fire had long since died out, and all that was left of it were the soft orange embers that continued to glow despite the evening breeze. Bianca welcomed the cool wind that caressed her burning skin.

"I don't know. I think so." She wiped the sweat off her forehead with the back of her hand.

"Your hands were on your neck," he said.

"What?"

"Your hands were around your neck . . . as if you were strangling yourself." Terrance frowned; she could see the concern in his dark brown eyes. Bianca looked away, not wanting him to see the fear that no doubt showed on her face.

"I heard your voice. I heard you calling my name. I kept trying to wake up. I tried. I just . . . I just can't believe Mirabel was forcing me to kill myself." Bianca's voice wavered. Never in her entire life had she ever had suicidal thoughts, even on her worst days. She enjoyed life and looked forward to the following chapter in her life. There was still so much she wanted to do, see, and learn.

"Is that what you were dreaming about?"

"That wasn't a dream; it was a nightmare," she whispered, so she wouldn't wake up David, Ming, and Ferdinand. Bianca yawned and rubbed her eyes. She was still so tired. How would she ever get any sleep after the experience she'd just had? Yawning again, she explained her nightmare to Terrance.

"Perhaps it's really Mirabel. I remember the stories my mother told me. Terrible and terrifying tales . . . she was capable of such vile things," Terrance said grimly after Bianca finished telling him about her nightmare.

"I thought Snow White had Mirabel executed."

"Yes, but remember where you are. My world is not like yours. Magic is part of our everyday lives. For all we know she could still be out there somewhere, casting her evil shadow everywhere she can," he said.

The thought sent a shiver down her spine. Even though every fiber in her being told her that what she had experienced in her dream was indeed very real, there was a part of her that wanted to believe it was just a nightmare. The rest of her was terrified.

The cool evening breeze rustled the leaves in the trees above them. She could've sworn she saw something glowing in the darkness.

Bianca gasped. "What was that?"

"Shh. There's nothing there that will hurt you," he said, doing his best to reassure her.

"God . . . I just want this to be over. I want to go home." Bianca drew her legs to her chest and rested her chin on her knees.

She could feel Terrance's eyes upon her. She felt so incredibly small. A far cry from the confident young woman she had been when they'd been in the woods. Out there with the sun shining high above them, she knew what she had to do. She'd had the confidence to make a plan and see it through. But here in the dark? She was just a frightened young girl who needed all the help she could get.

"Don't worry. This will all be over soon," he said.

Bianca nodded but wasn't too sure she felt comforted by his words. Terrance moved to go back to sleep on his blanket when Bianca grabbed his hand and squeezed it tight. The action surprised her more than it did him. She released her grip on his hand. She wrung her fingers together nervously.

"Terrance?" she whispered his name so softly that she wondered if he'd even heard her.

"Yes, Bianca?"

She felt her cheeks burn with embarrassment. She couldn't believe she was actually going to ask him this. "Is it okay . . . could you hold me for a little while? Until I fall asleep? Please?"

"Of course, I'll hold you all night long if I have to," he said with warm smile and an affirmative nod. He grabbed the shirt he'd rolled up into a pillow and shared it with her.

An immense amount of relief washed over Bianca as she felt Terrance's strong, warm arms around her waist. She felt certain that no more strange dreams or nightmares would plague her that night. And surely enough, within minutes they were both sound asleep.

When Bianca opened her eyes the following morning, she found she was still in Terrance's arms. She was surprised that he had kept his word and held her all night long. He held her tightly against his chest. He snored lightly, but she didn't find that annoying at all. If anything she thought it was quite possibly the most adorable thing ever.

Bianca tried to wriggle out of his embrace, but he snorted, muttered some incoherent words and held her even tighter. She wouldn't have minded it one bit if her bladder didn't feel as though it was full to burst.

"Terrance, wake up," she whispered as she nudged him on the shoulder with her free hand.

"Hmm? What?" He sat up still half asleep, never relaxing his grip on Bianca.

"Terrance, I need to use the bathroom," she whispered.

"Bathroom?" He frowned. He didn't seem to understand the word.

What else do you call a toilet? Bianca wondered as she searched her memory. "I have to relieve my bladder . . . umm . . . use the latrine," she explained.

"Oh." He nodded, finally understanding.

"Um . . . you have to let me go," she said unable to suppress the grin that appeared on her lips.

"Oh dear. I'm so sorry." He blushed and finally released his grip on her.

Bianca sighed and thought that Terrance was completely cute in the morning. She wondered if he was like this every morning, or if she was witnessing a rare moment.

She walked several feet away and stood behind a tree. She double-checked until she was sure no one could see and relieved her bladder. Ming soon followed and waited a few feet away for Bianca to finish.

"Morning, B," Ming said.

"Morning."

"I brought you your toothbrush." Ming handed Bianca a purple toothbrush and a small tube of toothpaste.

"Cool. Thank you." Bianca took these items from Ming.

"So . . . you and Terrance were looking pretty cozy this morning. Anything you wanna tell me? Hmm?" Ming wriggled her eyebrows up and down playfully.

Bianca groaned as she brushed her teeth. "I thought you were asleep," she said while the toothbrush bobbed up and down in her mouth.

"I'm a friggin' ninja, B. You know I have mad radar skills. You can't get anything past me." She took on a fighting stance and did a few air kicks. "Hiya!" she shouted.

Bianca rolled her eyes and spat the toothpaste foam out of her mouth. Ming then handed her a bottle of water. Bianca took it and used a mouthful of water, gargled and spat out the residue. She also rinsed her hands for good measure.

"Nothing happened," Bianca explained and then wiped the water off her chin with the back of her hand.

"Terrance is hot. Don't tell me you weren't hoping something would happen."

"I was having a nightmare last night, and Terrance woke me up," Bianca said.

"And then?" Ming smiled. She wiggled her eyebrows again, obviously hoping that Bianca was about to give her some juicy bit of information.

"He saw that I was strangling myself with my bare hands and couldn't wake up," Bianca admitted.

"Wait. What? You tried to kill yourself in your sleep!"

"Shh," Bianca whispered and then tried to cover Ming's mouth to keep her from making more noise. She didn't want anyone else to know about her dream, especially her father. The last thing she wanted to do was worry him.

Ming slapped Bianca's hands away and, just like that, her playfulness vanished. "No! You shh!" Ming snapped. "Don't shush me. This is too much, B."

"I know," she replied, her voice somber.

"I can't do this." Ming pulled on the ends of her jet-black hair.

"You wanna go home?"

Ming let go of her hair and nodded. "I don't want to die here, Bianca. I mean . . . working in the museum is one thing, but all this craziness with evil witches and now this? It's too much."

"I know," Bianca whispered.

"Listen . . . I'm not going to ditch you or anything like that right now. That would just not be cool. But you gotta promise me that we'll leave if it gets to be too overwhelming, okay?" Ming looked at her with pleading eyes.

Bianca shook her head. "I'm not leaving without my parents. But I do promise to find a way for you to go back home."

"I can't leave you here," Ming argued.

"You're gonna have to."

Ming sighed. "I think I'm going to let Future Ming and Future Bianca handle it when the moment arrives."

"I agree." But no matter what they said to each other, Bianca couldn't ignore the fact that the worst was yet to come.

15

AFTER TWO DAYS OF traveling in the forest, they all fell into a false sense of security. That night they decided to settle near the mouth of a small cave. Bianca had finally, albeit reluctantly, removed Red Riding Hood's cape for the night. She was scared that she wouldn't be able to find the right path again. Regardless, she let out a sigh of relief as she felt the magic peel itself off her body.

They all sat around the crackling fire, enjoying their simple meal of smoked venison, bread, and sweet wine, when the horses neighed and whined for no apparent reason.

Bianca jumped and placed her hand over her heart. It skipped several heartbeats. "What's wrong?"

Terrance grabbed both horses by the bridle and spoke softly to them. What he said to get them to calm down Bianca would never know, but within moments both horses relaxed. The horses had already gotten used to being around David so Bianca knew that it wasn't because of him.

"Is there something out there?" Ming looked into the darkness.

"I don't know. I'll go investigate. Stay here with the prince," Terrance said.

"Wait, I want to go, too," Ferdinand protested.

"Your Highness, please stay here and protect them," Terrance said.

"Very well." Ferdinand groaned.

"Be careful," Bianca said.

Terrance nodded and faded into the darkness.

No one made a sound. All of her senses were on high alert. She paid close attention to the crackling fire and the quiet creaks and snaps made by the burning wood. The rustling of the leaves. Her father's deep breaths. And after what felt like an eternity, they heard the rustle of branches. Ming grabbed Bianca's arm and shrieked. Bianca's heart leaped to her throat when she heard her father's snarl. All of his fur stood on end, making him look twice as large and much more menacing.

"It's me." Terrance stepped into the soft orange light.

"Did you see anything?" Bianca asked.

"Nothing, I'm sorry. Whatever frightened the horses is long gone," he replied.

"Somehow that doesn't make me feel any better." Ming nibbled on her lower lip. Her eyes darted nervously from side to side as though waiting for something to jump out from the bushes.

Bianca could tell that Ming was ready to have a nervous breakdown.

"It's okay. Calm down." Bianca hugged Ming and tried to get her to relax.

"Well . . . why don't we sleep in shifts? I can stay up with Dad and then Terrance and Prince Ferdinand can take the next shift and so on and so forth. At least until we're all ready to travel again. What do you think?" Bianca suggested.

"Sounds good to me," Ming replied with a sniff. She wiped away the tears that pooled on the corners of her eyes.

Terrance parted his lips, ready to protest Bianca's decision, but she quickly raised her hand and silenced him with a look.

"Don't say anything. You get some sleep. You know how to ride a horse, I don't. You know how to wield a sword . . . I don't. Can you do either of those things without sleep?"

Terrance narrowed his eyes. She could tell he wanted to argue with her, but instead he nodded. "Very well. I shall bid you a good night," he whispered.

"Good night."

"And please do not hesitate to wake me should something frighten you," he said.

"I won't," she promised.

Terrance rubbed his chin and shook his head.

He's probably trying to decide how stubborn I am.

She noticed he had a five o'clock shadow. She wondered how old he was and whether he spent the day thinking of her as much as she thought of him.

Terrance walked away and went to sleep. Whatever he wanted to say to her died on his lips.

Bianca grabbed a blanket and sat close to the crackling fire. David lay down behind her, and she rested her back against his great big, furry belly. She stared into the open flames, wondering what would happen next. Hours passed by and the only sound that could be heard was the chirping of crickets, the hooting of the owls, and the wood creaking and burning before her.

Bianca wondered if she stared into the flames long enough if she would see something. A premonition, her mother's face, or perhaps something completely unexpected. She mused with the idea of being able to catch fire. She giggled at the thought, yet something deep inside of her told her to try.

She took a deep breath and closed her eyes. She stuck her hand into the fire and closed her fist over the open fire. When Bianca retrieved her hand, she half expected to see it at least a little pink, but her hand was as pale as ever. She uncurled her fingers and to her amazement there was a tiny little flame on the palm of her hand. The flame was the size of her pinky finger. It danced and flickered its orange light from side to side as though trying to shimmy its way back into the fire.

"Whoa." She gasped.

Bianca threw the tiny spark back into the open flames and tried to make sense of what had just happened. She wished her mother had been there to see and give her advice on what else she should expect. Would her magical powers continue to grow? If so, into what? Would she be a powerful witch? What if she didn't want to go down that path? What would happen to her then? So many questions, never any answers.

She finally broke her silence, saying, "Dad?"

David grunted.

She still couldn't believe he was alive and close by. Even though he was a bear, it was still comforting to know that he was there with her.

"Daddy, I'm scared," she whispered. Her eyes blurred with the sting and promise of tears that would soon follow.

David let out a soft moan and licked Bianca's cheek. She curled up beside her father and burst into tears. Without realizing, she cried herself into a dark and dreamless slumber.

Bianca sat up and gasped. She had fallen asleep when she was supposed to keep watch over everyone.

"Don't worry. All is well." Terrance gently placed a hand on her shoulder.

"How long was I out?" Bianca rubbed the kink out of her shoulder.

"Several hours. Your father woke me and Prince Ferdinand. We resumed watch over our little camp," he explained.

"I'm so sorry. I didn't mean to fall asleep."

"Do not worry." He gave her a playful wink.

Bianca smiled, but no matter what Terrance said she still felt like she'd let everyone down.

They were on the third day of their journey, and Bianca could've sworn she heard something in the distance. Terrance stopped to listen, too. It sounded as though an earthquake had grown legs and was running toward them. David was gnawing on a smoked piece of venison; he dropped it and stood absolutely still. He too was bothered by the sound he heard.

Prince Ferdinand glanced at Terrance. "Did you hear that?"

"I'm starting to think that all bad things start with that question," Ming said.

Bianca's stomach dropped. She was certain that the ground would split open and swallow them whole.

David growled.

At least Bianca knew she wasn't losing her mind. The horses reared back and threw their passengers off their backs. They all fell clumsily to the ground and watched as the horses kicked up dust and dirt from the earth as they vanished into the thick forest.

"Crap," Bianca muttered.

"I'm getting kinda tired of being terrified," Ming said.

Terrance tensed. "We need to run and hide . . . now." The urgency and fear in his voice didn't escape Bianca.

"Who's after us?" Bianca asked.

"He's not so much of a *who* . . . he's more of a *what*."

"What is he?" Ming's eyes grew round.

"Wolf," he said.

"A wolf?" Bianca repeated.

Terrance nodded.

"As in the *Big Bad Wolf*?" she asked.

"Yes."

"Crap," Bianca and Ming said in unison.

Bianca's mind went a million miles per second as she tried to think of a plan. That was when she remembered the brick in her backpack.

"Hang on." Bianca opened her backpack and found the red brick sitting at the bottom.

"What are you doing? Why aren't we running?" Ming shrieked.

"Saving our butts, that's what I'm doing," Bianca said.

"I swear to God, Bianca, the horses have more sense than we do," Ming muttered.

"Shut up and do as I say," Bianca ordered.

"Not by the hair on my chiny, chin, chin." Bianca placed the red brick on the ground and took a step back after chanting the spell.

The brick trembled and quickly multiplied itself over and over again. It was as though a tiny group of invisible hands was building a house faster than the speed of light. This continued until everyone was standing in front of a large brick house. Bianca opened the door and corralled everyone inside the impenetrable walls of the famous home that had belonged to the third little pig. She locked the door behind her and let out a sigh of relief.

Hopefully we'll be safe from whatever is after us.

"Wow," Ming said as she looked around and took everything in. "B?"

"Yeah?"

"How is a brick house going to stop that giant wolf from squishing us to death?"

"This house is indestructible."

"Ooooh . . . cool," Ming said.

Then the house trembled as though bombs were falling from the sky. Ming screamed and ran to the furthest corner of the house. She covered her head with her hands and muttered several incoherent words. Ferdinand ran to her and held her tight. Ming accepted this bit of comfort and clung to him as though her life depended on it.

Bianca walked to the window. She wasn't sure what to look for, but it was better than rocking herself back and forth in a fetal position while sucking on her thumb. She saw nothing but pine trees and dried up leaves scattered on the ground. She assumed that the wolf Terrance spoke of was currently on the roof wreaking havoc on the little brick house, or at least he was trying to. She screamed when a huge yellow-green eye covered her view.

"Let me in," the wolf growled, his voice sounding like rocks falling down a mountain.

"No!" Bianca screamed.

"I'll let you have a swift end. Better for me to end your life than the witch," he snarled.

"I said no!" she shouted.

"You can't stay in there forever . . . even the pigs had to come out at some point." The wolf chuckled.

"Let me speak to him," Terrance whispered to Bianca.

"What? Why? Are you crazy?" Bianca frowned.

Terrance rested his hands on his hips and looked up at the ceiling. He ran his calloused fingers through his dark brown hair and finally said, "I'm his grandson."

"Grandson?" Bianca echoed. "How is that even possible?"

"I can't explain now, but trust me, anything is possible here in Everafter."

Bianca placed a hand on his shoulder. "Are you sure he won't eat you or worse? I don't want you to get hurt."

"You're very sweet to worry about me." He gave her the saddest of smiles. "But trust me. I'll be quite all right."

Bianca shook her head. This was wrong. She didn't want anyone to get hurt because of her. Angry tears of frustration escaped her eyes. She quickly wiped them away. She never liked it when people saw her crying.

"How do you know? How do you know everything is going to be okay?" she asked.

"I don't. I've never even met him before," Terrance admitted. "But he'll know my scent. I can only hope that it will be enough to keep him from tearing me apart."

"Terrance . . . I . . . " A lump formed in her throat. She couldn't even finish what she wanted to say.

"Trust me," Terrance whispered, and then he gently kissed her on the forehead. "I'll be right back."

Bianca could still feel the warmth of his kiss upon her skin. It burned with the promise of more to come.

Bianca snatched his hand before he touched the silver doorknob. "There has to be another way," she said.

He smiled and asked her to trust him once more, then Terrance took a deep breath and stepped outside. He closed the door behind him. Once Bianca heard the soft click of the door lock, tears came forth once more.

"What is he doing?" Ming snapped out of her nervous breakdown and joined Bianca by the only window in the entire house.

"He's going to talk to him," Bianca replied.

"Is he crazy? Did you try to talk him out of it?"

"Of course I tried. Do you think I want him to be out there talking to a giant wolf? Now be quiet. I want to hear what's going on outside." She gently pushed Ming aside and opened the window a crack.

The Big Bad Wolf was every bit as scary as Bianca had always imagined. He was completely black, darker than a midnight on a starless, moonless night. His gums were dark pink and his teeth were amazingly white. His eyes were bright yellow-green that held an indescribable flame. Where it came from, Bianca would never know.

16

THE WOLF'S MOIST, BLACK nose flared up as he took in Terrance's scent. The young man braced himself and stood completely still.

I'd do the same if this was my first time meeting the infamous Big Bad Wolf, Bianca thought.

The wolf took in the sight of his grandson. From where Bianca stood it looked as though he didn't know what to make of this hairless pup who stood before him as though he had a right to do so.

"You smell of my kin. Who are you?" the wolf asked as he narrowed his eyes with suspicion.

"I am your grandson, Terrance Connor," he replied.

"Ah . . . yes. William's son." He smiled, flashing his sharp white teeth.

"Yes, sir." He nodded.

"I will spare your life because you are my kin, but the others . . . they must perish," he said.

"But why?"

"It is what she wants," he growled.

"The witch?"

"Yes, it is what Lenore wants."

"Why are you doing her bidding? I never knew you to take orders from anyone."

Wolf snarled and slapped Terrance across the cheek, sending him flying against the door of the brick house.

Bianca jumped and shouted when she saw Terrance sail through the air. She was moments away from opening the door when Prince Ferdinand grabbed her hand and held her back. He slowly shook his head.

Terrance groaned as he massaged the back of his head.

The old wolf snarled. "Mind your manners, boy. I will demand the respect that is due to me. Remember, you may be my kin, but you're no full-blooded wolf. William dishonored his family when he ran off and looked underneath your mortal mother's skirt."

"Forgive me." Terrance wiped the bit of blood that spilled out of the corner of his mouth.

"Disrespect me like that again, and I will find it very difficult to spare your life . . . family or not," the wolf growled.

Terrance lowered his head and repeated his apology.

The wolf snarled and licked his nose with his long mauve tongue. He looked straight at Bianca. Her heart leaped to her throat as she stared right back into the wolf's menacing eyes. Never once did she look away from his yellow-green gaze.

"The witch threatened to destroy my family," he explained, finally pulling his gaze away from Bianca.

"And you believe her?" Terrance asked.

"She's no mere mortal. There is something frighteningly dark about her," he admitted.

"That is why we need your help, grandfather. We can stop her," Terrance said.

"I can't," he replied.

"Why?"

"I won't risk the lives of my children. I won't risk my wife."

"What can you do?" Terrance met his grandfather's eyes.

The wolf narrowed his gaze at his mortal grandson. "Four days," he stated.

"Four days?"

"If you haven't reached her castle in four days, I'll have no choice but to kill your friends," he said.

"Thank you, Grandfather." Terrance bowed. "Can you tell us exactly where her castle is?"

The Big Bad Wolf jerked his chin toward Bianca. "The girl knows the way. She has the red cape. It will take her where she needs to go," the wolf said.

"How do you know she has it?"

"No amount of time inside a wooden trunk will take away the smell of that girl. Little brat refused to die . . . but her grandmother certainly was tasty." The Big Bad Wolf then let out a low chuckle.

Terrance gave him a tight-lipped smile, and started to turn around to walk away but something the wolf said stopped him in his tracks.

"The girl . . . she smells just like her," the wolf said.

"I know," Terrance replied.

"Guard her well. She may be the one who can put an end to this madness." And with that having been said, the wolf vanished. He melded into the woods as though he had never even existed.

Terrance straightened his clothes as best as he could and knocked on the door. Bianca opened it immediately and pulled him inside the house.

"Are you okay?" she demanded as soon as he stepped inside.

"Yes, I'm fine, thank you," he said.

"What did he say?" Ming's voice held her worry.

"We have four days," he replied.

"Or?" Ming raised her brows.

"Or he'll kill us all himself," Terrance replied in a nonchalant tone of voice, as though this sort of thing happened to him every day.

For all Bianca knew—it did.

One by one they walked out of the brick house. Bianca pulled a single strand of hair from her scalp and tied it around the doorknob. The house disappeared and returned to its original form of a single red brick. Bianca noticed everyone staring at her as she put the brick in her backpack.

"What?"

"What else do you have in there?" Ming tried to peer into Bianca's bag.

"I can't tell you. It's a surprise," she replied.

"Come, we best be on our way," Terrance said.

Bianca put on the red cape and the path was shown to her once more. This time around she wasn't so overwhelmed when the magical veil fell over her body. She was getting used to wearing the cape.

"What did the wolf mean when he said kin? What does that word mean?" Ming whispered to Bianca.

"Kin is family," Bianca replied.

"So . . . Terrance is a wolf?"

"I don't know," Bianca said.

Ming shrugged her shoulders and kept walking.

They walked silently for many, many miles. Bianca quickly realized how lucky they had been to have horses in the beginning of their journey. After several hours of walking, Bianca was physically exhausted. Wearing the red cape was also starting to take its toll on her tiny frame. Luckily, everyone noticed and decided to set up camp for the night.

They built a fire and had some of Bianca's soup. Terrance had sneaked away to eat his food by himself. Bianca gulped down the rest of her meal, not caring that it burned the roof of her mouth, and went to find him.

He sat on an overgrown tree root. His bowl was empty and lay by his feet. Her heart ached for him when she saw his head hung low, his shoulders slumped downward. In the few days she had known him, she had never seen him like this. He always stood tall and proud; it made Bianca feel inadequate to stand next to him. She didn't like seeing him this way, so defeated.

"Hi," Bianca said.

"Oh, hello." Terrance turned and saw her. He smiled at her but she noticed that it didn't reach his dark brown eyes; their normal spark was almost gone. All she saw were faint embers of what was once there.

"Can I join you? I have some water if you'd like a drink." She showed him her bottle of water.

"Yes, of course," he replied.

Bianca climbed over the giant root and sat next to him. She unscrewed the cap and handed him the water. He took the bottle and studied it for a moment. Bianca then realized that he'd probably never seen a plastic bottle before. He took a long gulp and handed the bottle back to her.

"Are you okay?"

"Why do you ask?" He wouldn't meet her eyes.

"You've been quiet this whole time. Plus, I figured you might be a little traumatized from meeting your giant wolf grandfather for the first time . . . that can't be easy."

He nodded.

"Do you want to talk about it?"

"Why?"

She shrugged. "I don't know. I just thought maybe you wanted someone to talk to."

"Are you sure you want me to bore you with it?" Once more he gave her that heartbreakingly sad smile.

"I doubt you could bore me."

"I'm not like him," he said.

"Not like who?"

"Like . . . my grandfather."

"Oh, Terrance. I never thought for a second that you were anything like him."

"I'm also not a werewolf, no matter what you hear," he stated.

"Do you mind telling me . . . what it is you are?"

"I'm human. I'm a mortal man," he said in a forceful tone. He spoke in a way that led Bianca to believe that he wasn't just trying to convince her; he was also trying to convince himself that he was normal, just like everyone else. He shook his head and added, "Except that I have some heightened senses."

"Let me guess, heightened sense of smell and hearing?"

"Correct. But also heightened sense of sight, touch, and taste."

"Really?" Bianca scrunched up her nose. She sniffed underneath her armpits to see if she smelled bad.

Terrance laughed. "You smell wonderful, trust me."

"Could you smell me a mile away?"

"I could smell you if you were on another planet," he said.

"Now I know you're kidding," she said and giggled. She thought quietly to herself for a moment and then whispered, "Must be lonely."

Terrance nodded. He grabbed a fistful of stones and tossed them into the dark forest. Bianca wished the sun was up so she could see how far he had thrown those stones.

"Do you have any siblings?"

Terrance shook his head.

"Join the club," she muttered.

He turned to her with a confused look on his face. "Club?"

"Never mind that. What I mean is that it would probably help if you had someone to talk to besides your parents. Someone who is just like you."

"Spoken like someone who knows a little about loneliness." His eyes locked into hers.

She took a deep breath, looked away and fidgeted with her fingers. She avoided meeting his unfaltering gaze. She felt him staring at her and glanced at him with the corner of her eyes before quickly looking away.

"At least you found your father."

"Yeah, Mom will be very excited to hear about that. She's been searching for him for ten years."

"Ten years?" His eyes widened with surprise.

"Yeah." Bianca had enough of being underneath Terrance's microscope.

She wanted to know more about him. "What about your parents?"

"That is an incredibly short tale and just so you know my father tells it much better than I ever will. Having said that, my father, William, who happens to be a full-blooded wolf, saw my mother, Claire, walking in the forest with her family one day, and he fell madly in love with her.

"Every time he retells the story, he says that all he could see was her. He didn't notice the hundreds of scents the wind carried to his nostrils, nor did he care for the deer several feet from him. He forgot his hunger. His thirst. Everything. The world vanished . . . all he could see was my mother." He smiled. "Amazing? Isn't it?"

"What is?"

"That all he had to do was look at her . . . and immediately know that she was the only one for him. That no one would ever come close to the perfection he saw in her. He knew that he would love her and only her for as long as his heart continued to beat inside his chest."

"Sometimes things just work out like that . . . I guess," Bianca said. She didn't know anything about love. Sure she had kissed a couple of boys before, but she had never experienced that kind of feeling a person gets when they falls in love. All she knew was that she got butterflies in her stomach every time she looked into Terrance's eyes. Was that love? How was she supposed to know the difference? She shook her head and encouraged Terrance to continue telling the story of how his parents met.

"Well . . . he went to see a witch. He'd heard that she could perform transformative magic, the kind that would make him into a man. The price she demanded was the wolf skin he would shed when the spell was finished. He gave it willingly. It took him years, but he eventually made a name for himself as a merchant. He managed to garner entrance to the castle and gained access to the queen, for whom my mother is a lady-in-waiting. And they fell in love. No spells were needed for that to happen. Even now, years later, they are still madly in love and have eyes only for each other.

"My grandfather and uncles are ashamed of my father. They think he's a disgrace to his own kind. At least that's what he's told me. I've never actually spoken to any of the members of my father's side of the family, before today. But I can only assume that they love what they are: they love singing to the moon, hunting, their sharp claws and teeth." Terrance paused for a moment. "They couldn't understand why my father would willingly give that up. They would spare my life because none of it was my fault. But meeting my grandfather . . . he makes me feel ashamed of what I am."

When Bianca heard him talk about himself that way, it made her blood boil. She stood and said, "Don't be. I've only known you for a few days, and I can tell you're a good and caring person. If your father's family can't see that, then it's their loss. They're the ones missing out on you."

"You're very sweet to say such things," he said with a soft smile.

At least it's not that sad smile anymore.

She was glad she'd made him feel a little better. They sat silently side by side enjoying each other's company, but there was something that had been nagging her the entire time they had been traveling. She changed her mind several times as to whether she should ask him or not, then took a deep breath and finally decided to ask her question. "Terrance?"

"Yes?"

"What did he mean when he said I *smelled* like her? Who exactly? Did he mean my mother or Red Riding Hood since I was wearing her cape? What did he mean?"

"You wouldn't believe me if I told you," he replied.

Bianca laughed. After the rollercoaster her life had become in the past several weeks, she felt ready for just about anything. "Try me."

"How much do you know about your family?"

"Before she was kidnapped, my mom showed me our family tree."

"Then you know about your connection to Snow White?"

Bianca nodded. "But how do you know that? I've never said anything about it."

"You look a lot like her. The similarities are uncanny, and you smell just like her. It doesn't take much to connect the dots."

"Like Snow White?"

Terrance nodded.

"But how do you know? She's before your time."

"You're not the only one with items from legends and days of old." There was a twinkle in his eyes as he said this. He then explained that several kingdoms throughout Everafter had items that belonged to the famed princesses that the Brothers Grimm and other authors had written about.

"Like what?" Her curiosity was piqued. She immediately did a mental inventory of everything they had in the museum and began to compare the list of items Terrance gave her.

"Snow White's clothes, for instance, they stayed behind in the cottage that belonged to the seven dwarves. Prince Ferdinand's mother, Queen Felicia, has Cinderella's glass slipper and the dress she wore to the ball," Terrance said. "The other items, I'm not entirely certain what the other kingdoms have, they are very possessive of these items and they don't share them with the public."

"Wow. That's so cool. Mom will love to know that."

Bianca kept the fact that they also had Cinderella's slipper in the museum to herself. She wasn't sure her mother would appreciate her advertising their family secrets in Everafter.

Bianca then fidgeted with her fingers and thought about some of the things that Terrance had said about her smelling and looking like Snow White.

I'm still me . . . aren't I? At least . . . I sure hope so.

All of her thoughts seemed to jumble and stumble into each other, not a single one of them was a coherent and tangible thought. How was she supposed to know who or what she was supposed to be when there were people telling her that she was like someone else?

"You don't think I'm her . . . do you?" She blurted out, finally getting some of her concerns off her chest. She didn't sing everywhere, there were no dwarves or relatively short people following her around, and there was definitely no evil stepmother. She stared at Terrance and fidgeted with her fingers while she waited for him to answer her question.

"No." He shook his head and grinned. "You are most certainly your own person, of that I am absolutely sure. And I didn't mean to imply that you are exactly like Snow White, but there is something about you that carries an echo of what she represented and continues to represent to the world." He stretched his hand out and gently tucked a stray lock of hair behind her ear. "There's a spark inside of you. Something no one can touch."

He leaned over and kissed her on the cheek. Bianca closed her eyes and let herself enjoy the feel of his soft lips upon her skin. She let out a happy sigh when he pulled away from her.

"You are a very special young lady. I know I will see many great things from you," Terrance said.

"I hope I don't disappoint you."

"You could never do such a thing."

17

"WHAT'S GOING TO happen after we rescue your mother?" Prince Ferdinand inquired.

That was quite a loaded question. Bianca waited for Ming to respond. Her best friend just shrugged and shook her head. Which was her way of saying 'I have no idea, you decide.'

"I hope you guys don't mind me speaking for you," Bianca said, looking at Ming and her father, "but as far as I know, we all just want to get my mom and go back home."

Ming nodded in agreement, and David just huffed.

"Terrance?" The prince turned his attention to his friend.

Terrance's shoulders tensed for a second and then took a deep breath. "Go about our daily lives as usual . . . I suppose," he muttered.

They sat there contemplating their lives for several minutes when Bianca excused herself and placed the third little pig's brick down on the ground and chanted the spell that turned it into a sturdy, indestructible house. They had decided that there was no point in suffering out in the wilderness where they were vulnerable. Bianca hoped that the magic inside the brick didn't wear out.

Can magic get tired? Do magical items have an expiration date?

She stepped away from the brick and marveled once more over the magic block, at the way the house were being built out of thin air. Once everyone was inside the house, Bianca remained outside.

"Aren't you coming in?" Ming asked.

"No. I'm going to practice a bit of magic for a while," she replied.

"Alone?" Ming arched her eyebrow. It was safe to say that she was still a little skeptical of Bianca's magical abilities.

"Yeah, I'll be all right out here."

"Okay, but if you're not back in an hour, I'm going out to look for you," Ming said.

"Deal."

For a long while Bianca stayed outside practicing some of the magic spells her mother had taught her in the short amount of time allotted to them before Rose had been kidnapped. Bianca was getting better at conjuring fireballs, ice walls, and water. She had even memorized a few spells from Mirabel's book. She had a feeling they would come in handy at some point during their journey.

Eventually, curiosity got the best of her, and she decided to try a mirror spell to see if it would work in the little mirror she pilfered from the museum.

"Mirror, mirror in my hand, Pray tell,
Show me where the witches dwell."

The mirror flashed a bright green light that stung Bianca's eyes. She covered her eyes until the light vanished. When she lowered her hands, the mirror revealed a dark and filthy room. The bed was unmade; the once white bed sheets were gray with dirt. On the wall, right above the headboard, was a portrait of a woman who could only be described as serious and handsome. Bianca had forgotten her glasses so she couldn't get a good look at the woman's face. The night table was covered with black wax and crows feathers. Everything about the room screamed darkness and desolation.

"Who is there?" A familiar yet chilling voice cried out. Bianca's heart stopped beating momentarily in her chest. "Who dares spy on me?"

Then . . . Bianca saw Lenore sneering into her mirror.

That was when Bianca realized what happened. The mirrors were connected, allowing Bianca a one-way peephole into Lenore's depressing room.

Bianca whispered, "Enough," to the mirror and then all she could see was her own reflection. She quickly covered the mirror with a white piece of cloth and placed it back inside her backpack.

She studied the apple-shaped bruise in the palm of her hand. Bianca could've sworn it was getting bigger and darker with every day that passed. She was terrified over what was happening to her without her permission.

Once more she found herself inside a dark room. Her heart rate shot up as she felt herself being overtaken by fear. She fought to wake her body up, but no matter what she did she remained trapped in the nightmare.

She knew what came next . . . the mirror.

What is it with that mirror?

She couldn't help but admire the designs carved onto the frame. It seemed as though the artist had taken his time with every single detail and made sure he left nothing out. Each petal looked soft enough to touch and fool oneself into believing it was real. There were also vines, thorns and snakes that looked real enough. At the head of the frame was a regal crown. At the base were four crosses pattée alternating with four fleurs-de-lis.

She took a step toward the ebony-framed looking glass and saw her own reflection in the mirror. She reached out to see if she was real—at least as real as things could be in a dream.

Her reflection mimicked her movements although it wasn't enough to make her relax.

"God, why can't I just wake up?" She groaned.

She looked around her to see if anything else strange was going on around her. "What is going on?"

She scowled as she studied her surroundings.

Out of the corner of her eye she saw movement and looked into the mirror once more. She found her reflection screaming as it pounded on the glass. Bianca gasped in fear and jumped back a few feet.

Mirror Bianca looked nothing like her. This bizarre version of herself looked as though she were a wild creature. Her eyes were feral and bloodshot. Bianca shook her head in disbelief. Her body begged her to run away, but she remained rooted to where she stood.

That's not me. That will never be me. God, I have to wake up!

Mirror Bianca still pounded on the glass with all her might, still struggling to break free, when Bianca heard strange hisses and whispers all around her.

"Stop it." She covered her ears. "I said *stop it*!" she screamed and took her hands off her ears. Bianca took a few steps away from the horror she had just seen.

At that same moment the glass behind her exploded. Bianca covered her face to avoid getting cut with the shards of glass that torpedoed toward her.

"Finally . . . free . . . " Mirror Bianca smiled wickedly as she gazed at Bianca with strange, bloodied eyes. She tilted her head from side to side as though trying to decide what to make of her. Mirror Bianca stepped out of the ebony frame, the glass crunching and clinking beneath her feet. She grabbed Bianca and tried to pull her inside the frame.

"No!" Bianca struggled with Mirror Bianca with all her might.

Yet no matter how hard she fought, Bianca was dragged inside the mirror. The glass reassembled itself with Bianca on the other side of the looking glass. Mirror Bianca smiled and made faces at the young witch as she screamed and fought to be released from prison.

"No, no, no!" Bianca pounded her fists into the unbreakable glass.

Bianca woke with a loud gasp. She touched her forehead; she was covered in a cold sweat. She turned to her left and there, sleeping peacefully beside her, was Ming. To her right was Terrance, his chest rising and falling slowly and rhythmically. David and Prince Ferdinand were also close by, sleeping. She envied the serenity on their faces. Everyone was in a deep and peaceful slumber except for her.

What was that all about?

18

AFTER WALKING FOR several miles the following morning, they came across an amazing castle, the likes of which none of them had ever seen before. It was a castle built on a promontory on a cliff side. There was no curtain wall to speak of, and only one large tower with several windows and a crenellated crown, which had been roofed over in modern times. A large keep combined with a chapel overlooked the drop-off. Several smaller buildings were joined to the keep, and a couple of smaller towers were at the corners, with an unfilled moat.

"Wow. Who lives there?" Ming's eyes widened at the sight.

"I haven't the slightest clue. I didn't know this part of our world was even populated," Terrance replied.

"Really?" Ming was taken aback.

"I thought you knew everything there was to know about Everafter," Bianca said.

"Believe me, I know plenty about our world, but what this castle is or who lives here escapes me. Your Highness, what say you?"

"Terrance, if you do not know, then I most certainly do not. I say we go and knock on the door and sate our curiosity." Ferdinand had a wicked grin that let everyone know that he wasn't going to take no for an answer. Before anyone could convince him to stay with the group, he ran off toward the mysterious castle.

Bianca, who was still wearing Red Riding Hood's cape, watched as Ferdinand's footsteps burned bright red as he deviated from the path chosen by the blood red cape. She wondered about the price Ferdinand's distraction would cost her mother.

"Come on. Let's go get him. For all we know a freakin' giant lives there," Bianca muttered as she removed the red cape and hid it inside her backpack. The fewer people who knew the valuable magical items she carried with her, the better.

There was a collective sigh all around. Even David sighed, which Bianca found amusing.

Eventually they caught up to Prince Ferdinand who had already knocked on the massive wooden door several times.

"Your Highness, I think we should leave before we get into more trouble. We really don't know who lives in this castle," Terrance said, trying to reason with the prince.

"Nonsense, Terrance. I'm a prince. Why would anyone want to hurt me?"

Bianca put a hand on Prince Ferdinand's shoulder, ready to convince him to turn around when the massive oak door swung open. Bianca readied a fire spell and took on a defensive stance.

"Now, now. No need to set my perfectly good door on fire," said an old woman.

Bianca was surprised by how tall she was. The old woman was as tall as Terrance and Prince Ferdinand. Her face was thin, and dark tan as though she had spent every waking moment out in the sun. Her eyes were periwinkle, but clear and shimmering with youth and curiosity. Bianca wondered if it was only the outside that was made to appear old and withered while her spirit remained eternally youthful.

"You're late," said the old woman.

"Late? What are you talking about?" Bianca put out her fire spell.

The old woman clapped her hands. A loud, thunderous sound rippled all around them, causing the ground beneath their feet to tremble and quake. Bianca and Ming held hands to keep their balance.

The silence was deafening. Then everything stood completely still. The trees ceased to sway side to side. The birds remained suspended in the air mid-flight. The clouds stopped moving. Everything was frozen.

Time stood still.

"What is going on?" Ming's voice quivered in fear.

"Come inside. Your father as well." The old woman pointed a long, wrinkled finger at David.

"Wait, how did you know?" Bianca followed the woman inside the castle. She craned her neck as she tried to get a closer look at this strange new person who had unexpectedly been placed before her.

"It's not every day you see a man's aura swimming inside the body of a bear. Anyway, come inside all of you. The spell will wear off eventually. Either way, I've bought you all a few days' time at least."

"How?" Bianca walked briskly beside the old woman, following her through the impressive halls of the castle.

"I need to teach you a few tricks before you can face Lenore. You still have so much to learn," she said.

"Wait. What? Please stop," Bianca said.

The old woman ignored her and continued to walk.

Bianca stopped walking. She had questions. And she felt as though she was being dragged from one thing to the next with little explanation. She clenched her fists so tightly she dug her nails into the palms of her hands, leaving little red half-moons imprinted on her skin. She was tired of having no control over her life. She was tired of not knowing the truth or having things revealed to her late in life when she was supposed to know so much sooner. She was tired of the nightmares that had plagued her every night since her arrival in Everafter.

"Stop!" Bianca shouted. Her nostrils flared as she panted for air. She felt as though she had just finished running a marathon.

Finally, the old woman stopped walking and turned around to face Bianca.

"I'm sorry," the old woman said.

Bianca tried to calm herself down now that she had everyone's attention. "Now, before we go a step further, you are going to tell us who you are and what you want with us," Bianca demanded.

"I have no name. My creator didn't think I required one, but if you must call me something I will answer to Old Woman. And as for what I am? It's hard to say. I usually appear when someone is in an impossible situation that they cannot overcome on their own."

"Did the Brothers Grimm write about you?"

"Oh, yes, they certainly did. Very inquisitive, those two. I believe the title of the story was *The True Bride*. Poor girl, her mother beat her until there wasn't a bit of skin that wasn't bruised or bleeding. I helped that girl in every way I could."

"I thought it was her stepmother who beat her," Bianca said.

"No, it was her mother. The brothers changed that bit because it seemed too terrible a thing to have a girl be abused by her own mother. Either way, I played my part in her story and now I'm going to play a part in yours . . . if you'll let me," Old Woman said.

"How do you know I won't overcome this on my own?" Bianca asked.

Old Woman took a deep breath and lowered herself to meet Bianca's gaze. The intensity in Old Woman's gaze was enough to make Bianca take a step backwards.

"Trust me . . . you are way over your head. Now . . . you can either accept my help and live to see another day or you can walk out that door and face certain death. Your choice."

Bianca turned around and looked at her friends and father. She knew that she would do just about anything to make sure they all survived.

Bianca turned her attention to Old Woman. "All right. What do you want me to do?"

"Simple. Let me teach you what I know so you can survive this ordeal," she said.

Bianca thought about it for a moment, then nodded. "Okay."

"Very well. Follow me."

She led them through the long corridors of the castle and showed them to their respective rooms.

"If you need anything, let me know. Dinner will be ready at six o'clock." And with that she walked away and left them all alone.

Prince Ferdinand and Terrance shared a bedroom. David, Bianca, and Ming were placed in an enormous room together. There was a certain warmth to the space that surprised Bianca. She had half expected it to be dank and drafty and was given the exact opposite.

It had an incredibly high ceiling that seemed to go on forever. There were numerous tapestries hanging on the walls. Some were of famous fairy tale princes and princesses, like Snow White, Cinderella, Rapunzel, Sleeping Beauty, Jorinde and Joringel, and Hansel and Gretel. The one that Bianca was particularly drawn to was the Snow White tapestry.

It showed Snow White lying inside the glass coffin while the seven dwarves were on their knees praying—or weeping, she couldn't decide which. She walked toward the tapestry and gently ran her fingers against the fabric. It was amazingly soft. She could see the tiny glints of silver and gold fabric that the weaver had sewn into the pattern.

Snow White's face looked completely at peace. Serene even. Bianca wondered what she dreamt of during that time she was inside the glass coffin, waiting for someone to wake her up. Was she dreaming? Or was she trapped in shadows, pressing her face against the darkness, hoping to find an iota of light in the midst of it all? Bianca wondered all those things and felt herself becoming filled with sorrow for her ancestor. Sad for everything she had to endure on her own. She caressed Snow White's hair as though she could somehow comfort her from afar.

Bianca turned to Ming, ready to ask her what she thought about Old Woman and their new situation, but the words died in her throat. They melted away like snowflakes on a warm spring day. Ming was staring out the window, tears flowing freely down her cheeks. One thing Bianca could say about her best friend was that Ming cried prettily. Her face never contorted, nor became red. She didn't sob either. Her face remained perfectly still, and the only way anyone knew she had been crying at all was the fact that her eyes were ever so slightly pink.

"You okay?" Bianca whispered.

Ming nodded and quickly wiped the tears away with the back of her hand. "I'm just scared. I miss my mom, and I wanna go home."

"Yeah, me too," Bianca admitted. She shoved her hands in her pockets and rested her back against the cool stone wall.

"Really? You could've fooled me."

"Trust me, most of the time I just want to scream my head off and run in the opposite direction."

Ming sniffed and let out a gentle chuckle. "You would never do that. It's in your nature to help people."

"Only the people I like. Everyone else can suck it," Bianca replied.

Ming snorted and gave her the tiniest smirk. "You're crazy, B."

"I know."

Ming took a deep breath. "What now?"

"I guess we wait."

Several minutes later, there was a knock on the door. Bianca opened it; standing in the hall was Old Woman.

"You, come with me," she said as she pointed her index finger at Bianca.

"Where?"

"Outside, to the gardens."

"Okay. Hang on a second." Bianca turned around and asked Ming to find Prince Ferdinand and Terrance. She didn't want her to be all alone.

"Okey dokey," Ming replied.

She walked out of her room and followed Old Woman to the garden. Bianca was amazed at the amount of greenery and flowers that surrounded her. There were roses in every color imaginable: ruby, amethyst, pale lemon, ivory, and peach. Some were in colors Bianca couldn't name. In another part of the garden, there was nothing but sunflowers. They all shot out of the ground with large green stalks as though it were their goal in life to touch the sky. Some of the sunflowers were six feet tall, the shortest one reached Bianca's waist. Each petal seemed to mimic the color of the sun: yellow, orange, and fire-engine red.

"I've never seen a red sunflower before," Bianca whispered as she reached out and touched the soft petals of the flower.

"The red ones have always been my favorite," Old Woman said.

"My mom would love these."

Old Woman smiled warmly at Bianca. She stood on the tips of her toes, plucked a handful of seeds from the sunflower, and handed them to Bianca. She held the white seeds in her hands and thought of her mother and how happy she would be to have these.

"Shall we?" Old Woman gently coaxed Bianca out of her moment of sorrow.

Bianca nodded. She put the seeds in her pocket and followed Old Woman to the fountain in the middle of the garden. There was a statue of a winged woman holding a large stone basin on her shoulder. At first Bianca thought that it was an angel, but there was nothing angelic about the statue. Her face looked as though she had caused far too much mischief in the world. Trickles of water bubbled and dribbled over and over again. The statue's beautiful ivory face seemed at peace with this task.

"What have you learned so far?" Old Woman met Bianca's gaze.

Bianca explained everything her mother had taught her before she'd been kidnapped, and they picked things up from there.

"Attack me," instructed Old Woman.

"Huh?"

"You heard me." Old Woman grinned.

Bianca shook her head. She had a hard time wrapping that idea around her head, but instead of arguing, she shrugged her shoulders and said, "Okay, if you say so."

"Don't hold anything back," Old Woman instructed.

Bianca shook her head once more.

Is this really happening? she asked herself. She readied her magic and launched a fireball at Old Woman.

Seconds before the fireball would've struck her on the shoulder, Old Woman lifted her hand, and the fireball vanished in a puff of smoke.

Bianca scrambled to put her glasses on and was able to see the faint blue outline of an oval-shaped shield that surrounded Old Woman. It was as though a tiny blue spider had spun a web all around her at lightning speed, protecting her before anything could hit her.

"How did you do that?" Bianca's voice was filled with awe.

"I will show you," Old Woman replied with a mischievous smile.

Old Woman then led Bianca to another part of the garden. A section of the earth was filled with fragrant herbs and tiny flowers. Old Woman whispered and mumbled as she hunched over and one by one, plucked some herbs from the soil.

Bianca leaned over and listened. A deep frown appeared on her face; she couldn't understand what Old Woman was saying.

"What are you telling them?"

"Ah . . . so you figured out that I'm talking to the plants," she replied.

"Yeah."

"I'm thanking Mother Earth for allowing me to use Her bounty for your journey. I'm also asking for forgiveness because in essence I'm killing Mother Earth's children. But She knows that what we're doing is for a just cause. Mother will forgive us."

"How do you know? How do you know She will forgive us? Forgive me?"

"She's Mother Earth. She knows your heart." Old Woman reached up and tapped Bianca on the chest, right above her heart. "She knows every step you take above ground. Knows every tear you've shed. Every fear in your heart. Everything you love. Every worry that causes a frown to appear on your face. Trust me . . . She knows."

Bianca nodded, understanding what she meant.

"Now, enough chitchat. I believe we have everything we need. Protection spells are supposed to repel danger. All I've done is enhance my aura with certain herbs. I like the kind of magic that requires a helping hand from Mother Earth. Now, don't go thinking that this will stop you from suffering physical harm. If you're going to get stabbed by a knife or a sword, trust me, you'll get stabbed through and through."

"Good to know."

"But . . . I have a little concoction that will enhance any natural abilities you have."

Old Woman held up the herbs, and as she recited their names, she pointed to each one individually. "The herbs I've chosen for you are eyebright, mallow, mugwort, Saint-John's-wort, self-heal, speedwell, vervain, wormwood, and yarrow. All of these, put together, repel certain spells, but with a little of your magic and mine combined, you could keep some of Lenore's nastier spells at bay."

"Cool."

After a couple of hours, Bianca had a red pouch filled with crushed herbs that she tied around her waist.

"Now, let's put it to the test, shall we?"

"Um . . . okay . . . I guess." Bianca knew she had little choice in the matter.

Old Woman pushed the sleeves of her blouse up to her elbows and, with a smile on her face, launched a fireball the size of a basketball at Bianca. Her eyes widened in horror when she saw that giant fiery sphere headed straight towards her.

"Oh, God," she shrieked as she closed her eyes and chanted the spell that Old Woman had taught her. Slowly, she opened one eye and then the other. She was safe. Nothing had happened. The spell had worked. Before her was a white shield similar to the one Old Woman had created, like a million little interwoven spider webs. Smoke stung her eyes from the fireball that she had deflected.

Old Woman beamed with pride as she looked at Bianca. "Good. Now this time try to keep both eyes open."

"Oh, boy." Bianca muttered.

After several hours of training, Bianca finally got a much-deserved break. She looked at the bruise on the palm of her hand and decided to tell Old Woman about it.

"I need to show you something," she said.

Old Woman pulled her half-moon glasses out of her apron and put them on. She extended her hand and silently waited for Bianca.

Bianca clenched her fist and pressed it against her chest. Even now she was still unsure if she should tell or keep it to herself and deal with it her own way.

Old Woman smiled and waited patiently. That was all it took for her fears to wash away and trust her new trainer. Bianca took a deep breath and showed her the palm of her hand.

Old Woman drew in a breath and made tsk sounds. Her periwinkle eyes were hard and serious. "This isn't good."

Bianca looked at her hand and noticed that the apple bruise had grown in size since the last time she'd checked. It was now the size of a grape. She explained how and when it had happened and told her about the nightmares she'd been having since the bruise appeared in her hand.

"The one from a few nights ago almost killed me. She made me try to strangle myself. If Terrance hadn't woken me up when he did, I probably would've died." The thought still sent shivers down her spine.

"If you had come here sooner, I could've done something about it, but now all we can do is wait for her to show up and try to catch her then."

Bianca gave her an incredulous look. "Wait for who?"

Old Woman removed her spectacles. "You know who."

"Mirabel? But she's dead. She can't do anything anymore."

Old Woman chuckled. "It's a good thing I was never young and naïve. Stopped me from wasting so much time. Child, listen to me, and listen well. Just because you're dead doesn't mean life ends. There is another world where the spirit goes on to live a different life. Just because Mirabel is dead here doesn't mean she isn't alive and thriving on the other side of that very, very thin veil that divides us. That bruise is proof of that. But fear not. You'll rest easy as long as you are here. I'll try to bind it so that it doesn't get any bigger than that."

"Okay." Bianca nodded but remained confused by what Old Woman had told her.

"Come now, no need to dwell on things you have no control over. Let's get the others and have dinner. You'll need your strength and some rest. We have another day of training ahead of us tomorrow."

It had been a long three days. Part of her was grateful for the training; and another part of her was slightly annoyed because she didn't get to spend as much time with Ming, Terrance, Prince Ferdinand and her father as she would've liked. She was especially eager to get to know Terrance. She could feel his dark eyes on her everywhere she went.

Old Woman had taken her out to the garden every day and taught her about herbs and their natural healing and magical properties. Bianca also became adept at blocking all sorts of magic. Old Woman even taught her how to protect herself from certain elements like wood, rock, fire, and water. Bianca wasn't sure she could cram one more bit of information in her brain without her head spontaneously exploding. She could imagine the mess it would make: pink-gray chunks of brain matter everywhere.

Eeww.

They had been trapped in a perpetual state of twilight. The sky hadn't changed from its peach-pink tinge in three days.

The sky was . . . not completely lit . . . not completely dark either. Temporarily trapped in between.

Bianca was looking forward to seeing the sun finally sink underneath the horizon and see the moon and stars up in the azure sky. She took a moment to gaze up at the heavens. The entire time they were there, everything had remained frozen. She hadn't seen the moon in three days. The sun clung to the sky with jealous abandon. The trees remained exactly as they had left them. The red cardinal remained suspended in the air, waiting to be released from the cruel spell that kept it hungrily eyeing the worm on the ground.

On their last day at Old Woman's castle, they woke up rested and eager to continue on their journey. Old Woman smiled at each of them and then lifted her gaze toward the horizon. She seemed to be staring at something only she could see. It was as though Old Woman was having a conversation with an invisible being.

After a few minutes of silence, she finally blinked and nodded, then clapped her hands, releasing a thunderous sound that reverberated for miles around them. The earth trembled beneath their feet and time was restored back to its normal state and the wind resumed its trajectory. Trees danced lazily as though nothing had changed. The red cardinal swooped and finally caught its S-shaped meal.

"I guess . . . this is goodbye," Bianca said to Old Woman.

The ancient lady smiled, causing her skin to wrinkle and the corners of her eyes to crinkle. "No, sweet girl. Never goodbye. This is simply 'farewell for now.' This will not be the last time we shall see each other, of that you can be certain."

"All right . . . farewell," Bianca said and then embraced her.

Old Woman gently patted her on the back and whispered, "Good luck."

Bianca knew that she would need all the luck she could get.

19

ONCE THEY WERE FAR enough away from Old Woman's castle, Bianca donned the red riding hood once more and they resumed their journey. They walked until they reached the foot of a mountain.

David grumbled.

He shook his head and bit Bianca's shirt. He did his best to pull her back. It was obvious that he didn't want her to go up the mountain.

"Daddy, please stop. It'll be okay," she said, still unsure who she was trying to convince, her father or herself.

She patted David on the head. "Where are we?"

"This is Glass Mountain," Terrance replied.

"It's not really made out of glass . . . is it?" Ming's gaze traveled up the side of the mountain.

"Not anymore," Prince Ferdinand replied.

"I'm sure that there are still fragments of glass underneath the mountain somewhere. But right now, the mountain is more rock than glass," Terrance said.

"Why does this sound familiar?" Bianca mumbled. "Wasn't there a princess who lived on top of the mountain? Or was it a hill? I can't remember."

"Legend says that there's a golden apple tree at the top of Glass Mountain that can heal any wound and open any door."

Bianca stretched her neck as far as it could go.

The mountain seemed to go on forever.

How are we ever going to make it to the other side?

To her, it seemed an impossible task.

"So, what's the plan here?" Bianca looked to each of her companions in turn.

"It would take much too long to go around the mountain. It may seem daunting, but we have no choice but to climb over," Prince Ferdinand said.

"You're joking," she said.

Prince Ferdinand flashed a charming grin at her, nearly blinding her with his brilliant smile, and said, "Bianca, my dear new friend, this wouldn't be an adventure if we didn't have difficult and seemingly impossible tasks that we must overcome to rescue the damsel in distress."

"Oh God. Okay, I can do this." Bianca ran in place, shaking her arms and hands, trying to prepare herself mentally for the climb.

"Ready?" Ming sounded worried.

"No," Bianca replied in a small voice and shook her head.

"Well, it's not like we can go around the mountain. That would take longer," Ming said.

"Come on. No need to be afraid," Terrance said.

Bianca held her breath and then very slowly exhaled.

This sucks. But regardless of how she felt, she started climbing up the steep side of the mountain. *Okay . . . first one foot, then the other one. I can do this . . . I can do this . . . God . . . I hope I can do this.*

"Don't be afraid," Terrance whispered. He extended his hand out to her. Such a simple gesture but judging from the look in his eyes she understood that this was a big moment for him. His eyes begged her to trust him.

With her heart hammering against her chest at rapid speed she took his hands and interlocked her fingers with his.

Step by step they slowly began the climb up the mountain.

Bianca found tiny glinting pieces of glass scattered all over the mountain. "Wow," she whispered as she picked up a handful. They shimmered and glinted in the sunlight. If Terrance hadn't told her that it was in fact glass, she would've thought they were diamonds. She grabbed a fistful of them and put them in the smallest pocket in her backpack. She figured she might be able to put them on display at the museum.

"What are you doing?" Ming saw Bianca hunched over the ground.

"Picking up some souvenirs."

Ming shrugged her shoulders and said, "Weird. Come on, let's go."

Bianca nodded and continued with their steep trek.

It was after a lot of grumbling, muttering, panting, and sweating that they all finally reached the top of the mountain. Everyone seemed miserable except for Terrance. He had a smile on his face the entire time. He didn't look tired. If anything, he looked as though he could've gone even further.

A very sweaty Ming collapsed on to the rocky ground and rolled on her back as she tried to catch her breath. "I'm . . . so . . . out . . . of . . . shape," she said between pants.

"Tell me about it. My legs are killing me," Bianca complained.

David plopped down beside her and grunted right along with them. Bianca scratched his head and his chin without thinking. Then she remembered that he was her father, not a pet bear, so she forced herself to stop.

"Terrance?" Prince Ferdinand said.

"Yes, Your Highness?" Terrance said.

"You . . . get the honor of carrying me down the mountain," he said and then plopped down on the ground. He was drenched with sweat and his face was bright pink from exertion.

Terrance chuckled. "Certainly, Your Highness."

"Why is he smiling so much?" Ming looked from Terrance to Bianca.

"Dunno," Bianca replied.

"This place is twenty different kinds of crazy, B."

"Yeah . . . I know."

"I smell bad." Ming wrinkled her nose and sniffed underneath her arms.

She scrunched up her face as though she had just eaten a sour lemon.

"Yeah . . . I know." Bianca smirked knowing that she had teased her friend.

Ming gave her a raspberry and said, "If I could move my feet . . . I'd kick you."

Bianca laughed.

"Did Old Woman teach you how to conjure up water? Cuz I could sure use a bath."

"Not the kind of water you wanna use for a bath."

Ming shrugged. "Figures. I hope she taught you other useful stuff."

"I thought it was."

"What time is it?"

Bianca checked her watch. "Four o'clock in the morning."

"Old Woman freezing time really did a number on our schedule, huh?"

"Yeah, but we'll be all right. I'm going to set up the brick house. It would be good if we got some rest and got back on a normal schedule, you know what I mean?"

Ming nodded. "Sounds good to me."

Bianca got up and grabbed the third little pig's brick out of her backpack and set it down on the only bit of flat ground she could find. She got everyone to hold hands momentarily, and she chanted the spell that unlocked the magic inside the brick.

Terrance wandered off away from the group. His moment of elation forgotten, he had gone back to being shy and withdrawn. Bianca liked seeing Terrance smile. She liked the cheerful version of him a lot more than this strange recluse that walked away from her.

"Hey." Bianca quickly followed behind him.

"Oh, hello." Terrance turned around and gave her a smile that she knew wasn't genuine.

"Are you okay?"

"Fine, fine, perfectly fine. Why do you ask?"

"First of all, you just said fine, so that lets me know that you're not in fact . . . fine. Second of all, you tend to walk away from people when you're sad."

He shook his head. "Nothing gets past you, Bianca."

She shrugged her shoulders and shoved her hands inside her pockets. She balanced herself on the balls of her feet and said, "It's an annoying gift. So . . . you wanna talk about it?"

"It's not something you can fix if that's what your intentions are."

Bianca said nothing. She just stood there and waited for him to say what he wanted to say.

"I forgot," he whispered.

"Forgot?" She echoed and leaned forward, closer to him so that she wouldn't miss a single word he said.

"I forgot I was different from everyone else. For a single moment, I didn't think about who I was, who my father or grandfather is, or where I come from. All I could feel was the ground beneath my feet, the wind at my back, and the sky above my head. It's the only time I'm ever truly happy."

"I'm sorry," she whispered.

"Why are you sorry? It's not your fault."

"I still feel bad that you're upset," she said.

Terrance smoothed his hair back. He lifted his gaze toward the midnight blue sky.

Bianca smiled warmly at him and extended her hand to him. "Come on. It's getting late."

Terrance gladly accepted her hand in his and followed her inside the house.

They rested in the safety of the brick house and then early in the afternoon, they trekked to the other side of the mountain until they reached a canyon.

"Whoa." Bianca gasped in amazement as she looked down and saw the raging river and rocky ground below them. "How far down do you think it is?"

"I don't know thirty, forty feet? I'm not sure, I left my measuring tape at home," Ming said.

"Don't be a smartass. That's my job." Bianca narrowed her eyes and then pinched Ming lightly on the arm. Bianca looked around and found a huge oak tree. "That should hold us . . . right?"

"I think so. It looks strong enough," Ming said.

Bianca looked in her backpack and pulled out Rapunzel's hair.

Ming's dark brown eyes grew wide in surprise. "Is that what I think it is?"

"It sure is. Don't tell my mom. She'll kill me."

"I'm not saying anything. I'm not getting involved in this craziness."

"Umm . . . Terrance?" Bianca said.

"Yes?"

"How good are you at tying knots?"

"Not good at all, actually. But Prince Ferdinand may be of some assistance. Your Highness?"

"Hmm?" The prince turned away from the scene before him and gave his attention to his friend.

"You've been sailing," Terrance said. "Do you think you could help us with some knots?"

"I feel confident enough to say I can tie a knot secure enough to hold all of us," he replied.

"Awesome." Bianca handed him Rapunzel's braided hair.

Prince Ferdinand took a moment to study the famous hair he held in his hands. Bianca saw the way he marveled over each strand of hair. How it glinted in the sunlight. Each strand brighter than the last.

"You okay?" Bianca watched the prince's face soften.

"You read these stories . . . they are a part of our history—at least here in my world, and you feel as though it couldn't possibly be true and yet . . . here's proof." He had an awestruck look on his face as he continued to gaze at Rapunzel's hair.

"I know exactly how you feel," Bianca replied.

Prince Ferdinand shook himself back to the present and tied a knot around the tree trunk. He tested it by pulling as hard as he could.

"It'll hold," he announced.

Bianca took the hair from the prince's hands and chanted the spell.

"Rapunzel, Rapunzel

Let down your hair

So that I may climb

The golden stair."

The hair then grew four times in length. She walked to the edge of the cliff and threw the thick lock of blond hair off the edge. She stood and watched as it twirled and performed a snake-like dance all the way to the bottom.

"What about your dad? He can't climb down . . . " Ming said.

"Crap." Bianca turned her attention to her father. "Dad . . . oh, God. I'm so sorry, I forgot."

He shook his head and nudged her toward her friends. "But what are you going to do?"

He sat down by the tree and growled. He opened his mouth wide, revealing perfect pink gums, a long mauve tongue and row after row of sharp white teeth.

Nothing was going to get past him, of that Bianca was certain. "Stand guard? Make sure no one touches the hair?"

He nodded. Bianca thought about it for a moment, then decided she was going to stick to her no-one-gets-left-behind plan.

"No, Dad. We'll figure something out." Bianca turned to her friends. "Any ideas?"

Ming's eyes grew large as an idea came to her. She jumped up and down and raised her hand in excitement.

"Yes?" Bianca said.

"A harness! We can use the hair like a rope and tie it around your dad," she said.

"He weighs a ton. Are we all strong enough to lower him all the way down?" Bianca replied.

"Oh . . . yeah." Ming looked defeated.

"Hey." Bianca patted Ming on the shoulder, "it's a great idea, but we gotta find a way to make it work so Dad doesn't get hurt."

Bianca put her arm around Ming and gave her a gentle squeeze.

David walked to the edge of the cliff and looked down. Bianca frowned. *What is he looking for?* She then noticed that his eyes were focused on the river at the bottom of the canyon.

"Daddy . . . no. We'll figure something else out."

David huffed and walked away. Bianca let out a sigh of relief and tried to think of other ways they could all get down safely when a black blur ran past her and jumped from the side of the canyon.

Bianca screamed and ran after her father. "No, no, no!" She stopped at the very edge of the cliff and reached out as though she could somehow catch her father mid-flight and pull him back to safety, but all she touched was air and empty space. Her stomach dropped. She watched in horror as her father soared through the air and landed right in the middle of the river with a huge splash. Bianca stared at the river and willed her father to float up to the surface. She covered her eyes and shook her head.

This isn't happening. This isn't happening.

"Oh, my God. He's dead, isn't he? I can't look. Is he dead?" Bianca whimpered.

"No, he's fine. He's finally out of the water." Ming giggled. "He's shaking the water off his fur like a puppy on shore."

Bianca pried her hands off her eyes and looked to where Ming pointed. And just like Ming said, there he was safe, alive, and looking very satisfied with himself.

"You're crazy!" Bianca shouted.

His reply was a mix between a bark and a laugh.

"Not funny," Bianca shouted back. She turned her attention back to Ming, Terrance and Prince Ferdinand. "All right, well, at least we got that part figured out."

"I'll go first," Terrance offered. He took a deep breath and climbed down the cliff. He was quick, which surprised no one. When he reached the bottom safely, Prince Ferdinand was next, followed by Ming and lastly it was Bianca's turn.

She wasn't a fan of heights.

"It's okay . . . I'm just using indestructible hair as though it were any regular ol' piece of rope. No safety harness to make sure I don't fall down and die," Bianca muttered as she slowly climbed down.

Bianca took a moment and looked at the emerald hills and the aquamarine sky. She memorized every detail so she could draw it the moment she returned home. She was finally hitting her stride and becoming comfortable climbing when suddenly a gust of wind caused her to slam against the side of the canyon. A sharp edge sliced through her right arm, and she shrieked with pain. She then made the fatal mistake of looking down. Her vision swirled and her heart dropped to her stomach. Bianca closed her eyes tightly and wrapped herself around the long braid of hair, hanging on for dear life. She took several deep breaths and then opened her eyes. She needed to snap out of it, fast.

"I think I'm gonna throw up!" she shouted as she looked down to where her friends were.

"Don't blow chunks down here, B. I didn't bring any shampoo so if I smell like vomit I'm gonna have to stop being friends with you for a while. I mean it," Ming shouted back.

"I'll try."

Ming cupped her hands around her lips and shouted, "Don't . . . blow . . . chunks!"

She had to agree with Ming. It would suck if Ming had to spend the rest of their journey smelling like Bianca's bile. She thought of other things that made her happy as she climbed down. Warm jeans when they come out of the dryer on a cold winter's day. Hot showers. Snowball fights. Hot chocolate with marshmallows on a snowy day. Her mother's laughter. She couldn't help but smile when she thought of Rose. She focused on thoughts about her mother. She thought of everything she wanted to say to her. She even had an imaginary conversation with Rose inside her head as she continued her climb down the side of the cliff. Before she realized it, she was at the bottom.

"I made it," she said nearly fainting with relief.

"And you didn't throw up on me. Good job, B." Ming patted Bianca on the shoulder.

"God, that was scary," Bianca admitted.

"What about Rapunzel's hair?" Prince Ferdinand asked.

"I guess we have to leave it here. It'll be all right. I can't worry about that right now. Come on, let's go," Bianca replied.

Without even glancing back at the long, lustrous lock of hair that dangled gracefully in the wind, she headed toward the unknown: Lenore's castle.

20

LENORE GATHERED ALL the saliva in her mouth and spat into her black cauldron.

"Stupid little bitch! Spying on me. She probably thinks she's so smart. I'll show her. I'll show them all!" She snarled.

Lenore made her way down to the dungeon. There was one final ingredient she was going to need to complete the spell she was working on. She unlocked the door and opened it wide. In the middle of a tiny pool of light was Rose Frost, her prisoner. She never thought she would ever see the day that she would finally bring down the Frost family. Now, it looked like she would finally achieve what Queen Mirabel could never do.

Rose lifted her battered face and stared at her captor. The hatred she held for Lenore burned in her emerald eyes.

For the longest time neither of them said a word to each other. The anger swam around them freely in that tiny cell. It was almost a tangible thing.

Lenore pulled out a silver dagger from the sheath tied around her waist. She showed it to Rose and wiggled it before her. The blade glinted menacingly in the little sunlight that squeezed into her pitiful holding cell.

"Curious?" Lenore whispered.

Rose's eyes widened with fear and understanding. There was a heartbeat of silence between them before Rose exploded into a violent struggle against her bond, kicking and struggling to free herself from the chair she was tied to. She tried to use a fire spell that would incinerate the ropes that bound her. Lenore moved faster than a snake. She grabbed Rose by the hair and pressed the dagger to her throat. "I wouldn't do that if I were you," she hissed. "You didn't think I'd bring you all the way here, just so you could escape and murder me under my own roof, did you?"

Lenore slapped Rose across the cheek and released her from her grip. She rested her elbow on Rose's head.

"I want you to think of this cell as a giant invisible mirror. Any spell you cast . . . will simply bounce right back to you. So if you thought you could burn the rope off your hands, all you'd do is set yourself on fire. Now . . . as much as I would love to see you burn yourself into a pile of ashes . . . I need something from you first." Having said that, Lenore cut a straight line on the palm of Rose's hand and used a silver goblet to collect all the blood she needed to complete her spell.

Lenore could see Rose suppressing the urge to scream in pain. It seemed that Rose wasn't going to give Lenore the satisfaction.

"You think you're proving something by staying quiet? Trust me, when I'm through with you . . . you're going to beg for me to end your life," Lenore whispered.

Lenore laughed as she walked out of Rose's cell. The door closed, and Rose was left alone with her thoughts, pain, and misery.

21

BIANCA HEARD STRANGE murmurs, a series of hisses and whispers as she struggled to open her eyes that morning. No matter how hard she tried, she couldn't wake up. She tried to move her hands and feet all to no avail. It felt as though someone had bound her limbs into place.

Something isn't right.

Then, everything turned pitch black, and she stood alone in the darkness. Her stomach dropped; this was an all-too-familiar darkness, but she couldn't help but feel there was something different this time around.

"Hello? Anyone there?" she shouted. No response. All she heard was a faint echo of her words.

She fought the urge to stand still and walked instead. Oddly enough, she felt the ground beneath her feet changing even though she couldn't see. At first it felt she was going up a steep hill, then her feet sank a little, almost as if she were walking on sand. The ground was constantly changing; the only difference was that she couldn't see it. Either way, she kept moving.

Bianca heard a familiar voice screaming and shouting for help; it sounded far away and faint.

"Hello? Daddy? Ming? Terrance? Prince Ferdinand? Can anyone hear me?" Bianca cried.

"Bianca?"

She let out a sigh of relief when she heard her best friend's familiar voice. "Ming?"

"Yes!"

"Where are you?"

"I don't know. I can't see anything," Ming replied. Bianca heard the desperation in her friend's voice. She could only imagine how terrified Ming was.

"Keep talking. I'll try to follow the sound of your voice," Bianca suggested.

"Okay." Ming's voice trembled.

But before they could follow up on their plan, Bianca heard a gut-wrenching scream.

"Ming!" Bianca ran toward her friend, still unable to figure out where she was going. She stopped, hearing Ming's screams from all directions.

Which way do I go? She wondered desperately as she spun around in search of her friend's voice. Her heart hammering against her chest from the fear of losing her best friend . . . her only friend in the world.

She closed her eyes and focused on finding Ming. Where is she? She stretched her arms out and tried to get a feel for the energy surrounding her.

As soon as she decided which direction she wanted to take, the darkness lifted like a fog, and she found herself in a garden that looked as though it hadn't been tended to in years, perhaps decades.

"Ming?" Bianca whispered as she carefully navigated her way through the strange garden. There were roses everywhere: ruby, ivory, pink, yellow, and onyx. The roses that had once been bright and colorful were now wilted, grayish, and frayed at the tips. But that wasn't what concerned her. What worried her was the fact that those once-beautiful roses were growing out of ebony-colored vines. They were covered by sharp and dangerous-looking thorns.

In the middle of the garden, a comatose Ming lay in a bed made up of cotton candy pink hydrangeas.

A dream within a dream. Is this even possible?

"Ming, please wake up. Open your eyes." Bianca gently shook her friend on the shoulder.

There was a lump in her throat; she was trying so hard not to cry. She thought of ways she could wake Ming. She searched her memory for every fairy tale that involved a girl trapped in a sleep-like state. Then she remembered the story of Sleeping Beauty.

True love's kiss. Maybe Prince Ferdinand can help. He might not love her, but his kiss could break the spell.

She wondered if Prince Ferdinand and Terrance were trapped in this nightmare as well.

"Terrance!" She waited several minutes in silence for any type of response.

"Bianca?" Terrance cried.

It looks like we're all trapped in the same dream.

"Terrance! Where are you?" Bianca searched for him. Silence.

No movement.

"I don't know. I can't see anything. Is Prince Ferdinand with you?"

"No. Ming is with me, but she's unconscious. I can't get her to wake up."

"Stay where you are. I'll find you."

"Keep an eye out for my father. I haven't seen or heard from him. And find Prince Ferdinand if you can. I think he's the only one who can wake her."

"I'll do my best," he replied.

Again, she waited in silence. Then she heard a soft rustling sound. Bianca frowned as she studied her surroundings.

"Terrance? Prince Ferdinand?" she whispered.

She gasped in horror as she watched black vines slither toward her, almost as if they were onyx pythons and she, their prey.

"Oh, my God." She was surrounded. Everywhere she looked there were dozens of vines, all of them closing in on her and Ming.

Bianca tried to cast a spell, anything to help defend herself and the unconscious Ming, but nothing happened. Her magic didn't work in a dream—or nightmare.

"Huzzah! Unhand her, foul beasts!" Prince Ferdinand shouted as he burst out from behind the bushes sword in hand ready to attack.

"Prince Ferdinand?" Bianca said.

He nodded and shook his blond hair out of his eyes.

He swung his sword and attacked all the vines. He sliced left and right with a bright smile on his face, almost as if his body were made for combat. It was a brutal, strangely graceful dance, and in a matter of minutes, the fight was over, leaving him the victor.

"A fine adventure indeed, Bianca. I'm so glad we ran into each other." He put his hands on his hips and let out a happy sigh before extending his hand out to help her stand up.

This crazy prince is actually enjoying every moment of this.

"Your Highness, I'm so happy you're here. By the way . . . thank you for saving us . . . again," she said.

"You're welcome."

"Where is Terrance?"

"I don't know."

Bianca glanced around as though expecting Terrance to appear at any moment the same way Ferdinand had.

"Terrance?" Bianca cried.

No reply.

"Damn it," Bianca muttered.

"What's wrong?" The prince had a deep frown of concern for his friend.

"Terrance was trying to find you the last time I spoke to him," she explained. She wanted to go and look for Terrance at that very moment, but then she remembered that Ming was still fast asleep.

She took a deep breath. *Okay. One thing at a time.*

"You really are a prince, right?"

"Of course, I'm a prince. Why would I lie about that?"

She wasn't about to explain to him that people lied about all sorts of things. "Can you wake her up?"

"I–I'll try," he stammered. For the first time since they met, he seemed unsure of himself.

Bianca closed her eyes, crossed her fingers, and hoped that the kiss would work. Ferdinand took a deep breath and sheathed his sword. He walked up to Ming, shook her shoulders, and shouted into her ear, begging her to wake up.

Oh geez. "Not like that, you idiot," Bianca shouted as she punched him on the arm. "Kiss her. Like in the story of Sleeping Beauty."

"Oh, my apologies." At least Prince Ferdinand had the decency to blush and look slightly embarrassed.

He leaned over and kissed Ming gently on the lips. Bianca waited with bated breath. Ming finally stirred, her dark brown eyes fluttering open like the wings of a butterfly.

"It worked," Ferdinand whispered, amazed.

"W–what happened?" Ming murmured, clearly confused.

"You tell me," Bianca replied.

Ming massaged her temples and shook her head as though trying to shake something off. "I don't remember. Why is he looking at me like that?"

"You just got the Sleeping Beauty treatment," Bianca replied.

"What? Whoa, hang on a minute . . . did we just kiss?"

"Yep," Bianca said.

"Man, I missed it. I didn't feel anything," Ming complained and touched her lips as if to verify that she did indeed get kissed.

"Didn't feel anything?" Prince Ferdinand sputtered.

"Come on. Time to focus. You'll have plenty of time to kiss and make up once we get out of here," Bianca said.

"Challenge accepted! I shall kiss you once we wake up, fair maiden, and then we shall see whether you feel anything." Ferdinand rubbed his chin and shook his head in confusion. "Not feel anything, my horse's arse," the prince muttered quietly to himself.

Ming rolled her eyes and sat up. "Where are we?"

"I don't know. But wherever we are, it's a bad place to be trapped. We have to find Terrance and my dad, and get our bodies to wake up," Bianca explained.

"Maybe your dad isn't here," Ming said.

"Why wouldn't he be here? He's with us inside the brick house," Bianca said.

"Maybe the spell saw him as an animal? I don't know."

"You could be right." Bianca nodded.

They held hands and searched for their missing friend in the abandoned garden. They walked in circles for what felt like an eternity, but eventually they reached a part of the garden they hadn't explored. A scream escaped Bianca's lips when she saw an unconscious Terrance on the ground. He had black vines wrapped all over his body and they were slowly dragging him into the darkness.

"No! No! Leave him alone!"

She released Ming's hand and ran to him. She tried to pull the vines off Terrance's body, but she wasn't strong enough. The thorns sliced through the skin on the palms of her hands, but no matter what happened she wasn't going to stop fighting them off.

"Your Highness! I need your sword or a knife," she shouted, continuing to struggle with the seemingly indestructible vines.

Ferdinand pulled a small knife out of his boot and handed it to Bianca. She grabbed it and began to cut all the vines as quickly as she could. Ming jumped in and did what she could to help while Prince Ferdinand unsheathed his sword and swung it with reckless abandon to help his friend. Once he was free, they pulled him into safety.

"Terrance?" she whispered as she carefully tapped his cheek with the palm of her hand. Without meaning to, she left bloodied imprints of her hands on his skin.

Prince Ferdinand picked up his friend's hand and then dropped it; it was completely limp.

"He's out cold," he said.

"No, no, no. Terrance, wake up," Bianca pleaded as she gently patted his cheeks.

"Do you think he's awake in the real world? If you can call that crazy place . . . real," Ming said.

"Wouldn't his body have vanished though? Besides I'd like to think he'd be trying to wake our bodies up." Bianca reasoned.

"That makes sense," Ming said.

"Bianca?" the prince said.

"Yes?"

"May I be so bold as to suggest that you try waking him with a kiss?"

"But . . . I'm not a princess," she whispered. She looked at her clothes and her bloody hands, she was the most non-princess girl she knew.

"You do not need to be a princess to be one's true love."

She gave him a sad smile. "That sounds like something Terrance would say."

"I do spend a lot of time with my friend . . . some things are bound to rub off on me."

"Here goes nothing," Bianca whispered.

Tears stung her eyes as she looked upon Terrance's face for a moment. She knew . . . in that instant that she would do anything for him.

Please let this work.

She gently combed his dark brown hair with her fingers. She marveled over how soft it was. He looked so peaceful in his sleep. It was strange to see him that way, so vulnerable. Helpless. She realized that she would've done just about anything to have him open his eyes and look at her.

She took a deep breath and leaned over to kiss him on the lips.

His dark brown eyes opened while Bianca was still pressing her lips against his. He reached his hand out and ran his fingers through her hair. They forgot where they were for a moment and deepened their kiss. The world vanished. There was nothing except the two of them and their kiss.

22

SLOWLY, ONE BY ONE, they roused themselves awake. David licked Bianca's face until she patted him gently on the cheek and reassured him that she was okay.

"Are we back? Did we make it?" Ming rubbed her temples as she carefully sat up.

"I think so." Bianca threw the sheets aside and got out of bed, staggering a little as she tried to regain her balance from the nightmare they all had shared. She made her way toward the only window in the brick house.

She gasped when she looked outside. "Oh. My. God."

The brick house was completely covered in black vines and thorns. Bianca couldn't even see the sunlight. She couldn't believe that this was actually happening to her.

"It's like being trapped in a twisted version of Sleeping Beauty. They kind of skip her reaction when she wakes up to a castle covered in thorns," Bianca mumbled. "Of course, they also left out what happened to Sleeping Beauty after she married the prince."

Ming groaned. "What are you muttering about? Speak English."

"Nothing. Story for another time," Bianca replied.

"What's going on out there? Why is it so dark?"

Ming rubbed her eyes and stood next to Bianca. "What is that stuff?" Ming shrieked, "Is it what I think it is?"

Bianca nodded, and said, "I think they stopped growing." She was, trying to make the best out of a sticky situation.

"Yeah, but we're still surrounded. How are we going to get out of here?"

"We might have to cut our way out of this one," Bianca suggested.

"That could take forever. Don't you know any spells? Check the spell book and see if you find anything in there that can help us," Ming said.

Bianca shook her head. She was going to save the book as a last resort. She opened the window and used every one of the few spells she knew. Nothing worked. Not fire. Not ice. Neither did wind nor water. Nothing she did made the black thorns disappear.

Bianca felt like she had no choice but to listen to Ming's suggestion. She reluctantly opened her backpack and pulled out the spell book. Chills ran up and down her spine as she opened the book. She hadn't realized that she was holding her breath until her chest began to ache. She let out a shaky breath and searched each page carefully until she finally found a spell to control the thorns. Her hands trembled as she held the book in her hands and read the words written on the page.

"Black thorns
Beneath my feet,
Hear my call,
Hear my plea,
Obey my words
And return to the place
Whence you came."

As Bianca chanted the spell, she could feel a part of her soul begin to darken, like a bruised fruit, just before it's about to go bad. But to everyone's amazement, the ebony-colored thorns hissed and trembled as it slowly receded back underground.

The spell worked . . . but at what cost?

Ming ran out of the house as soon as the thorns vanished. She headed for the trees and began to hyperventilate. She placed a hand on her chest as she tried to slow her breathing. The entire experience had obviously left her shaken. Bianca chased after her and tried to offer her some comfort.

"Leave me alone, B." Ming pushed Bianca away when she got too close. Bianca opened and closed her mouth a few times. She was speechless.

Ming had never spoken to her that way. Ever. Her words stung.

"Ming . . . I'm so sorry," Bianca whispered.

"I know. I know you're sorry. I know this isn't your fault, but I just can't look at you right now."

Bianca shook her head and turned away from her oldest and dearest friend. The promise of tears swam in the corners of her eyes. She sniffed and wiped them away before anyone could see her cry.

Prince Ferdinand patted Bianca on the shoulder and walked up to Ming. Bianca stood by, feeling empty and useless as she watched the prince comfort her friend.

"Are you all right?" His voice was soft and kind.

Ming turned to him and sobbed into his chest. His blue eyes widened in surprise. His hands hovered over her back as though uncertain if he should embrace her or not. The way her body trembled with every sob that raced through her body, he quickly overcame his shyness and held her tightly against him.

"There, there. We made it out all right. No one got seriously hurt," he whispered.

Ming shook her head and sobbed even harder.

Prince Ferdinand kissed the top of her head and let her cry all she wanted. She was scared, pure and simple. This was his world. He knew to expect strange adventures and obstacles that could shake your entire being to its core.

"I want to go home. I've had enough," she said.

Prince Ferdinand gently lifted her face by placing a finger below her chin. He looked into her dark brown eyes. "Then we shall make it so. Please, don't cry."

Ming took in a shaky breath of air and wiped the tears that gathered at the corners of her eyes. She gave him a single nod and tried to smile.

Prince Ferdinand chuckled. "That has to be the saddest smile I have ever seen."

"I think this is the best I can do under the circumstances."

"Come, let us talk to Bianca about how we can get you back home."

"What about you? Don't you want to go home?" Ming looked into the prince's eyes.

"Heavens, no! I'm having the time of my life," Prince Ferdinand replied, unable to stop himself from smiling. His voice softened and he said, "But for a lady such as yourself? This is no place for you. You're wise in your desire to return home."

"What about Bianca?"

"She will understand."

"You think so?"

"Come, I'll prove it to you."

Bianca took that as her cue to walk away and left them alone. She went back to the brick house and waited for them to return.

Together, Ming and the prince walked through the front door.

Ming nibbled on her lower lip nervously as she stood in front of Bianca. "I'm sorry for pushing you," she whispered.

"That's okay. I know you didn't mean it," Bianca replied. Ming nodded and tucked her hair behind her ears.

"Home?" Bianca gave Ming a half-hearted smile.

Ming nodded.

"It's okay. I understand."

"Are you sure?" Ming's voice was laced with a mixture of relief and guilt.

Bianca grinned. "You're my best friend. The last thing I want is for you to get hurt. I'm not mad. I'd leave too if I could. But I can't leave my mom here."

Ming nodded once more.

"When I get back, we'll go shopping and have some of your mom's famous dumplings."

"Promise?" Ming sniffed a few times and wiped her eyes with the sleeve of her shirt.

"I promise. I'll even buy you that lipstick you were eyeing last time we went to the mall okay?"

"Okay." Ming stifled a sob.

"Shh, it's okay," Bianca whispered.

Ming burst into tears and embraced her best friend. Bianca couldn't remember a moment in time where they weren't together. This was different though; this was a matter of life and death. There were risks.

"Bianca?" Ming whispered.

"Yeah?"

"What if we never see each other again? What if you never come back?"

Bianca shook her head. That was such an impossible scenario that she wanted to erase it from her thoughts, for fear that she could accidentally conjure it and make it real.

"You don't really believe that? Do you?"

"I . . . I . . . I don't know," Ming said between sobs.

"I need you to believe that we're all gonna get back home safely. Okay? I'll be back home before you know it," Bianca promised.

Bianca stayed outside and thought about what she was moments away from doing. She was going to send Ming home. Sure, David, Terrance, and Prince Ferdinand would still be by her side but, she knew they weren't going to be enough. Ming was the only one among them who completely understood her quirks and sense of humor.

Once more she had to use Mirabel's book to find a spell that would send Ming back home. Bianca rubbed her temples; she felt the pangs of an oncoming headache. She couldn't remember the last time she'd had such an achingly sharp and painful throbbing in her head. She took a deep breath and tried to clear her thoughts.

"Here it is," she whispered. She turned to Ming. "Ready?"

Ming shook her head. She wanted to at least say goodbye to David and her new friends. She took a moment and hugged everyone farewell. Bianca grinned when she saw Ming hugging the prince for a few moments longer than everyone else.

Ming blushed slightly when she walked away from Prince Ferdinand. "I think I'm ready now," Ming said.

"Wait!" Prince Ferdinand shouted.

Ming arched an eyebrow and gave the prince a perplexed look. Bianca shrugged and waited.

Prince Ferdinand walked right up to Ming grabbed her by the waist, drew her to him and kissed her passionately on the lips.

When their lips finally parted, Ming had to take a minute to catch her breath. Prince Ferdinand looked rather pleased with himself.

"Anything?"

Ming blinked a few times and blushed. "You kiss by the book, Your Majesty."

Prince Ferdinand gave her a blinding smile. From where Bianca stood, he looked like he wanted to kiss her again, but decided against it.

Ming straightened her already perfect hair and nodded. Bianca wondered if the kiss was enough to make her reconsider her decision, but Ming turned to Bianca. "Ready."

"Later, alligator," Bianca said.

"After a while, crocodile," Ming replied with a wink.

Bianca took a deep breath and chanted the spell:

"Find the shortest distance between,

My home and the faeries' green.

A place for clear days and starry nights,

Put this door within my sight."

She felt the strange pull of magic coming from her and transferred that energy to the door that started to take shape before their eyes. With an ache in her heart, Bianca turned the knob and opened the portal. Tears stung her eyes as she watched Ming step through the door.

Ming looked over her shoulder and gave her a little wave. Bianca waved back and Ming took another step. In a flash of light she vanished. Just like that, her friend was gone.

Bianca stared at the spot where the door had been. She realized she hadn't blinked in several moments and shook herself out of it. She prepared herself mentally for the final leg of her journey, then looked through her backpack until she found one of the metal spoons she packed.

Bianca used her spoon to dig a hole in the ground. When the hole was big enough, she threw the spell book in it and covered it up. The book was the only bit of leverage she had against Lenore. She did everything she could to make the earth look normal and inconspicuous.

Bianca looked at the sky and saw there was still plenty of daylight left. It was time to go.

23

AFTER SEVERAL HOURS OF walking in a lush, green forest, they came across barren ash-colored trees. It was almost as though someone had drawn an imaginary line across the forest and everything beyond was decaying.

"What happened here?" Bianca wondered.

"Lenore happened. She poisoned the land with her magic. We're getting close," Terrance said.

"Everything here is dead," Prince Ferdinand commented.

"Except us," Bianca said. *But for how long?*

She didn't dare utter those words out loud. Everywhere they looked they saw lifeless trees, pale as ash. Even the soil was covered with ashes. Then, when there were no more trees to protect them or give them coverage, they finally saw Lenore's castle. It was gray, imposing, and terrifying, even from a distance.

Bianca stopped walking.

"What's wrong?" Prince Ferdinand asked.

"My mother is in there . . . somewhere," Bianca replied.

Terrance held her right hand, and Prince Ferdinand took her left. David remained close behind. Bianca took a deep breath. She felt braver now that she had her friends and her father close by. Together they forged ahead.

"What is that?" Bianca asked as a fog formed and quickly covered them from head to toe. She felt their hands slip away from hers.

"Daddy? Terrance? Prince Ferdinand?" she cried. She looked all around her but saw nothing. She moved her hands, searching blindly, hoping that she would at least touch someone. Her hands remained empty.

When the fog finally cleared, Bianca stood alone.

"I didn't think you'd make it this far. I was hoping you would die sooner," Lenore said as she materialized before Bianca in a swirl of gray smoke.

Bianca resisted the urge to gasp but took a step backwards in surprise. "Where are my friends?"

"Out of the way . . . for now."

"Where's my mother?"

"Where's the book?" Lenore narrowed her eyes.

"Safe."

"Where?" Lenore snarled.

"When I get my mother back, I'll tell you where it is," Bianca said.

"Insolent little brat! I make the demands here. Not you!" Lenore roared.

Before Bianca could react, Lenore attacked her from every direction imaginable. Bianca raised one hand and with the other she clutched the leather pouch around her waist. She did her best to remember the shield spells that Old Woman had taught her. A large, oval shaped shield formed itself around her, strong as the silk threads of a million invisible spiders. While it wasn't indestructible, it was strong enough to keep Lenore's spells at bay.

Lenore slammed her fists against the shield. Her black eyes filled with rage at the fact that she couldn't get through Bianca's shields.

Bianca didn't know how much longer she could keep it up. It took all her concentration and strength to keep her shields in place. She needed to be able to cast an attack spell of some sort; otherwise, there was no way she could survive Lenore's attacks.

Lenore finally took a step back and wiped a thin coat of sweat off her forehead. "Fine. This is how you want to play? I'll show you a new trick you've never seen before."

Bianca took a moment to catch her breath; holding the shield up was a tiresome task.

Lenore crouched down and picked up a large chunk of caked up earth. She flashed Bianca a menacing look as she muttered a spell. Lenore then threw the piece of earth towards Bianca, it landed with a loud splat between them. The mass of light brown dirt trembled and quaked. Bianca let out a tiny shriek when it sprouted a large hand and pulled itself out of the ground.

"Oh, my God," Bianca gasped.

She couldn't believe her eyes. The creature continued to pull itself out of the soil until it was fully formed. Lenore had given a huge chunk of earth . . . a body. It looked like a mix between a gorilla and a man, and he—or it—was staring straight toward Bianca. She concentrated all her power and energy on her shield. The creature looked around. It scratched its dirty head as though it had been woken up from its nap.

Lenore clapped her hands, and the creature turned its attention to her. Lenore needed no words to give her command—all she did was point her finger at Bianca.

Before she could react, it was on top of her, pounding its fists against her shield.

She screamed in horror as she felt the vibrations on her shield. It felt as though her body was trembling from the inside out. She desperately thought of ways she could get this thing off her. She wondered if an air spell would work, but the most it could do was blow the creature a few feet away from her and would only make it angrier. Then she remembered something Mrs. Lee, Ming's mother, once said after their house flooded several years ago. She'd quoted Lao Tzu. "Nothing in the world is more flexible and yielding than water. Yet when it attacks the firm and the strong, none can withstand it, because they have no way to change it. So the flexible overcome the adamant, the yielding overcome the forceful. Everyone knows this, but no one can do it."

That was when Bianca realized what she had to do; she had to make it rain. It was the only way to destroy the earth creature dead set on killing her. She had to do the one thing that seemed unthinkable to her. She released her shield and quickly cast a thunderstorm spell. Before the earth creature could pound its heavy, meaty fists upon her, she put her shield up once more and she hoped that her spell worked.

Several long minutes passed, and nothing happened. Bianca thought about something else she could do to stop this monster dead-set on ending her life. Then to her great relief and surprise, she heard the rumble of thunder. She had braced herself for the worst when she saw a huge droplet of rainwater bounce off her shield. The earth creature finally stopped attacking her long enough to look up just as a downpour fell upon them.

Bianca let out a whoop of delight and watched as the earth creature was reduced to a puddle of mud within minutes.

Bianca released her shield and stood up. Every bone in her body ached.

Using magic was more taxing than she had first thought.

Lenore narrowed her eyes. "Very impressive."

Bianca locked eyes with her enemy. She took a moment to catch her breath as the rain she'd conjured, drenched her from head to toe.

"I want my mother back," she demanded.

"So do I," Lenore replied.

Lenore waved her hands, and Bianca was enveloped in darkness.

24

BIANCA OPENED HER eyes with a start. It was pitch black. She gave her eyes a moment to adjust to the darkness. She wasn't sure where she was, but she suspected it was a dungeon.

Oh, good, a dungeon . . . that's classy. It's usually how these things work. At least now I know she's a villain who goes by the bad guy rule book.

Water dripped from the ceiling, rats scurried in the corner, and she heard cockroaches skittering under the dirty bed. A bat swooped over her head. She gasped, covered her head and ducked. The last thing she needed was a bat tangled in her hair.

"Well, well, well. You don't look powerful from where I'm standing," Lenore said as she emerged out of the shadows.

Her heart almost burst out of her chest. Bianca let out a string of curse words and pressed herself against the cold stone wall.

"Where is my mother?"

"Still alive . . . barely. If you can call what she's doing breathing, then you have nothing to worry about." Lenore's voice dripped with nonchalance.

"I'll tell you where the book is if I get my mother back . . . alive. And we get to leave safely back to our world," Bianca demanded.

Lenore smirked. "So many *demands* from someone so young. How do I know you're not lying to me?"

"Um, you're the evil one who kidnapped my mother and turned

my dad into a bear. If anyone has any reason to lie . . . it's you," Bianca said, feeling more confident.

Lenore cackled. "I was just like you when I was your age. Naïve, stubborn, and ultimately . . . foolish."

Bianca narrowed her eyes. "I highly doubt that. I'm nothing like you."

"In time you'll see that we have more in common than you think. You're going to end up all alone, just like me," Lenore taunted.

Bianca felt rage boiling below her skin, flushing her face. "That's not true!"

"Do you see anyone else in this dungeon with you?"

"Someone will come find me." Bianca spoke those words as though they were a prayer. She kept repeating it over and over in the back of her mind.

"Your mother said the same thing last week. She's still waiting." Lenore patted Bianca on the head and smiled. Then she stopped and inhaled the air around Bianca. She bared her yellowed teeth into a wicked smirk.

That look sent a chill down Bianca's spine.

"She's marked you," Lenore whispered.

Bianca shook her head in denial. She didn't want to admit the truth, least of all to Lenore.

"You see, little one? You really are just like me." Lenore then lifted her hand. She had the same apple-shaped bruise on the palm of her right hand. Except that hers covered the majority of her palm and it had sprouted tiny veins all around it as though seeking to further imbed itself into Lenore's being.

"No." Bianca shook her head, trying with all of her might to erase the image of that black and blue apple out of her mind. "You're wrong."

"We shall see who is right and who is wrong at the end of the day."

Bianca threw her head back and spat on Lenore's face. The witch slapped her on the cheek so hard she fell on the floor. Her head connected with the corner of the tiny bed. Her vision swam as she struggled to sit up. She gingerly touched the side of her head. Her trembling hand came back slick with blood.

Lenore squatted and looked into Bianca's eyes. She tried to look away; she didn't want to know what horrors lay within those black orbs. Lenore snarled and grabbed Bianca's chin, forcing her to look at her.

"I'm going to let you stay here and think about things for a while. When I come back . . . we'll have a little chat," Lenore said.

"You'll get the book . . . when I get my mother back."

"We'll see about that."

Then without warning, Lenore vanished.

Bianca wasn't sure if she'd used the door or not because she fainted before she could figure out whether she was hallucinating.

Bianca fell into a strange dream. She fell through a dark hole. She half expected to see the white rabbit appear, but no such luck. She would've chosen a Wonderland filled with a Mad Hatter, March Hare, and the Queen of Hearts any time of the day. Anything would've been better than the hellish dungeon she found herself in at that moment. She thought she was going to fall straight on through to the other side of the world when a hand with skin as white as snow reached out and grabbed her. It was that ethereal hand that pulled her out of the darkness and into the light. She closed her eyes and waited until her sight adjusted to the sudden burst of brightness.

When she opened her eyes, she stood in the middle of a beautiful apple orchard. She could see tiny red apples growing on each branch. They would be ready to be picked in the fall. She extended her hand to gently caress the bright red apple.

"Hello," a sweet voice said.

Bianca withdrew her hand and hid it behind her back. "Hello? Where are you?"

A woman wearing a robin's-egg blue empire dress stepped out from behind one of the apple trees. She had long black hair that cascaded past her shoulders, vibrant indigo eyes, and perfect rose red lips.

"Who are you?" the woman repeated Bianca's question.

"I'm Bianca Frost."

"Lovely name," she replied.

"Thank you."

Bianca frowned and whispered, "Snow White?"

She gave her the warmest of smiles and nodded. "That was one of my many names."

"What other names do you have?"

"Daughter . . . wife . . . mother . . . witch," Snow White replied.

"I never thought of them as names."

"Ah, they are the most powerful names. They mean more than you think."

"Names don't matter anymore. We're all going to die here," Bianca muttered.

"Now, now, that sort of talk isn't allowed." Snow White wagged her index finger and gently scolded her.

"What are you doing here?"

Snow White's smile vanished. Her eyes became distant and somber. "I've been trapped here for years. I . . . don't even know how long it's been. All I know is that you are the first person I have seen since Mirabel put me here."

"Me?" Bianca pointed to herself.

"You," Snow White confirmed.

"That's . . . insane."

"Now the question is . . . who exactly are you?" Snow White's blue eyes bore into Bianca.

"I don't know if you'll believe me." Bianca chewed on her thumbnail.

"Please . . . who are you?"

Bianca gave her a small smile. "I have reason to believe that I'm your great-great-great-granddaughter."

Snow White's eyes grew wide with disbelief. Her face crumbled. She fell to her knees and rested her hands on an apple tree.

"Snow White, are you okay?" Bianca rushed to her youthful-looking ancestor and sat beside her.

"So many years lost," Snow White whispered as she shook her head.

Bianca said the only thing that came to mind. "I'm so sorry."

"Don't be sorry. None of this is your fault."

Bianca sighed. "Doesn't make me feel any better."

Snow White smoothed out her hair and her dress. She stood up and held her hand out to Bianca. She promptly took her ancestor's hand and got up. There was a spark in Snow White's blue eyes. A fire that reignited Bianca's urge to fight back with everything she had.

"Tell me everything you know. I want to know what I've missed in my time in exile."

Bianca told Snow White every bit of information she could think of. She started from the very beginning. Bianca loved Snow White's reactions to everything. Her face was a palette of facial expressions.

"I wish there was something I could do to help my mother."

Snow White became pensive. "Perhaps there is something you can do."

"What? What can I do? How can I stop Lenore? I'm just a newbie, and she's too powerful." Bianca covered her face and sighed. She felt a giant black cloud hovering over her head. She failed to see a way out of her situation.

"How old do you think I was when I had to face my stepmother?" Snow White placed a hand on Bianca's shoulders.

"I don't know . . . I think Mom said you were seventeen? I can't remember . . . that conversation feels like it happened a million years ago."

"I was twelve years old when I ran away because the huntsman told me that if I ever went back home, my stepmother would kill me. But no matter how well I hid, she found me, even though I had the protection of my seven dear friends, who sacrificed everything to keep me hidden." Snow White hesitated a moment, then continued, "Mirabel could always find me . . . no matter what I did. I was only thirteen when she tried to kill me the first time with ribbons. The second time she came back, I was fourteen and that time she used the poisoned comb, and when I was sixteen she finally killed me with the poisoned apple. I was about your age when I finally defeated her all on my own."

It was one thing for her to hear her mother tell Snow White's story, but it was an entirely different experience to hear it from Snow White's lips.

"Where are we?" Bianca gazed around.

"A place neither here nor there. Some people call it limbo. I like to call it a reminder."

"Why a reminder?"

"I've been trapped here for centuries, unable to move on toward wherever I'm supposed to go. Heaven? I don't even know anymore. Wherever we are, Mirabel has made certain that I never get out." Then she became pensive and whispered, "All I know is that I want to go to wherever he is. I can't see him anymore. I can't even remember what he looks like anymore."

Snow White looked at Bianca, then seemed to remember herself and why they were there. "No matter what happens we must continue to fight Mirabel and protect our family. I can't allow her to extinguish our light. You can't let her win."

"I don't know how to do it. I'm not strong enough." Bianca began to cry. The tears silently slid down her cheek and clung to her chin before falling to her feet. She kept going over what Lenore had said. She knew the witch was wrong—there was no possible way that Bianca would become anything like her. And yet . . . there was a part of her that kept wondering if Lenore was right.

"She said . . . I'm just like her." Bianca spoke so softly that she was amazed her lips even moved. She lifted her hand and showed the mark to Snow White.

Her ancestor tenderly looked over the bruise and made little tsk sounds.

"It could be worst. She could be controlling you like a marionette. If she were, you wouldn't be here with me right now."

"Will it go away?" Bianca studied the apple-bruise.

"If we defeat Mirabel."

"What if my magic isn't strong enough? What if I mess things up and just make things worse?"

Snow White smiled, her blue eyes shimmered with infinite knowledge as she spoke, "Silly girl. Of course your magic is good enough. Magic isn't about control or power. Magic is all about believing in the impossible. Magic is believing in things you can't see or touch. The desire . . . the will . . . to make something true despite the laws that bind us all to the material world."

"I never really thought of that," Bianca said.

"Do you believe you can save your mother?"

"I think so."

"Now, you know that's not the answer I wanted to hear. Now let's try again, do you believe you can save your mother?" Snow White repeated.

"Yes," she whispered.

Snow White stood up to her full height. She looked larger than life when she did. In a commanding voice, she said, "Say it and mean it, Bianca Frost."

"Yes," she replied firmly.

"Good. Now it's time for us to wake up."

"Us?"

"I'm coming with you. I have reason to believe that you're the way out of here."

"I don't understand." Bianca frowned.

Snow White walked up to Bianca and gave her a kiss on the forehead. She stood beside her and held her hand. "You don't have to understand, dear girl. Just close your eyes . . . and believe."

Despite her confusion, Bianca did as she was told. She closed her eyes and thought about everything that had led her to this moment, to this place in time. She believed that she was in fact holding Snow White's hand. That they were going to get out of here. That they would defeat Lenore.

25

BIANCA SAT UP AND immediately felt better. Refreshed. Every sad and depressing feeling that she had been plagued with vanished. She felt as though her soul had been scrubbed clean. Had that really happened? Did she really meet Snow White in that orchard? Then Bianca heard a soft humming close to her ear. Bianca was going to take that as a yes.

I don't know what Snow White packed into that kiss on my forehead, but this is a little weird. Actually, I take that back . . . this is A LOT weird.

"Whoa," she whispered. She rubbed her eyes a few times, wanting to make sure her eyes weren't playing tricks on her. Bianca saw the intricate web of spells that Lenore had carefully woven into the walls of her cell. She was surrounded by a kaleidoscope of mirrors. It was designed to boomerang any attack spells Bianca might use against Lenore should they both be inside Bianca's prison.

"Huh . . . interesting." Bianca couldn't help but be impressed by Lenore's work.

Magic is all about believing in the impossible, Snow White's words echoed in her mind.

"Here goes nothing," Bianca muttered. She waved her hand and imagined the mirrors destroyed, and to Bianca's surprise, that's exactly what happened. The mirrors exploded and shimmered out of existence.

Cool.

Now she needed to focus on opening the door. She looked through the keyhole. She saw the hallway. Her vision was limited, so she didn't know if there was someone standing next to her cell door, but there didn't seem to be anyone out there.

Bianca placed her hands on the door. She thought of winter and everything it represented. Snow. Icicles. Blizzards. Ice. When she pulled her hands away, they were blue and trembling with cold. She rubbed her hands and blew warm air into them until they regained their natural color. The door was frozen solid. Bianca hoped that what she had planned in her head would work; otherwise she was going to be trapped in her cell until Lenore returned. Bianca gave the door a hard, swift kick, and it crumpled to the floor into a thousand pieces.

Awesome.

She stepped out of her prison and looked up and down the hallway.

All clear.

She opened some of the doors, searching for her mother, but she stopped when she came upon a door that was locked.

"Mom?" she whispered.

She waited with bated breath. No answer. She took a step back and was ready to walk away to check the next door when she heard a soft whimper coming from the other side of the door.

"Who's there?" a deep feminine voice asked.

"My name is Bianca Frost. Who are you?" Bianca whispered.

"Luna, but I highly doubt you know what that name means," she replied.

"What are you?"

After a long pause, Luna whispered, "Wolf."

"I think I've met your husband."

"You've spoken to my mate, and you lived to tell the tale. Are you a powerful witch?"

"If I can open this door, then . . . yeah, I guess so. Stand back," Bianca instructed.

Bianca froze the door and kicked it down the same way she had with her cell door. The massive oak door shattered and fell into a messy pile on the gray-black stone floor.

A large white wolf sat in the furthest corner of the cell, staring at Bianca with thoughtful hazel eyes. Even though her fur was matted and covered with dirt, she reminded Bianca of a wild queen.

Queen of Wolves. That wouldn't be too far from the truth.

"Impressive," Luna said, studying the remains of the door. She lifted her gaze and openly stared at Bianca. She tilted her head from side to side as if that would somehow change what she was looking at. "You are a child," she finally said.

"I'm not a child," Bianca said in a defensive tone.

The wolf barked a sharp laugh. "Now I know that you definitely are a Human Girl."

Bianca stepped over the mess she'd made to Luna's side. "Are you okay?"

"I will be . . . once I tear that bitch apart limb from limb." Luna growled.

"You'll have to wait in line because I get to go first."

"Why are you here?"

"I'm looking for my mother."

"Follow me." In two long leaps, Luna was in the hallway, ready to show Bianca the way to her mother's cell.

They walked quietly side by side and stopped only so Luna could sniff every door they passed by. The only sound that could be heard was the click of Luna's long black talons. Luna stopped in front of a door and sniffed frantically.

"I smell . . . a human woman . . . smells like you." Luna stood on her hind legs and scratched softly at the oak door that separated Bianca from her mother.

Bianca pressed her ear against the door. "Mom?"

"Bianca?" Rose spoke, her voice weak.

"Mom, it's me," Bianca cried.

"Oh, thank God." Rose sobbed.

"Stand back, Mom."

"Okay."

"Luna, you should stand back, too."

The white wolf gave Bianca a single nod and did as suggested.

Bianca froze the oak door. She had never wanted to kick a door down as badly as the one in front of her. She let out a nervous giggle when she saw the shattered remains lying before her feet. She carefully stepped over the frozen, broken door pieces and walked into her mother's prison. This was the place Rose had been kept prisoner for the past ten days. There was a dirty cot pressed against the left side of the room. In the middle was a weathered wooden chair with bloodied lengths of rope hanging on the sides, claiming its innocence even though Bianca clearly saw it was guilty of unspeakable horrors. She didn't have to wonder whether the blood belonged to her mother. Bianca had a hard time believing that Rose, her mother, had been locked away in here. The woman who had shooed the monsters out of her closet. The beautiful woman who had sung lullabies to her when she couldn't sleep at night, who had held her every time she'd cried, who had made her laugh with quirky jokes. Rose hadn't had anyone to shoo away the monsters for her. She had been trapped in this hell all by herself.

"Momma?" Bianca whispered as she searched for her mother in the darkness.

"Hi, sweetheart." Rose stepped into the only source of light that was in her cell.

"Oh, God." Bianca covered her mouth to keep herself from crying out in shock.

Rose was almost unrecognizable.

Bianca took a closer look. Her mother's left eye was swollen shut. There were vicious cuts all over her face. Bianca carefully inspected her mother and noticed the untreated cut on the palm of her hand. The skin was still open and covered with puss.

"I'm going to kill her." Bianca vowed.

"Shh. Don't talk like that," Rose whispered.

"I mean it, Mom." She took a deep breath and ran her fingers through her hair a few times.

"Human Girl, is there anything I can do to help?" Luna poked her head inside Rose's cell.

Rose gasped in surprise and took a step back. Her body trembled in fear as she looked upon the large white wolf.

"It's okay, Mom. She's a friend." Bianca gently put her hand on her mother's shoulder. "Luna, do you think you can find my backpack?"

Luna nodded. "What is this backpack?"

"It's a black sack. It smells like me and may even smell a little like magic because of the items inside."

"I will find this and bring it to you," Luna replied, and then without making a sound, she was gone.

"You've made some interesting friends while I was gone," Rose said.

Bianca waved a dismissive hand. "Never mind that, let me take a look at you."

"It's okay. It looks worse than it really is. Let's just get out of here."

"Wait." Bianca closed her eyes. She wanted to know if she could do anything about her mother's wounds.

Snow White, I hope you're close by. I could use some help here.

She felt the ghost of a hand above her own. She closed her eyes and concentrated on her mother. She thought of all the times her mother had healed her cuts, scrapes, and bruises. It was time to repay in kind. Bianca thought of the love she had for Rose, her mother and friend. The one person she trusted above all others. She opened her eyes a little and noticed that her hands were glowing with a soft white light. She held her mother's hands and healed her as best as she could.

"What are you doing?" Rose whispered.

"Shh."

"Feels warm. First time I've felt warmth in almost two weeks."

When Bianca opened her eyes, almost all of Rose's wounds were healed. Some bruises were still visible, but the important thing was that Rose wasn't in pain anymore.

"Where did you learn that?" Rose gently prodded at her left eye.

"Long story, let's get out of here."

"Gladly," Rose replied.

They stepped out of Rose's cell. Bianca couldn't wait to go outside and leave this place behind. She held her mother's hand and carefully walked down the hallway. Every once in a while, they looked behind them to make sure they weren't being followed.

Finally, they reached the steps.

"Stay here. I'll go take a peek and make sure it's safe to go up," Bianca whispered.

Rose nodded.

Very carefully Bianca went up to the steps. She looked up and down the hallway. Nothing. Empty. She let out a sigh of relief and waved at her mother to join her.

I hope Luna found my backpack. I hope nothing bad happened to her.

Bianca then heard a soft clicking sound. There was a rhythm to it. She concentrated on the sound, and little by little the clicking got closer until it suddenly stopped. Bianca held her breath and waited.

"Human Girl." A voice that sounded like silk over steel spoke.

"Luna?" Bianca whispered.

"Yes." Luna finally emerged from the shadows with Bianca's black backpack hanging from her jaws.

Bianca was glad to have Luna on her side. She didn't want to know what it would feel like to be caught between Luna's sharp white teeth. She tried hard not to shiver in fear as Luna walked toward her and gave her the backpack.

"Where was it?" Bianca asked, unable to hide her curiosity.

"I'm not familiar with the names you humans give to each room, but there was a lot of food in this place and a great big steel thing that was very hot to the touch," Luna replied.

"I think you were in the kitchen."

"What now?" Rose murmured.

Bianca squatted and opened her backpack. If what she had in mind was going to work, she needed to make sure everything inside was more or less intact. Bianca smiled. Everything was still in her backpack. How could Lenore have missed seeing the magic mirror, the brick, and the red cape?

"What are you looking for?" Rose looked down at Bianca.

"Nothing, just making sure I didn't leave anything behind. Kind of my Plan B in case we bump into her," Bianca explained.

They all walked pressed against the wall, doing their best to make as little noise as possible. They made it as far as the dining hall when Bianca heard a slow clap. Every clap caused her heart to jump and her blood race through her veins. Luna took on a defensive stance, bared her fangs, and let out a fierce snarl.

Lenore sat at the head of the table, her eyes zeroed in on Bianca. It was as though no one else in the room existed.

"Impressive," Lenore said.

"Get out of our way," Bianca demanded.

"More demands? I've never met anyone, save your mother, that tasks me as much as you." Lenore shook her head and clicked her tongue against her cheek. "I'm afraid your attempt at a rescue ends here, little one." She stood up from her heavy wooden chair.

Luna snapped her jaws and did something that Bianca could only describe as a mixture between a bark and growl.

"Silence!" Lenore shouted. She waved her hand and from cracks in the stone black vines snaked through, binding Luna's paws and muzzling her snout shut.

Luna whined and struggled to free herself.

"Bianca, you're not ready," Rose whispered into Bianca's ear.

"If I were you, I'd listen to your mother." Lenore chuckled.

Not an ounce of confidence from her own mother. There wasn't enough time to explain to Rose that she was more than capable of saving them all. She could bring them all home. Snow White believed in her as did Old Woman. If they had faith in her, then there was no doubt in Bianca's mind that she could defeat Lenore.

"Mom, I can do this," Bianca replied. Never once did her eyes leave Lenore.

"All right," Rose said.

"Excellent, I get to kill you both at once," Lenore said.

"We'll just see about that," Bianca replied.

Lenore attacked first. She took the dagger she had in the sheath and made it multiply itself over and over until there were several dozen silver daggers hovering in front of her. She waved her hands, and they all launched themselves toward the Frost women.

Bianca's eyes widened in surprise as a wave of daggers headed straight toward them. Thanks to quick thinking on her part, she created a wall of fire and melted the daggers. She used the molten silver and made a shield. Mother and daughter hid behind the silver shield.

Lenore screamed in frustration and continued to throw daggers at them. Bianca used the daggers that struck the shield and made it even stronger. "You weren't kidding when you said you learned some tricks," Rose said.

Bianca smiled and nodded. She could tell her mother was impressed with her new magic skills.

"What next?"

"I'm thinking . . . mirrors," Bianca said.

"Mirrors?" Rose echoed. "What for?"

"Just . . . keep her busy. I'll let you know when I'm ready," Bianca replied.

"Okay," Rose said with a nod.

Rose threw an ice spell at the ceiling, creating stalactites that covered the entire top part of the room. She clapped her hands and watched as huge chunks of ice fell on Lenore. The witch spent the majority of her time dodging them, which gave Bianca the time she needed to prepare.

Bianca pulled Mirabel's little hand mirror out of her backpack. She took a deep breath and held the mirror in her hands. Then . . . she grabbed the frame and pulled it apart.

At first Rose was confused. Her green eyes widened in surprise when she noticed that Bianca was making the mirror bigger. By the time Bianca was finished, it was half her size. She then created ten replicas of the mirror.

Bianca handed the original mirror to Rose. The other nine she tossed in Lenore's direction until they had scattered all around the evil witch.

"What game are you playing at here, brat?" Lenore spat. "Do you think you know mirror magic just because you had my mistress' spell book for a week? You know nothing!"

Lenore slammed her fist into the two mirrors in front of her. Tiny fractions of glass rained down on her feet. A thousand miniature reflections looked back at her from the floor. She growled and stomped on the mirrors.

"See ya later." Bianca jumped into the mirror her mother held in her hands.

"Bianca!" Rose cried out in surprise.

She found herself in a hallway with seven mirrors showing Lenore in different angles. The wicked witch looked at her surroundings and frowned at the mirrors that surrounded her. Bianca felt a surge of hatred run through her body. This was the woman who had ruined her childhood. This was the witch who had taken her father away from her mother. Bianca's arm shot out and grasped Lenore's filthy dress. Lenore gasped as she was pulled inside the mirror.

There was a scuffle inside the hallway of mirrors as Lenore wrestled the young witch, trying to escape. Lenore growled and shrieked as she tried to claw Bianca's eyes out but Bianca pushed her off with all the strength she didn't know she possessed. She kicked Lenore in the face and heard the satisfying crunch of bones being broken. When she stepped back, she saw a spray of blood all over Lenore's face.

Bianca stood by the edge of the mirror's frame and narrowed her eyes at Lenore. She wanted nothing more than to leave her in this place to rot.

A flash of horror crossed the evil witch's features when she realized what Bianca's intentions were.

"You can't leave me here," she said.

"Yes, I can," Bianca replied.

"No. No!" the witch shouted.

With little remorse, Bianca jumped out and made the other mirrors vanish with a loud pop, leaving only the original mirror that Rose continued to hold in her hands.

"Thanks, Mom. I'll take that now," Bianca said.

Rose furrowed her brows, obviously confused, then handed the three-foot tall mirror back to her daughter. Bianca took the looking glass and concentrated as she pushed it down until it shrunk back to its original size. Bianca realized she'd done it just in time since she could hear Lenore's screams from within the mirror.

"Not so powerful now, huh?" Bianca said.

"She's trapped in there?" Rose asked.

"Yep. Wanna see?"

Rose nodded and took the little hand mirror from Bianca. She looked into the mirror and instead of her reflection she saw Lenore's angry face. She heard her screams and felt her fists pounding on the cold, hard glass.

"Good riddance," Bianca muttered as she placed the little hand mirror in her backpack.

"We're going to have a serious talk about this when we get home," Rose said.

"You don't think she deserved this?" Bianca asked.

"I think there was a better way to take care of her."

"Like she was going to do with us, you mean? You think she wasn't going to do everything in her power to make sure she tortured us to death before finally killing us? Do you honestly think she would've shown us any type of mercy? Because if you think she would've, then please tell me now and I'll set her free." Bianca frowned, unable to understand why her mother was arguing with her.

"All right," Rose whispered, finally conceding to Bianca and the decision she'd made.

26

"STAY STILL," BIANCA gently scolded Luna. The large wolf groaned and did as requested.

Bianca and Rose had to use a combination of knives and magic to set Luna free from the impromptu prison Lenore had made.

"Finally." Rose sighed as they cut the final vine off Luna.

The female wolf got up and stretched. "Thank you."

"You're welcome," Bianca replied.

"Quiet . . . I hear something." Luna's ears twitched and moved as they followed the sound.

Bianca listened and heard a faint familiar voice.

"Who's that?" Rose looked from Bianca to the shadows where the voice came.

"Terrance?" Bianca called back.

"I'm confused." Rose frowned.

"Shh, I can't hear him," Bianca whispered.

"Bianca!" Terrance cried as he finally came into view at the end of the hallway along with Prince Ferdinand.

Bianca smiled and ran toward Terrance.

Rose and Luna quickly followed suit and trailed behind.

Suddenly, Bianca felt herself being hoisted up in the air by her neck. Her stomach lurched as she felt her feet leave the floor. Her vision swam as the ground beneath her grew farther and farther away from her.

"Bianca!" Rose cried.

"You stupid little brat! You just had to keep interfering," a cold feminine voice hissed into Bianca's ear.

Luna growled in response.

"Who's there? Show yourself!" Prince Ferdinand demanded as he flicked his sword nervously from side to side.

"Show yourself, you coward!" Terrance shouted.

The voice laughed in response to their demands. Bianca helplessly dangled in the air as though she were being held by an invisible noose. She fought frantically to free herself, but nothing worked. She kicked and tried to wriggle herself free all to no avail. Out of the corner of her eye she saw a series of black ribbons. She knew they were similar to the ones Mirabel had used on Snow White.

"Mom." Bianca choked the word out as she struggled to breathe.

"Silence!" the voice said.

"Mirabel?" Rose wondered aloud.

"That's *Queen* Mirabel to you." She spat.

Slowly they were all able to see what they were up against. Hovering in the air was Mirabel's ghost. Her once beautiful face was contorted with hatred and anger as she looked down at everyone. Her feet were bright red and covered with blisters. Her blond hair was knotted and frayed at the ends.

"Don't worry, little one. Soon you won't feel a thing," Mirabel said with a fake saccharine tone of voice.

For the first time in her life, Bianca was frozen with fear. She was too high up. No one would be able to reach her. At least not in time to save her.

"I'm coming, sweetheart," Rose said.

Bianca heard her mother, but she had no idea what she was doing or how she planned on saving her from this horrible situation. Bianca struggled to breathe. Her vision slowly darkened. She felt her limbs beginning to go numb.

"Enough!" Snow White bellowed.

"At last," Mirabel whispered.

Bianca's heart dropped to her stomach when she felt the black ribbons around her neck vanish like a fog. She braced herself for a fatal fall that would surely kill her. Terrance caught her moments before she crashed onto the cold, hard floor. Bianca gasped for air.

Rose quickly scrambled down the cabinet she'd been trying to climb to reach her daughter. She ran to Bianca and gently touched her forehead, the way she used to when she was younger. She kissed her cheek, her forehead, and the very top of her head.

Rose then examined Bianca's hand. The apple shaped bruise on the palm of her hand was the size of a half-dollar coin, and it had tiny red veins that sprouted out of it as though trying to latch onto Bianca's fingers.

"Why didn't you tell me about this sooner?" Rose wondered aloud. Bianca, unable to speak, only shook her head.

"Come on, let's get out of here," Rose said.

Terrance stood up, with Bianca safely in his arms. She buried her face into his chest and breathed in his scent as they all made their way toward the castle doors. When they reached their way out, Rose touched the massive wooden door and cast a fire spell. The door burst into flames as though it had been doused with gasoline.

"Bianca?" Terrance whispered her name as he lay her down on her ground. They were at a safe distance from the castle. The grass was burned the color of ashes, a sharp contrast to Bianca's pale skin.

She opened her eyes and gazed at Terrance. She'd been afraid she would never see him again. He smiled as he smoothed out her hair and tucked it neatly behind her ears.

"Hurts," she whimpered, gingerly touching her throat.

Terrance studied the bruises on her neck. Prince Ferdinand joined them and sat down next to Bianca. Luna sniffed Terrance and then reluctantly sat several feet away from the odd group.

"I can't believe a ghost can cause so much harm to a single human being. I'm amazed your neck isn't broken," Prince Ferdinand whispered.

Bianca tried to sit up, but grimaced in pain and slowly lay back down.

"Shh, don't worry. You're safe now," Terrance said.

"Mom?" She croaked, her eyes searching for her mother.

"She's on her way here. She's setting the castle on fire . . . at least that's what it looks like from where I'm sitting," he explained.

Bianca smiled even though it sent a shock of pain down her neck. *Good riddance.*

Rose finally returned to the group and sat down beside her daughter. She frowned and after several minutes of silently studying Bianca's wounded neck, she finally said, "I hope this works."

She cast a spell and healed most of Bianca's wound. It still hurt to turn her head from side to side, but at least she could speak without sounding like a toad.

Bianca frantically looked around, frowning. Where was her father? "Terrance?"

"Yes?"

"Where's my dad?"

"The last I saw of him he was taking care of some of the guards at the main entrance of the castle," Terrance said.

"You found your father?" Rose's voice cracked.

They called out to David until he finally appeared.

He took slow steps, literally dragging his feet beneath him. It was as if he was embarrassed to be seen in that form.

Rose fell down on her knees when she saw the great black bear. He gingerly took steps closer to Rose. She couldn't stop staring at him. She opened her mouth to speak but all that escaped her lips was a series of sobs that threatened to shake the earth to its core. Tears poured out of her eyes as though she were a river, the greedy soil welcoming her gift of tears. She reached out and caressed his face. After ten years of searching, she'd finally found him.

"David," she whispered. A word. A name so charged with love that it was electrifying. Out of a land that was barren, their love was able to create life . . . or at least the promise of it. The sky was brighter, flowers bloomed on the soil where Rose's tears had landed, butterflies fluttered around them, curious and wanting to be a part of the love that surrounded David and Rose. At that moment, anything was possible.

Rose smiled as she gazed into David's ice blue eyes. There was no denying that he was in there somewhere. David licked Rose's lips and face.

"Not exactly the type of kiss I was looking for, but it's better than nothing," she said with a smile.

The first genuine smile Bianca had seen on her mother's face since her father's disappearance. Everyone remained silent. Bianca was there to witness true love in its rarest form. She had never seen anything like it.

27

"HUMAN GIRL."

"Yes, Luna?" Bianca replied.

"I must leave you now."

Bianca smiled and told her that she understood.

"I will be eternally grateful for what you have done."

"I'm just glad I was able to help."

Luna studied her closely and quirked her lip, what looked to Bianca like the wolf equivalent of a smirk. "Anyone else in your position would demand as many favors from me as possible. You are a strange human."

"Yeah . . . I get that a lot."

"Should you ever need me, just call my name to the North Wind. I will hear you. Goodbye, Human Girl." Luna gave her a short bow.

"Goodbye, Luna."

The great white wolf walked up to Terrance and studied him for a moment with her inquisitive hazel eyes. "Why do you smell familiar to me, Human Boy?" She sniffed the air that surrounded him and gave him a quizzical look.

"We share the same blood, you and I," Terrance explained.

"Do we now?" Luna's ear perked.

"My father is your son . . . William."

"I see," she whispered.

Terrance chuckled softly when Luna licked his face and hair.

"Tell my son that his mother misses him," Luna said.

"I will." Terrance nodded.

"Farewell . . . Grandchild." And having spoken those words, Luna finally left.

28

BIANCA STOOD AND gazed at Lenore's castle. Half of the building was engulfed in flames.

"Mom? Am I finally going crazy or do you see what I'm seeing?" Bianca squinted.

Rose sighed and searched in Bianca's backpack until she found her glasses.

"Here." Rose handed the wire-framed glasses to her daughter.

Bianca groaned but put the glasses on. It felt good to have her mother back. It was a welcome relief to have someone take care of her for a change. Finally able to see better, she saw that she was correct: there was a figure emerging from the flames.

"Look." Bianca pointed to the entrance of the castle. Rose and Bianca got as close as they could. They were precariously close to the fiery building, but Bianca wanted to get a closer look.

Amid the flames, she saw two ghosts, Snow White and Mirabel, standing before each other.

"I'm weary of all this nonsense, Mirabel," Snow White said. "Aren't you tired of fighting?"

"You ruined my life, you little whelp. From the moment I set foot in your father's castle, I not only had to compete with you for your father's affections, but I also had to compete with your mother's bloody ghost!" Mirabel sneered. "Everywhere I looked there was a portrait of her or some memento your father refused to get rid of no matter how hard I begged."

"That was not my fault," Snow White replied.

"You ruined my life. Now I'm going to destroy everything and everyone you hold dear."

"You know very well that what you plan to do is impossible. They are strong." Snow White looked at Rose and Bianca and smiled.

Mirabel contorted her face in anger and screamed with rage. She then threw an emerald green energy ball at Snow White who deflected Mirabel's sickly energy by barely lifting her hand.

"I am not a terrified little girl anymore, Mirabel. While you have been hiding in the shadows, feeding off everyone's nightmares, I was living my life and learning and practicing my craft. I know things that would astonish you . . . if such a thing were even possible."

Mirabel launched herself into the air like a panther. Snow White grabbed Mirabel by the throat in midair. Bianca gasped when she saw the look of fierce determination on Snow White's perfect face.

"You will plague my family no more," Snow White said.

A flash of white light burst up toward the sky. Bianca covered her eyes as the light became brighter. When she uncovered her eyes, the castle was burnt to the ground and the flames that had engulfed the building had been extinguished. All that remained were ashes and puffs of smoke that curled into careless tendrils caressing the sky.

"Where did they go?" Bianca whispered.

"I don't know," Rose replied.

"Well . . . they were dead before. But I think Snow White finally killed Mirabel's spirit," Bianca guessed.

"You are correct," Snow White said, emerging from the ashes like an ivory phoenix. She walked toward her kin. "You fought well, Bianca. Rose, you should be very proud of your daughter. She was very brave."

"Oh, I am." Rose put an arm around Bianca and kissed her on the cheek.

"Bianca?" Snow White turned to her great-great-great-granddaughter.
"Yes?"

"I need you to give me the little hand mirror."

"Um . . . Lenore is in there." Bianca admitted.

"I know. I'll take care of it."

Bianca looked through her backpack until she found the mirror. She handed it to Snow White. How she was able to hold onto something material when she herself was a ghost, Bianca would never know. All she knew was that she felt an immense sense of relief as she passed on the responsibility to someone else.

"Don't feel bad. You did what you had to do to protect yourself and your loved ones," Snow White said, almost as if she had read her mind.

"I know . . . it's just . . . I can't help feeling bad." Bianca shrugged her shoulders.

Snow White nodded but remained silent. There were no words of comfort she could give her. Bianca knew it was something she had to deal with on her own.

"I must go now," Snow White said.

"Wait. Where are you going?" Bianca asked.

Snow White let out a happy sigh. "I finally get to rest. I can finally go home now."

A massive, regal white door appeared several feet away from them. "Will we ever see you again?" Bianca called out.

"When it comes to our family? Never say never, but I have a feeling that you will be just fine without me," she replied.

"Thank you for all your help," Bianca said.

"You're very welcome."

"Goodbye."

Rose echoed the same words and waved goodbye to the most famous woman who ever lived.

"Farewell," Snow White said with a bright smile on her face.

The white door then swung open and waiting on the other side was a man dressed in princely finery. He had light brown hair and kind, light green eyes. Snow White ran to the man and embraced him. She rested her head on his broad shoulders and allowed herself that moment with him. She lifted her gaze toward him and gave him a chaste kiss on the lips.

"Is that . . . "

"Prince Charming? I think so, yes," Rose replied.

"Wow," Bianca whispered.

She wondered if she would live happily ever after once she walked through that door. Would she remember her life, what it was like to be alive and in love? Would Snow White remember the pain she lived through? Would she remember Bianca? She wondered all those things as she watched Snow White disappear to another world, someplace she couldn't follow.

29

THEY ALL RETURNED to the spot where Bianca had buried Mirabel's spell book. She dug it out, searched for the portal spell and ripped the page out of the book.

"What are you doing?" Rose asked, horrified at what Bianca had done.

"What *you* should've done years ago." Bianca folded the piece of paper and shoved it in her jeans pocket.

Then, much to Rose's shock, she watched as Bianca lit a match and set a corner of the book on fire. Before Rose could mutter a water spell, the old musty book burst into flames, falling curled and singed to the ground within moments.

"That book was a priceless part of our history," Rose shrieked.

"Trust me, it has a price. A hefty one too. It almost cost us our lives. We almost died because of that stupid piece of crap. Look at what it did to me, Mom. Look at my hand!" Bianca showed Rose the palm of her hand. It still bore the apple-shaped mark.

"It's shrinking," Rose whispered.

Bianca nodded. She rubbed the bruise with her thumb as though doing so would make it go away faster.

"You didn't have to burn it," Rose said.

"And do what instead? Put it back in the hole I found it in? Wait until some other vengeful witch comes knocking on our door looking for it? Can you go another ten years without Dad?" Bianca's questions came flooding out.

Rose's breath caught on her throat. She shook her head. Bianca had never talked back or questioned her before. She had always been a meek and obedient daughter. So much had changed in such a short amount of time.

"Sweetheart . . . I'm so sorry."

"I wish you'd have told me sooner," Bianca whispered.

"I'm sorry," Rose said.

Bianca wanted to yell and scream. She wanted to ask her mother why she'd let this happen to her? Why she'd let this happen to them? But as much as she wanted to put the blame on Rose, on anyone, it wouldn't fix anything. It wouldn't change what had happened. It wouldn't give them back the ten years they'd missed with her father. And even though every fiber in her being wanted to run away in the opposite direction, she stayed with the group instead.

"Are you okay?" Rose whispered.

"I don't know," Bianca muttered.

"You wanna talk about it?"

Bianca sighed. "No. I'll be okay. Come on. Let's get out of here."

"Where are we going?" Prince Ferdinand turned to Bianca.

"We have to go back and get Rapunzel's hair," she explained.

Rose's gaze snapped to her daughter. "What do you mean get Rapunzel's hair?"

"I brought it with me," Bianca replied.

Rose sucked in a breath of air. "What else did you bring?"

"The brick, Red Riding Hood's cape, the little hand mirror, and the red dancing shoes," Bianca admitted.

Rose sighed and said, "We'll talk about this when we get home."

Bianca groaned. *Great, more talking.*

They gathered the few items they possessed and walked away from the barren land and the castle that had once stood there.

Things settled into a strange sort of routine by the second day of their journey to retrieve Rapunzel's hair. They walked all day, taking short breaks when necessary, and they slept in the third little pig's brick house.

On the third night of their journey, they all decided to sit outside around the fire and enjoy the moonlight and the shimmering stars. Suddenly, Terrance stood up and flared his nostrils as wide as they could go. It was as though he wanted to fill his lungs with as much air as possible. The hairs on the back of Bianca's neck stood on end, and her skin was covered with goose bumps.

"Terrance, what's wrong?" Bianca whispered.

"Shh." He gently patted her hands.

In a loud, forceful voice, he said, "Hello, Grandfather."

There was a soft rumble, a chuckle that came out of the darkness. It seemed to come from all around them; there was no way to pinpoint its exact location.

"Your sense of smell is getting much better, pup." The Big Bad Wolf emerged from the shadows. With one giant paw after the other, he got closer to their camp.

David jumped in front of Bianca and Rose and took a defensive stance as he growled at the ancient wolf.

The wolf licked his lips playfully. He looked directly at Bianca. "Tell your father to calm down. I come in peace."

"How's Luna?" Bianca carefully walked away from her father's massive body.

"A little thin and her coat needs to be cleaned, but she will recover. I wanted to thank you for your help. I am grateful," he said.

Bianca smiled. "We were headed in the same direction. I would've done it even if you hadn't asked."

"Nevertheless, should you ever need my aid, all you have to do is call my name," the wolf said with a low nod.

"What is your name? I mean . . . is it really The Big Bad Wolf?" Bianca asked.

Once more the enormous wolf chuckled. "No, that is not my given name. My name is Magnus. Call it to the North Wind . . . I'll hear you."

"I'll be sure to remember that," Bianca said.

"Farewell, little one. I expect to hear great things about you." Magnus gave Bianca a playful wink. He then turned his attention to his grandson.

"Terrance."

"Yes, Grandfather." It was obvious to everyone that he was nervous about what his very dangerous grandfather was going to say to him.

"Tell your father . . . tell William . . . he is missed," he whispered.

Terrance nodded and promised to deliver the message to his father. The old wolf vanished into the darkness of the forest.

"That was terrifying," Rose said. She shuddered and tried to rub the goose bumps off her arms.

"Then you should be happy you haven't seen him angry," Bianca replied.

"Really?"

"Really, really."

"Tell me everything." Rose clapped her hands excitedly.

Bianca sat down with her mother. It was funny to have the roles reversed. Bianca was now the storyteller and Rose, the eager listener.

The sky above them was midnight blue, and the stars were twinkling and shimmering with delight. The cool wind brushed over everyone, reminding them that it would be a cold night.

"Wow," Rose said once Bianca finished telling her incredible story.

"Yeah," Bianca said.

"You did all of that?"

"We all did."

"And you really stayed in the castle of the True Bride?"

"Yeah. Old Woman kept us there for a few days and taught me a few things: how to use herbs, stones, and a couple of useful shield spells."

"Did you explore? Did you see the cellar door where the True Bride's mother fell down to her death?"

"Not really. I was kind of tired after all my training. All I did was eat, train, and sleep."

"That sucks." Rose pouted. If it was one thing Rose lived for, it was details. The more accurate, the better.

Rose yawned.

"Going to bed?" Bianca smiled.

Rose was still yawning as she forced a nod out of her exhausted body.

"I forgot to tell you, I have some clean clothes for you in my backpack."

"Oh, God, you're an angel!" Rose kissed Bianca on the cheek and thanked her.

"You're welcome."

"Good night."

"Night, Mom."

Soon everyone except Terrance and Bianca were inside the little brick house. Bianca turned toward him, ready to ask him something—anything—she just wanted to enjoy another moment with him before she had to go back home with her parents.

"For God's sake, man. Kiss her already!" Prince Ferdinand shouted.

Bianca turned around and all she saw was the top of his wavy blond hair at the bottom of the window.

"Ever heard of a little thing called privacy, Your Highness?" Terrance shouted back.

Ferdinand chuckled, and he stretched his neck as far as it would go so he could spy on the budding couple. Once his sky blue eyes came into view, Bianca stuck her tongue out at him and gave him a raspberry. She grabbed Terrance's hand and together they walked away from the brick house and prying eyes.

The inky blue sky and the sparkling stars were above them. The only visible light came from the silver moon, giving them both a pearlescent sheen upon their skins.

"Bianca . . . I . . ." Terrance's words died before he could finish his sentence.

Bianca stood on the tips of her toes and kissed him. She certainly caught Terrance by surprise. His hands hovered behind her back as though he were afraid of his own actions if he touched her. As their kiss deepened, he ran his fingers through her hair. She was over-whelmed by the butterflies that fluttered wildly in her stomach. For a moment she wondered if she would float away from the joy she felt at that moment. This was the first time she'd felt like herself since she arrived in Everafter. There was no one else she had to rescue. No one she needed to fight or defend herself against. She could finally let go. When they finally came up for air, they were both panting and doing their best to catch their breath.

Terrance tucked her hair neatly behind her ear. "Do you really have to go?" he whispered.

Bianca nodded as she wiped the tears that gathered on the corners of her eyes. She didn't want to cry anymore, but regardless of what she wanted, she still sobbed. There was no way she would be able to stay in Everafter. Her parents, especially the one who was still human, would never allow it, no matter how hard she begged.

Terrance caressed her cheek and kissed her on the lips. This time they didn't rush into it. They took their time and enjoyed the feeling of each other's lips.

"Stay, Bianca," he whispered into her ear.

Feeling his hot breath so close to her skin sent a tiny shiver down her spine. She would never be able to make a decision if he said things like that. Of course she wanted to stay. The only things that waited for her back at home were homework, a weak social life, and a return to her normal day-to-day.

No Terrance.

No magic.

No adventure.

She would be invisible to everyone once more.

Do I really want to go back to that?

"Do you have to go?" Terrance repeated.

Do I really want to answer that question?

Bianca shook her head. She wanted her head emptied of all the confusion and all the thoughts buzzing in her head nonstop. She gently placed her fingers over Terrance's soft lips and said, "Shh. No questions. Don't ask me anything anymore. Just hold me . . . please."

Terrance remained quiet. And did as she wished; he kissed and held her. That would have to be enough for the night. At least for the time being they forgot where they were and the decisions they had to make in the morning.

30

THE NEXT DAY, ON the final leg of their journey, Bianca was quiet and pensive throughout most of their walk through the forest. The sun hung above them, taking with it the magic of the previous evening.

"You okay?" Rose nudged her daughter.

"Yeah," Bianca replied unconvincingly.

"Right . . . and the sky is purple, and the moon is made out of cheese." Rose laughed, placing her hand on Bianca's arm. "I'm your mother, remember? I know better."

Bianca said nothing.

"So . . . tell me about Terrance. He seems nice."

Bianca blushed as she remembered the previous night. They'd kissed until they were too exhausted to even hold each other. She was pretty sure that it had been way past midnight when they'd crept inside the brick house.

"He's great," Bianca said.

Her mother waited for her to say something else about the elusive young man. Bianca was sure that she noticed Terrance rarely spoke unless it was to Prince Ferdinand or Bianca.

"Mmm hmm. And?" Rose made a hand gesture to encourage Bianca to continue talking.

"And . . . " Bianca shook her head as she tried to find the right words to describe Terrance. "He's kind, smart, handsome, and sweet.

He's an amazing kisser, and I wouldn't mind it one bit if I spent the rest of my life making out with him."

"Really?"

Bianca nibbled on her lower lip. "Now I wish I had kept that last part to myself," Bianca muttered as she covered her face in shame.

In the distance, she heard Terrance chuckle.

"Just because you have super hearing doesn't mean you should eavesdrop on private conversations," Bianca shouted.

That comment only made Terrance laugh even harder.

"God, will this ever end?" Bianca groaned.

"At this rate? Who knows, sweetie . . . who knows?" Rose put her arm over Bianca's shoulder and kissed to the top of her head.

"We're here," Prince Ferdinand announced.

Once they stepped out of the woods, they had a clear view of the cliff they'd climbed down not too long ago. And dancing in the wind like a long blond snake was Rapunzel's hair.

"So . . . you left it there?" Rose ground her teeth.

"Our only other choice was to leave Dad behind. Lucky for us he cannon-balled his fuzzy butt into the river we just crossed," Bianca replied.

"You can undo the knot and retrieve it without climbing up."

Bianca had a deadpan expression on her face. It took her a moment to remind herself to blink. "You mean . . . we could've avoided this *three-day trek*?"

"Do you really want me to answer that question, or do you want me to lie to you?"

"You can't answer a question with another question, that's cheating."

"Then I don't know what to tell you, sweetheart. Besides, I'm sure that I taught you the spell. I guess you were overwhelmed with all the stuff we talked about that day."

"Whatever," Bianca muttered. She ran her fingers through her hair and sat down on a flat rock. She was beyond exhausted. All she wanted was to go home, lock herself inside her room, and sleep on her bed. She also wanted to stay with Terrance and get to know him better. Why couldn't she do both?

"Rapunzel, Rapunzel,
We have climbed your golden stair
Please return your hair
To its original form."

Bianca watched as her mother coiled the hair around her elbow and thumb until it was a perfect oval and neatly tied up.

"What else didn't you tell me?" Bianca raised a brow at her mother.

"What do you mean?"

"I mean, what else did you keep from me? Stuff that was for my own good." Bianca made air quotations with her fingers.

"Did you think I wanted this to happen to you? Is that it? You think I wanted to get kidnapped, tortured, lose my husband and have him turned into a bear, and almost lose you? For what? A crash course in magic? Do you really think I'm that horrible? That cruel? That I would do that to you?" Rose cried.

David sat beside Rose and whined as he rubbed his wet nose at her hand. She wiped the tears that inevitably escaped out of her eyes and waited for her daughter to speak.

Bianca remained silent. There was nothing she could say. She knew better. She knew that had her mother anticipated anything that happened in the past few weeks she would've prepared her for the worst. The truth of the matter was that there had been no time. Even Bianca herself had been overwhelmed by the amount of information given to her. She could easily imagine her mother forgetting a detail or two.

"Never mind. I'm sorry, Mom. It's just . . . it was a lot to take in, you know what I mean?"

"I know exactly how you feel. I was overwhelmed when I found out. And however harsh my mother was to me, at least she prepared me for the worst. I'm sorry I didn't do the same for you. I just wanted to protect you so much." Rose sniffled. "I was foolish . . . and it almost cost me a price much too high. The last thing that I ever wanted was for you to get hurt. Do you understand?"

Bianca nodded.

"From now on . . . no more secrets. I'm an open book to you. Anything you want to ask me I will answer, okay?" Rose said.

"Really? You mean it?" Bianca sat straighter.

"Absolutely."

"Okay." She took Rapunzel's hair from her mother's hands and put it away in her backpack.

"Do you want a moment to say goodbye to your friends?" Rose looked at the two young men.

Bianca nodded and turned her attention to Prince Ferdinand and Terrance.

"We have to go," Bianca said.

"I know," Terrance whispered. He gazed at the ground as if afraid to look at Bianca.

She knew that neither one belonged in the other person's world. Bianca couldn't stay, and Terrance couldn't go with her.

"Terrance . . . Prince Ferdinand, I just wanted to say thank you," Bianca said. "Thank you so much for helping me rescue my mother. I'll be forever grateful to both of you."

"It was our pleasure," Terrance replied.

After a moment of standing stoic in front of each other for far too long, Prince Ferdinand threw his hands up in the air and shouted, "For heaven's sake, do I have to do everything around here? Must I really command you to kiss her?" He rolled his eyes and muttered, "I am very disappointed in you, Terrance. Really, really disappointed."

Bianca blushed.

Terrance grinned sheepishly.

"Very well . . . seeing as you leave me no choice." He cleared his throat dramatically and said, "I, Prince Ferdinand Anthony Charles

Ash, command Terrance and Bianca to kiss and embrace each other goodbye."

Bianca laughed. She turned to her parents and shrugged. "A little privacy, please?"

Rose winked at Bianca and walked away a few feet. David reluctantly followed his wife.

"You too," Bianca said as she pointed at the prince.

"But it was my command, I must see that my wish is fulfilled," he argued.

Bianca made a little running man with her index and middle fingers and shooed him away. It took some coaxing, but he eventually followed Rose and David.

She sighed and took Terrance's hand in hers. She turned it over and traced the lines on the palm of his hand. They were riddled with tiny scars and cuts. This was the hand of a young man that worked every day of his life. She tried to remember a book about palm reading her mother kept in the house. She knew that the thumb represented Venus, the index finger represented Jupiter, the middle was Saturn, the ring was Apollo and the pinky was Mercury. She knew that the line that started below the index finger and ended below the pinky was the line of the heart. But other than that, she didn't know what the others meant.

There was no way for her to predict what would happen to Terrance once she left Everafter.

All she knew was that she wanted to remember every single detail. She wanted to be able to close her eyes and see Terrance, his smile, his dark brown eyes, and his long brown hair. She didn't want to leave him behind. All she wanted to do was sit, have him wrap his arms around her and tell her everything about himself. She wanted to know why he had scars on his hands. What he'd been like as a child, what his fears were, and what his dreams were—everything.

"I wish you didn't have to go," he whispered.

"Me too," she replied.

Bianca hugged Terrance and breathed in his scent. Earth. Ozone. A hint of sweat. She wanted to take a tiny part of him, however minuscule, with her back home.

"Don't forget me. Promise me you won't forget me," she whispered into his ear.

"Never," he promised.

They held each other for a moment longer and painfully pulled themselves apart.

"I guess this is goodbye," Bianca said.

"Not goodbye . . . farewell."

There was no use in prolonging the inevitable. They kissed each other gently, softly as though they had all the time in the world to feel each other's lips. Then, before they realized it had even happened, their lips parted, and the kiss was over.

It was time to go home.

"We absolutely must find a minstrel to write a song about us," the prince said as he rejoined them.

Bianca smiled; she was going to miss them.

"Ready?" Rose gently patted her daughter on the shoulder.

"Yeah." She forced the word out of her mouth. It left her throat dry and with a bitter taste. It felt wrong to lie. She wasn't ready. She didn't think she would ever be.

"Find the shortest distance between,

My home and the faeries' green.

A place for clear days and starry nights,

Put this door within my sight."

The portal door appeared. The ghost-like door stood a few inches above the ground, waiting patiently to be opened. As if it was a living entity. Magic that was tangible and defied everything Bianca knew about time and space. It made her feel small and slightly insignificant. Almost as though there was still so much for her to learn and even if she reached old age she would never know as much as that door standing before her did.

Bianca turned around and waved goodbye to her new friend, Prince Ferdinand, and Terrance, the young man who could be the love of her life.

She wondered if she would ever see them again.

31

WELCOME BACK TO Normalville, USA, she thought as she stepped out of the portal and into her backyard. Everything was familiar once more.

This is so weird.

Bianca let out a shriek as her father fell to the ground with a loud thump.

"Daddy!" Bianca cried.

David's transformation began the moment the portal behind them closed. His growl quickly turned into a human scream as his bones popped in and out of place, taking on a more human appearance. His black fur dissolved and revealed his olive toned skin. His sharp black claws retracted and became hands. His fangs sank into his gums and reappeared as normal teeth. He let out a blood curdling scream and curled himself into a fetal position as he continued to change back into a man.

Bianca saw the muscles move underneath her father's skin. She covered her mouth with her hands as she watched her father's painful transformation. By the time he was finished with his change, he was trembling and drenched with sweat even though it was a cool summer evening. Rose grabbed a towel from the clothesline and swiftly tied it around his waist. He then stared at his hands as though he were looking at them for the first time in his entire life.

"Oh, God. David? Are you okay?" Rose whispered as she stared at the half naked man in her backyard.

"Rose? My Rose?" His voice was hoarse from all his time living as a bear.

Bianca grinned as she watched her parents embrace for the first time in a decade.

"David . . . I missed you so much," Rose said softly.

"I thought about you every single day," he said as he ran his fingers through her bright red hair. He kissed her on the lips several times. Then his lips traveled all over her face.

He finally turned to Bianca and opened his arms to her, welcoming his daughter into a long awaited embrace. For the first time in a decade, Bianca got the feeling that they would be able to move on. That it would actually be okay for once.

"Come on, let's go inside. I'm sure everyone can use a nice hot shower and a hot meal," Rose said.

"Hot shower? What's that?" Bianca joked.

"I got dibs. I haven't had a hot anything in ten years," David said.

"I think we can let you go first. Right, Bianca?"

"Yeah. I can stay stinky for a couple of minutes longer," she replied.

Bianca used the key they hid underneath the frog figurine to unlock the back door. All eyes were on David as he stepped into his home. It was as though he didn't know what to look at first. So much had changed since he had been taken from their lives. His little girl was no longer a child. His wife, although still beautiful, held so much sadness in her eyes.

"The kitchen is different," he whispered.

He walked into the dining room; it too was different for him, Bianca knew. Everything had changed. Everything but him.

"Daddy? Daddy, are you okay?" Bianca noted the distress in her father's eyes.

He quickly nodded. "Yeah . . . I'm okay. It's just . . . a lot to take in."

Bianca knew her father was lying.

"Bianca . . . why don't you go up to your room. I'm going to set up a nice bath for your father." Rose held David's hand and gently guided him upstairs. Bianca stood in the middle of the living room and watched her parents slowly make their way up the stairs. She knew they had some more hardships ahead. Challenges to overcome. She hoped that they could jump through those hurdles unscathed and unharmed.

At least they have each other.

It was a small consolation, but it was better than being alone.

Bianca called Ming on her cell phone the following morning. After one ring her best friend answered the phone. It felt good to hear her voice, to finally surround herself with familiar sights and sounds.

"B?" Ming's voice was a welcome sound.

"I'm home," Bianca said.

"I'll be right over. Don't move." Then she hung up.

Ming arrived at her house in record time. Bianca watched her car pull into her driveway from the kitchen window. She wondered how many stop signs Ming had flown past to get to her house. Ming jumped out of the car and didn't bother to close the door. Bianca opened the door before Ming could raise her hand to knock.

"B!" Ming threw herself into her best friend's arms, making them tumble onto the floor.

"Hey, how the heck are you?" Bianca tried to sound casual.

"You're alive!"

"Yeah, we all are."

"Really?" Ming squeaked.

"Yeah."

"Is your dad still a bear?"

"Nope," Bianca replied, unable to mask the huge grin on her face.

"Hey, Ming," David said as he walked into the living room with a cup of coffee in his hands.

"Yay!" Ming clapped her hands with excitement. She stood up and ran up to David. He smiled as he hugged her.

"I'm so glad you're back Mister Frost," Ming said.

"Me too," he replied.

"Come on. I promised you we'd go shopping when I came back," Bianca said.

"And my mom's dumplings for dinner," Ming added.

"Of course." Bianca nodded.

"Are you sure? Don't you want to spend time with your parents?" Ming lowered her voice.

"I want to give them some time alone. They've got ten years' worth of making out to catch up on. Trust me . . . I don't want to be anywhere near the house when they finally get it on."

"Cool. I'll wait for you to get ready," Ming said.

"Okay."

Bianca went upstairs to her room to put her makeup on. She grabbed her purse and keys. She was amazed how easy it was to fall into old routines.

"Have fun, you two. Please wait at least a few months before you tell me I'm gonna have a little brother or sister. Use protection!" Bianca teased as she headed downstairs.

"Very funny," Rose said dryly.

"Love you," Bianca said as she walked out the door with Ming.

"Love you, too," Rose and David said, their voices woven into one.

Bianca beamed as she closed the door behind her. She stood on the porch for a moment and let that sink in. Both her parents were alive, safe and sound. They were home. She took a deep breath and followed Ming to her car.

"So . . . tell me. What happened after I left?" Ming pulled out of the driveway.

Bianca told her everything that had happened after Bianca had sent Ming home. Thankfully, Ming drove the speed limit. Ming wove in and out of traffic as she listened to her best friend's story. By the time Bianca was finished, Ming had pulled into the mall entrance.

"Wow," Ming said when she finally parked the car.

"Yeah."

They walked for a while and bought a few things. Eventually they ended up at the food court.

"What about Terrance and Prince Ferdinand?" Ming popped a French fry into her mouth.

"Ferdinand was sad to see you go. He likes you."

"You think so?" Ming wrinkled her nose.

"Yeah."

"What happened with Terrance?"

"Nothing," Bianca lied. She couldn't help but blush at the very vivid memory of them kissing.

Ming gasped. "You lie! Tell me."

"We kissed," Bianca admitted.

"And?"

"Nothing."

"Nothing?"

"What was I supposed to do? Stay? I don't belong there," Bianca said.

"He was crazy about you. A blind man could see that," Ming said.

"I know. I was crazy about him, too. Believe me, the last thing I wanted to do was leave."

"That sucks."

"So . . . anyway . . . what did I miss? How did it go for you?" Bianca changed the subject.

"Well, I opened the museum like you asked me to. Not too many people came. But the ones that did show up kept asking when you and your mom were coming back. Seriously, B, what do you guys do there all day?"

"Don't worry. We're gonna take over from now on. Thanks for covering our butts though," Bianca said.

"No problem."

"What did your mom say?"

Ming moaned. "She asked me a million, billion, zillion questions!" She mimicked her mother's soft and wispy voice. "Where were you? Where is Bianca? Where is her mother? Where are you going? Why do you have to open the museum? Blah, blah, blah, she just wouldn't stop."

Bianca laughed. Ming rolled her eyes and then, because Bianca's laughter was so contagious, she laughed as well. Amid all the laughter, Bianca couldn't help but miss Terrance. She wondered how much time would pass before she would finally be able to move on with her life and when the ache in her heart would stop.

32

ON TUESDAY MORNING, the Frost family opened the doors of the museum. Bianca was surprised to see that there was a group of people standing in line.

"Why are all these people here?" Bianca whispered to her mother as she unlocked the doors.

"I called the newspaper a couple of days ago and had them put an announcement in the paper," Rose replied. "I also explained that we were gone due to a family emergency, that the first week back would be free of charge, and that all items in our gift shop were twenty-five percent off."

"Wow . . . I'm impressed," Bianca said.

Rose smiled.

Bianca took her regular post behind the gift shop counter. To everyone's relief and joy, Rose resumed her storytelling duties. Once more the Princess Room was filled with toddlers and little girls dressed up as fairy tale princesses. Everyone, including the parents, sat on the floor and listened to Rose tell the story of Cinderella. Her melodic voice once more enchanted everyone in the room.

David hid in the office to look through their papers and documents to reacquaint himself with what had been going on in the museum for the past decade.

Bianca grabbed a book from the shelf above her and read while she waited for a customer. She was reading a Grimm's fairy tale book. She turned to the story of Snow White and Rose Red. She wondered if it was the same Snow White in both stories; if so, it would explain why Rose had bright red hair and Bianca had jet black hair.

Maybe I have more in common with my mother than I thought.

She was three pages into the story when someone walked up to the counter. Bianca marked her page with a bookmark, closed the book and put it away.

"Good morning. How can I help you?" Bianca smiled politely.

"Good morning. I'm looking for David Frost. I believe he's your father."

Bianca studied this woman before she told her anything. She had perfect blond hair, cut into a stylish bob and wore a white blouse with a black pencil skirt and patent leather high heels.

"Depends on who you are and what you want." Bianca crossed her arms over her chest.

The woman smiled and flashed her bleached white teeth. "My name is Aspen Fisher. I'm with the Daily News. Your father has been missing for ten years and all of a sudden he's back. I want to interview him."

"I'll tell him you stopped by."

Aspen narrowed her brown eyes and pursed her lips. "Okay. Here's my card."

"Thanks," Bianca said as she took the card from her.

Weird.

As soon as Rose was finished with story time, she went to the gift shop to check up on Bianca.

"How's it going on your side of the world?" Rose sat on the stool next to Bianca and rested her elbows on the glass counter.

She looked happy to be back, Bianca thought. For better or worse, the museum was a second home to Rose. Bianca was afraid to tell her about the reporter for fear that it would ruin her good mood.

"Fine, everything is fine. Everyone's taking advantage of the sale,"

Bianca replied. She lied by omission. She wasn't any good at lying, any kind of lying, white or black, or any other color lies came in.

Rose frowned.

"Great." Rose nodded. She studied Bianca; she could tell something was going on. Rose stood up and walked away.

Rose took three steps when Bianca said, "Mom?"

Rose chuckled softly. No matter what had happened in Everafter some things simply didn't change. Rose turned around. "Yeah?"

"Some reporter . . . journalist lady dropped this off. She wants to interview Daddy." Bianca sheepishly handed the business card to her mother. She was going to tear it up and throw it away, but she was worried that it would only encourage Aspen to chase after them in search of a story. She was happy to hand the card off to Rose. One less thing for her to worry about.

"Yikes. News around here travels fast. All we did was go to the supermarket. Someone must've seen him." Rose sighed. "Well, we have to come up with something before we call her up."

"Why do we have to call her?"

"Because it'll look suspicious if we start avoiding her. Best thing we can do is call and come up with something. It'll be in the news a day or two and then we can move on with our lives."

"Okay," Bianca replied as she shook her head in disbelief. She couldn't believe her mother was going to lie to a reporter.

"All right, I'm gonna go and get some coloring sheets and crayons for the kids. I'll come and check up on you later," Rose said.

"Okey dokey."

Bianca turned her attention back to her book. She had put it down when the reporter appeared and completely forgotten about it.

The way the story of the two sisters ended didn't surprise her. Almost everyone got a happy ending. Snow White married the prince and Rose Red married the prince's brother.

Isn't it that the way these stories always end? Marry the prince and all your problems are magically solved. What if you don't fall in love with the prince but his very handsome friend? What's the solution to that problem?

Oh . . . and he happens to live in another dimension.

"How about you answer those questions? How about a solution to that little problem? Hmm? Anything, Brothers Grimm?" Bianca muttered to the book in her hands.

The book remained silent.

Figures.

Several weeks went by and slowly they fell into a strange sort of routine. David was still getting used to being a man again, but some mornings Bianca would find him sleeping outside or using a tree to scratch his back. His sweet tooth was completely out of control, especially when it came to honey. Whenever Rose made tea, he would use half a bottle's worth of honey to sweeten his tea.

Bianca thought it was hilarious. Rose worried he would develop diabetes.

David promised to try harder.

One day, while Bianca was eating her lunch in her backyard, a door appeared. It was very similar to the one she had opened not too long ago. She dropped her sandwich and readied her magic to fight whatever it was that was coming from the other side. The door opened and a familiar figure appeared at the edge of the magical entrance. Terrance was on the other side smiling at her. Her heart skipped a beat and almost burst out of her chest.

Love. Pure and simple. The agony and ecstasy of love coursed through her veins.

"Terrance?" she whispered with a smile.

He nodded and extended his hand out to her. He was more handsome than she remembered. His smile was broader. His dark brown eyes seemed brighter. His brown hair tickled his shoulders in careless waves.

Bianca took several tentative steps and wondered if she could even do such a thing. Could she do it? Did she dare? Could she take his hand and leave everything she knew behind? Every night since her return, all she had done was think of Terrance. Often, she wondered if people could die of a broken heart. Would she be able to live without him? She gazed at his hand. Calloused and riddled with tiny scars, she wanted to know the story behind each mark. She wanted to kiss him and simply be by his side.

What about her parents? What would they say? What would they think?

Would it be all right if she left them a note? Was there enough time?

She took a deep breath. Too much. Too many thoughts racing through her mind. Too many hearts to break. Too many decisions.

Not enough time. Never enough time.

Terrance stood before her, still patiently waiting for the answer to his unspoken question.

Could she do it?

Did she dare?

Yes, she could.